TERRSCOPE

The October Society

Season Two

Written, Directed, and Produced by
Christopher Robertson

Copyright Christopher Robertson 2022.
Cover Design by Derek Eubanks, Copyright 2022.
Interior Artwork by Matt Taylor, Copyright 2022
Edited by Bret Laurie.

The October Society is a work of fiction. Any resemblance to persons living, dead, or trapped in The Dark are purely coincidental. No part of this book may be copied, distributed, or shown on a broken TV in a dark attic without permission of the author and/or TerrorScope Studios.

A Note from the Producer

This season of The October Society contains subjects and situations some may find upsetting and disturbing, including references to self-harm, death, and child abuse. Please refer to the Producer's Notes after the Credits if this is likely to upset you.

Also from TerrorScope Studios

R-Rated:
My Zombie Sweetheart
Virgin Night
The Cotton Candy Massacre
Goons and Grease Paint – A Short Story
The Comeback Kid - A Short Story

PG-13:
The October Society – Season One

Tune in and Listen to the Soundtrack Here

Or search for The October Society: Season Two on Spotify.

Contents

Previously On The October Society…   1

Opening Credits   4

Episode One   11

   The Dreamer's Date Night   18

Episode Two   47

   The Reel Midnight Spookshow   54

Episode Three   87

   The Song of Sorrow   91

Episode Four   128

   The Unkindness of Ravens   134

Episode Five   178

   Those Quiet Bones   183

Episode Six   231

   The Fear Factory   234

Credits   271

"Every day is Halloween, isn't it?"

Tim Burton

Once again for each and all,

Who smile as the leaves begin to fall.

The October Society

Are

Derek Chardea Braden

Gwennie Rascal Morgan

??? ???

Previously On The October Society...

Once upon a time, at Halloween, they gathered: The October Society. They wear their masks, and tell their tales. Though the members change, one among them remains constant.

A quiet, intense boy wearing a yellowed, chipped hockey mask stares into the fierce, singed orange of the Hallow Fire, shadows dancing across his mask.

Their stoic leader, Derek. He's seen those who find their way to the fire through good times.

A boy in a pumpkin mask and backward baseball cap leaps into a hopping jig as a girl in a devil mask frightens him. Despite his fright, there's joy in the air.

On the ground, a Dachshund pounces on and covers a tiny fairy-like girl in a witch mask. He lashes her with doggy kisses as she squeals in delight.

A tall boy in a werewolf mask and the same slight girl walk hand-in-hand towards the fire, giggling lovingly.

Reaching into the fire and pulling her hand out unscathed, a girl with multicolored mermaid hair stares in awe as she finds a white and red Japanese fox mask in her hand. "A kitsune...what does this mean?" she asks, and the boy in the hockey mask answers, "Welcome to The October Society."

And the not-so-good...

The October Society, all six of them, and the haughty Dachshund sits around the Hallow Fire. Each looks to the boy in the werewolf mask, who holds a black leather-bound book in his hands.

"I guess what I'm trying to say is: goodbye."

"Dino!" the fairy-girl with wispy near-white hair in the witch mask, gasps.

"My brothers," the werewolf boy says, "my sisters." He looks at each of them and offers a resigned smile, finally coming to terms with what he has to do. "The girl I love more than life itself," he says to the witch, "it's time to say goodbye."

Dino announced his departure from The October Society, and it broke poor little Gwennie's heart.

Taking his mask off, Dino hands it to his sweetheart, telling the little witch to hang on to it, to give it back to him when it's her turn. Gwennie shatters like glass and gives her boyfriend one last kiss.

She vowed, at that moment, to find him again. That neither The Light nor The Dark will stand in her way. But even at her most courageous, fear infests her heart...

The girl in the kitsune mask, Morgan, seems confused by the solemn tone of the occasion. It feels more like a funeral than a farewell.

Gwennie wasn't the only member to find their world upheaved without warning.

"Where do you think you are?" Derek guides Morgan to an earth-shattering revelation as a ghostly figure emerges from the shadows beyond the fire.

The October Society, each of them, dead. Not quite ghosts, something else. They are The Lost in The Dark, haunted by their tragic deaths, trapped between life and death, drawn to the Hallow Fire. To tell their stories, feed them to the flames, and someday find the peace to move into The Light.

Morgan approaches the figure in the shadows. "It wasn't your fault," she says, and those words bring comfort to the amorphous form.

Dino says his farewell to the group, and as he moves into The Light, he winks at Gwennie. "See ya later, Dolly."

They come together, the five that remain and the little dog too. Arms around shoulders, they watch the fire crackle and glow well into the night.

In the morning, there's scorched earth and discarded trash where they once sat—broken, discarded furniture instead of chairs made from tree stumps. A smashed TV lies on its back, the cord dangling in tatters. It's like the children were never even there.

And so, once more, they gather...

Opening Credits

The clang of a bell unleashes a tide of demons, ghosts, and monsters. They flow through a door, masks askew, braying like feral nightmare creatures catching the scent of chaos and candy in the air.

As the pandemonium parades through the streets, arching rolls of toilet paper through the air and pouncing upon one another with screams and boos, one amongst them lingers behind. Standing within the relative safety of the school walls, in a handmade Superman costume—blue pants and a t-shirt, with a ripped red blanket for a cape—the boy waits. Unlike the hero, whose face adorns a cheap plastic mask with a broken string that he clutches tight, this boy knows fear. Fear that comes with being powerless. Fear that's amplified on this of all nights, when that which torments us runs wild.

Storm clouds close in, moving fast, and thunder follows as thick gray titans clash in the sky.

He knows he should wait; experience has taught him this, but the near-instant drone of thick, heavy rain drowns out all thought and sound. There's been talk of flooding all day, but till the skies turned dark, he didn't believe it.

They won't still be waiting for him, not in this rain, the boy tells himself, so he runs for it. Within two steps, he's soaked to the bone; within five, he realizes his mistake.

Two bikes skid to a halt in the rain before him, kicking up sprays of dirty water that splatter the boy with a strike of black spots. Both riders wear their hoods up, their mouths covered with half-masks. One a set of vampire's teeth, dripping blood, and the other a rotting zombie's jaw, hanging crooked with bugs crawling between torn flesh. Their eyes glint with malice.

He runs—the boy knows it's futile, but hope exists purely in spite. The slick playground works in his favor, causing his pursuers some delay as they turn their bikes to follow. Their wet sneakers lose purchase on the pedals as the boy pounds through the rain. He takes a sharp corner, keeping tight to the old sandstone building, and one of his pursuers aquaplanes—the bike and rider sliding on their side as the second rider makes the turn.

There's nothing but a long straight now, and the second rider catches up, pumping enough power into the bike that he can coast the remaining distance. The rider kicks the boy's knee, sending him splashing face-first to the ground.

He hears the squeal of wet brakes, quick steps sloshing through puddles, and before the boy can pick himself up, there's a foot digging into his back.

The other bike catches up and clatters as it's ditched. Footsteps race through the rain to the clack of the wheels slowing.

The second rider puts a running kick into the boy's side, rocking him over with a painful oof.

While the boy recoils, the other two raid his backpack, emptying books and pencils to the ground. Of all the things so carelessly discarded, it's a worn paperback the boy cares for most and he reaches to save the book from watery disintegration. As his fingers brush the cover—a giant mantis in the middle of a street—the sole of a sneaker crushes them. The boy cries with a sharp breath, but it's seeing the pages turn to mushy pulp and drift away in the downpour that hurts the most.

A second later, the boy's thrust up against the wall, pinned in place by one of them as the second ransacks his pockets. A thick torrent pours on his head, flowing down from a broken drainpipe. He wishes the rain would sweep him away.

They find nothing worth taking in his pockets, so they give the boy something instead, a quick punch to the gut with a chorus of laughter. At least it'll be over soon. They've checked everywhere and given him a beating; what else is there? He finds out.

Futile protests accompany the boy's quick journey toward one of the school's dumpsters. He hears talk of putting the trash where it belongs. Already he can smell the stench of rotting leftovers and sour milk. From experience, the boy knows that unless the bin's at least half-full, he won't be able to climb out, though, with this rain, it's only a matter of time before it overflows.

The thought of soaking in the foul slurry and swimming in garbage soup is too much. Revulsion sparks rebellion and the boy finds the courage to kick, punch, scratch, and do whatever it takes to get free.

He's on the ground, then, scampering and hobbling. Running for his life. There's no way he can outpace the two older boys, even without their bikes, so he looks for another option.

A narrow window of opportunity presents itself, literally. Along the ground side of the old school building, a line of small rectangular windows peer into the basement.

Tales about this basement cause the students to fill with dread whenever a teacher sends them there on an errand. Right now, though, the boy would prefer risking a run-in with imaginary ghosts to the real-life monsters on his back.

The boy hits flush to the wall above one window and kicks at the glass. It's ancient and solid, as old as the school, but the putty holding it in place is rotten, cracked, and weak. Instead of breaking, the whole window falls away, shattering on the floor below. The boy drops down and crawls through, head first. He's almost inside when hands grip his sneakers. He kicks wildly and then falls free suddenly, landing hard on the floor, socks overhead.

Threats call through the window, almost drowned by the rush of water flowing through behind him. The boy finds himself in two inches of water. All around the basement it leaks in through loose brickwork and broken pipes.

The boy splashes through the ankle-deep pool, weaving through a maze of boxes overflowing with seasonal decorations, damaged stage props, and faulty AV equipment till he reaches a staircase leading up. He nearly loses his footing as damp socks skitter on wet, bare stone, but the boy makes it to the top only to find the door locked.

No big deal, he thinks. He'll wait down here for the bullies to leave and then move enough boxes till he can climb out. He'll be frozen and soaked to the bone, but at least he'll be safe.

The basement fills with painful scraping, the agonized cry of metal dragged across stone. Darkness covers the window, inch by inch, and as the boy plods through rising, shin-deep water, he realizes what they're doing. His eyes fall upon the window as a dumpster's pushed in front of it, barely blocking the water flow but completely cutting the boy off.

Trapped and desperate, the boy races back to the steps, and this time falls as he races up. He doesn't let a busted lip deter him, and he scrambles to the top—pounding on the door, calling for help.

As the water level rises, his pleas fall on empty halls beyond, and the only two people who know he's there ride away into the storm. The water reaches the second step and begins to encroach on the third. It will take some time, but the basement will fill.

One last time the boy screams for help, and this time it comes.

A TV comes on across the basement, high on a shelf in the back. A TV, the boy knows, is broken. He recalls a bang, smoke, and nose-singeing burn of melting plastic the last time his teacher used it.

Flickering light fills the room. Something in that glow calls to the boy—lost between the static, an image forms. Something like a dancing fire. The boy's drawn to it, taken away as—

A rolling viewpoint moves through a cornfield to the steady drum of a beating heart on the cracked TV screen. Tall, skeletal stalks brush aside, and in the brief glimpses of a moonlit night in between, there's a suggestion that something else is there—a freshly covered grave mound in the dirt: the ground shifts as something buried beneath stirs.

We dolly through, too quick to be sure we saw anything, to a stand where a scarecrow once stood, but no longer. It's just your imagination that it feels like the camera lingers, like it's surprised there's nothing there.

We move through a farmhouse into the kitchen, and the heartbeat picks up. The door to the cellar creaks closed as we drift past and up the stairs. Tiny shadows, might be fingers, grip the edge, but just as we notice, they slip into the dark, and the door slams.

Moving through the dark house like ghosts, we find ourselves inside a lamplit girl's bedroom. An imposing, ornate dollhouse stands in the corner, and as we flow through a tiny window, we find ourselves in a model of the same room, only it doesn't feel right. A hairy hand reaches out from under the bed; gnarled feet peek below clothing hung in an open closet; we see them both, but not for long. Through the back of the dollhouse, we find a hole in the wall; it can't possibly be a peephole. Inside the walls, we weave through cobwebs and torn-off doll heads till we find our way to another room. The sound of roaring flames, the ghosts of ashes, and wispy smoke haunt the room.

We're out the window, which only looks like a pair of sinister eyes, then over a dark well, where the rushing water doesn't sound like someone calling for help.

Beyond the house, there's a forest, deep, dark, and never-ending. Like a sea of blackness, except for a brief glimmer. A glimmer we zoom towards as the heartbeat races faster and faster. Whipping through gnarled branches, we reach a campfire surrounded by seats carved from tree stumps. We settle on the dim fire; tiny red embers pulse in The Dark. The flames flicker like they're struggling and suddenly erupt to life in a blaze of orange and red. A surge of green smoke billows from the fire and—

—cut to static, again, though something jarring and raw sounds. Almost like something laughing—something wickedly delighted—something you might glimpse between the lines of static before—

The credits resume as a title appears in the green smoke:

The October Society

Episode One

Oaks reach through midnight forest air that cackles with hoots of fearless joy and undying amusement. Look how their swaying branches dance through shadows that caress them, like old sweethearts.

Cries of terror and joy call from little mouths, squealing with wild delight above a living fire surging once more. The one place they do not come from is the mouth of the girl in the witch mask. She sits alone in The Dark, the joy of the coming festivities like needles under her fingernails.

The season approaches once more. Halloween looms ahead with distant promise like the first sliver of a moon in the night sky. Gwennie, as always, feels the call, as they all do. She felt something else as she arrived to hear laughter and cries of joy from the clearing. A hesitation, no...resentment. How dare they be so happy...

So, the little witch with the near-white hair sits alone in The Dark and waits. Though for what, who's to say?

Dead leaves crunch somewhere else, moving toward the clearing. Gwennie watches the girl with jet-black curls and a winking devil mask appear from The Dark, striding with fearless confidence.

Then another follows, moving with less grace, more caution. Gwennie spots the white and red of the girl's kitsune mask through gaps in gnarled, twisted dead trees. She sighs. Soon she'll have to take her place amongst them once more—even if it's the last place in the world she wants to be.

"Right, so, like the kid goes up this massive chimney thing," an overexcited boy in a grinning pumpkin-face mask with a backward baseball cap explains.

An enthralled girl with messy red hair tumbling from below her own forward-facing cap listens.

The boy's arms fly up. "And there's like these smoky ghost kids at the top–only. No, wait, I'm messing it up."

"Nothing new there, Braden," the devil girl jokes as she enters the clearing, feeling the warmth of the Hallow Fire embrace her. She reaches out, tickling the flames with shiny, manicured fingernails.

"'Sup Char-Char." Braden nods to the devil. "Just telling Holly here 'bout Dino's wicked good story from last year."

Chardea takes notice of the new girl sitting very close to Braden. There's nothing on Holly's face save soot, a few Band-Aids, and the biggest smile. That poor girl, she thinks with a pang of unease. The scent of ash and pain fills the air, and to make things worse, Braden's latched onto her like a barnacle.

"Howdy, the name's Holly," the girl waves. "You must be Chardea. Braden's told me all about you."

"Lies and hearsay," Chardea snorts. "No doubt."

"Oh, he said you told the most wicked story last year..."

Chardea shoots a glare at Braden, and the boy fires her some finger guns while winking under his mask. The little rat.

"Heya," the girl in the kitsune mask says from outside the circle and waits as though seeking an invitation.

"Morganna! Mor-go-girl! Whatcha waiting for?" Braden leaps up and waves her over.

"I dunno." Morgan rubs her arm. "After last time..." Her eyes fall on the new girl, and still wrestling with knowing the truth about The October Society, she cuts herself off. It was hard enough for her to find out how she died, but at least the others let her walk into the revelation when she was ready to.

"It's cool," Holly giggles. "We're all the dead kids," she says in a creepy monotone.

"You told her?" Chardea glares at Braden, actual anger boiling. "That's—"

"I know, against the rules." Braden shrugs. "The boss man says you gotta figure it out on your own, but that didn't go too well last year. Sorry, Morgan, I figured I'd help a sister out, you know?"

"Hey, I mean, I was trapped in a fire. Doesn't take a genius to work out. Not many ways outta that kinda predicament, y'know?" Holly shrugs.

"Took dingus here nearly two seasons to click," Chardea nods to Braden.

"What was it like?" Morgan takes a seat on one of the carved stumps. Five of them surround the Hallow Fire, with a large, blackened throne-like stump making up the sixth chair. "I can't remember much about how I..." she gulps, "died."

"I know what you mean; it's Morgan, right?" Holly crosses over and kneels beside her. She touches Morgan's hand, smiling up at the girl. "Your hair is so cool, by the way. Did you do it yourself?"

Morgan runs her hand through her rainbow-colored hair and smiles. "No, my sister did it for me. I miss her."

"It's beautiful; she must have loved you lots."

"I...she did. I know that now. Thanks to these guys and the fire."

Holly looks over her shoulder at the dancing flames of the Hallow Fire and begins to feel it—the presence of the thing. It's alive, truly alive.

"I was scared, couldn't breathe, crawling through The Dark, and then I found Braden," Holly says, staring into the flames.

"You poor child," Chardea grumbles as Braden strikes a heroic pose.

"And I wasn't afraid anymore. I just knew I could trust him, that he was like me in a way I couldn't put into words."

"It was the same for Dino and me."

The sound of someone approaching silences them, all but Holly gulping in the awkwardness of the timing. Though small in stature, the girl in the white dress who appears from The Dark emits an aura of bitter coldness. It's so unlike her it takes them all a moment to notice her once-long wispy hair cut short, sitting atop her witch mask in an angry spiked bob.

"Hey, Gwen..." Braden's words fail as he notes her new, more aggressive look. "Cool-cool hair."

Gwennie says nothing to the others and takes her seat like she's picking a fight.

All of them, even the new girl, get a sense something's wrong with the little witch. None want to risk poking the bear, though.

With Gwennie's arrival, they're all here, bar one.

"Where's Derek?" Chardea asks, noting how odd it is their leader's not here.

He's always the first to arrive: him and his little demon Dachshund, Rascal. She looks to Braden for an answer.

"I dunno." He shrugs and looks at Holly. "There was nobody here when we arrived, right?"

Holly nods.

The Hallow Fire cracks, a flame whips out almost like a hand pointing, and it draws Chardea's eye to the main chair, the gnarled wooden October Throne. Sitting where their leader should be, is the black leather-bound book where the tales from The October Society are collected. Chardea can hear the pages whisper for her to take them up, and as she does, she notes words carved into the throne.

Odd that she has never seen them before, but then again, this is Derek's chair.

Here sits the master of fright; the bringer of Light; the one who challenges The Dark, the night; and leads The Lost to what's right.

Though she reads the words silently, the voice in her head isn't her own. It's inhuman, primal, surging with erratic energy. It's, she imagines, how a fire might speak.

"Woah, is that the book?" Braden snaps Chardea out of her daydream as he reaches for it. She holds it aloft, high above the boy's reach. "No fair! I wanna see!"

The Hallow Fire flickers like it's waiting.

"I think it's telling us to start," Morgan says with great confusion. "I dunno how I know that."

"It speaks to us," Chardea points out, holding Braden at arm's length as he fights for the book. "The longer you're here, the clearer it gets."

"But Derek?"

Chardea looks into The Dark for any sign of her friend. "Maybe he can't make it tonight. The fire needs feeding, though." She takes the book to heart and brushes Braden aside.

"I'm guessing sticks and leaves don't hit the spot, huh?" Holly jokes.

"Somebody's gotta fill in." Chardea looks to the others.

"I vote for President Braden! A vote for Braden's a vote for truth!" Braden pounds a fist into an open palm. "And my first order of business will be a full-scale, no expense barred investigation into the greatest scandal to ever rock The October Society! Just who started the Fart War!"

"Hashtag Fartgate?" Morgan giggles.

"Sounds like a government cover-up," Chardea snorts. "We all know it was you."

"I...one of these days, I'm gonna prove it and make you all beg for forgiveness. And I'll look down and—"

"Rip one, 'cause you started the Fart War," Chardea says without her usual venom. The book feels heavier in her hand. "I think it wants me…we should vote, though."

"I'm new. I don't think I should," Holly waves it off.

"Makes sense to me," Morgan adds. "I mean, it's just for tonight, right?"

"I hope so." Chardea doesn't want to think the alternative's even a possibility.

"Fine!" Braden pouts. "I mean, you are the oldest."

Chardea turns to the last remaining member, sitting quietly in her chair, arms crossed over her chest. "Gwen?"

"Sure." Gwennie shrugs, barely peeking around the silent wall she's put up between herself and the rest of The October Society.

"Okay," Chardea says with a heavy heart and takes one last look into The Dark. "Where are you, Derek?" She takes a seat on the October Throne and feels far too small for it.

"Um, so welcome everyone to this meeting of The October Society. Since we have a new face, and the rules say potential members go first, I guess—"

"Woah!" Holly panics. "Like I've got to tell a story *tonight*?"

"Yeah," Chardea questions. "Didn't Braden tell you?"

"Knew I forgot something!" He slaps his knee. "My bad!"

"I'm sorry, I didn't. I mean, I don't even have an idea—"

"You know what, it's fine. It's my fault for thinking BRAT-en did a thorough job." Chardea shakes her head.

"Glad to hear you take some gosh dang responsibility," Braden jokes.

"It's not like we're doing this by the book anyway." Chardea ignores Braden's snort at her unintentional pun. "I've got a story that works."

"Oh, awesome." Holly plops into her seat with excitement. "Braden's told me all about your stories."

"He has?" Chardea worries.

"Yeah, he says they're all stabby but full of passion. Like a dance with the devil, you know you shouldn't, but boy does he know how to do a mean worm."

Chardea's taken aback by the compliment and the idea that Braden would speak so highly of her when she's not around. It makes her uncomfortable in ways she doesn't quite understand.

"He's right," Gwennie finally speaks up. "Let's hear it."

Again, this doesn't seem right. Gwennie's not usually so forward.

"Look, I'm not saying he's not, but the words Braden and right don't go together." Chardea shifts in her seat. "Okay, this story is about what we think we know about people. First impressions and long-held conceptions can be wrong. They can be deadly."

Chardea clutches the black book to her chest and speaks into the Hallow Fire. "My October Fellows, time to clean up and put your best clothes on, 'cause you're going on…"

The Dreamer's Date Night

Built for fun, Dreamland was the place to be. You could bowl to hit songs.

Bowling pins loom as a pink and white marbled bowling ball clunks to the lane, spinning as it speeds towards the stack. Neon blues and purples reflect in the shine of the ball and waxed boards, whirling like a kaleidoscope. It hits right in the middle, clattering all ten pins into a clunking explosion.

Still holding the throwing pose, the bowler cheers as STRIKE appears on a screen above their lane, and a girl leaps on him. Wrapping him in her legs and arms, they spin together, cheering wildly below a new caption: PERFECT GAME.

Waste all your quarters at the arcade.

Two girls dance in sync, consistently hitting perfects on the Dance Dance Revolution cabinets behind them. Inside a large arcade cabinet covered in pictures of lurching zombies, a couple screams through their smiles as they point plastic guns at the screen, blasting undead abominations away together.

Grab a burger at Doc's Diner.

A group of teens squeezes into a corner booth at a retro-styled diner, the rest of the alley visible behind them. One boy in a varsity jacket taps a girl on the shoulder. When she looks that way, the boy leans around the side and dips a fry in her shake. She catches him before he can eat it, biting it from his fingers with a smirk.

Play some pool on tables the color of distant galaxies.

A boy leans on his pool cue, sweating under the purple overhead lights. His eyes flit from the girl lining up her shot to the pile of money resting on the table's edge. She takes her shot, sinks the last ball, and snatches the prize money just like that, leaving the boy to hang his head in defeat.

Or win a prize for your sweetheart at the claw machines.

A boy bites his protruding tongue in sheer concentration as he maneuvers a claw over a stuffed robot dog inside a Zoozie the Space Pirate claw machine. He picks it up, gets it towards the shoot, and slams a palm down in frustration as the toy slips free, glancing off the edge of a transparent plastic barrier, and falls into a pile of identical robo-dogs. The boy immediately starts pumping more coins into the slot, as the girl he's with sighs and walks away.

Braden: Amateur! I got a system. See, my cousin Caleb would sneak around back and—

Morgan: You're missing the point, dude; the trying shows you care.

Holly: I'm with Braden. Outsmart the game. Smart is cute.

I'm gonna pretend you didn't use either of those words in the same orbit as BRAT-en and continue, 'kay? Dreamland was the perfect place for a first date. All the noise and distractions filled in those painful, awkward silences. But, for the same reason, it was the perfect place to hide your true intentions, to get away with doing something terrible in plain sight, bathed in neon and flashing lights.

Outside, in the shadows below the massive twinkling sign for Dreamland, a single pinprick of red ignites, showing a glimmer of something dangerously handsome. Only somewhat seen, lost in Dreamland's glow, a small plume of smoke follows it as a boy in a leather jacket lights up, taking a draw. He exhales and smiles as he watches a solitary girl make her way through a sea of parked cars and other teens keeping the party going outside Dreamland's doors.

The boy in the leather jacket has to admit, she's cute in her own way, even if she has the same vibe as the last puppy left at the shelter. Pity and sadness come together into something endearing, though he keeps that to himself. He's been doing this long enough to know how the game's played. And this is hardly his first time.

"All right, here we go," he says, flicks his cigarette away, and sticks his hands into his pockets. Kicking off the wall with one heel, he heads to the door but takes his time. He wants to keep her waiting. It does him no good to seem too eager, and it'll make her needy, make the night all the more enjoyable.

The guy in leather weaves through the crowd of friends and lovers. They don't even notice he's there. Effortlessly passing as one of them, but he's not. No, he's something else altogether.

A couple nearly collides with him at the door. They fall through, so wrapped in one another's joy they don't even notice the boy in the leather jacket. He steps aside with the instinctual grace of a predator. The couple race away, desperate to get to their car and drive into a night full of possibilities.

The boy in the leather jacket feels a pang of jealousy. He wants what they have, even if he knows he can't. Besides, he's getting a bit sick of Dreamland. It's not like there's any other place in town with anything going on, not for him, and it's not like he has many choices. Needs must when the devil drives, or so he's heard.

"What is going on with my hair!"

The girl stares at the messy mane in the mirror. Above her small, round face, wild mounds of coppery auburn hair flow almost vertically.

"I look like a clown, like a damn clown caught in a hurricane."

She rummages through her bag and produces a hairband; it won't match her yellow floral-print dress, but at least it'll stop her from looking like an electrified hairball.

"Okay, Ally, you got this." She poses and tries to talk herself up. "Just be cool, be yourself; you can do this." She smiles and doesn't believe her own hype.

"Oh, who am I kidding," she sulks, but just as she's sinking into premature defeat, she finds a vein of confidence buried deep down.

"No! You got this!" She fires herself up and accidentally turns the tap on full blast—water gushes everywhere, soaking her dress.

"Damn it! Great! Good going, Ally, now you look like you've wet yourself."

Other girls stare in confused wonder at the scene, edging away as though they can sense something's wrong.

Holly: That poor girl!
Braden: If it was me, I'd pee myself in solidarity.
Morgan: She didn't pee—
Leave it. He doesn't need an excuse. So, by the time Ally manages to dry herself, she's added the thought of her date showing up, not seeing her at the diner, and leaving to her list of worries.

Ally steps out of the restroom and feels her heart race so fast it could crack her ribs.

There he is, all alone at a side booth in Doc's Diner, looking the other way at the row of lanes. The donut-shaped clock above the diner bar says she's ten minutes late, and Ally thanks her lucky stars; he didn't ghost her.

She has plans for this boy. Tonight he's all hers, and he's sure to remember it.

"Carson?"

He turns and meets her eyes with those impossibly black ones that make Ally weak at the knees. The boy's charm hits her despite her best efforts, like a warm summer breeze. She can't help but admire him and melts, entirely against her will.

God, you're pretty. She can stop herself from saying it but not thinking.

"Hey." He nods. "Was getting worried you stood me up."

"Me! Stand you up!? As if I could!" Ally flusters, frustratingly so, as she takes her seat, knocking over the salt and pepper shakers on her way. Smooth, Ally, very smooth; what happened to keeping it cool?

Carson smirks; he kinda likes that she's a klutz. It's cute.

Ally chastises herself and then puts the shakers back where they belong. Carson squints as Ally sprinkles some salt into her hand from the shaker. "Spilling salt is bad luck; you gotta toss some over your shoulder to counter it."

Carson watches as Ally flicks the salt over her shoulder, and it hits the face of a guy behind them just as he's drawing in a breath. A mighty sneeze follows, and he shotguns his date's milkshake right into her face.

"What the hell, David!" the other girl screams and stands up, whipped cream and strawberry syrup painting her like a sloppy Dairy Queen clown.

"Babe, it was an accident! Babe!" the other boy protests as his girlfriend storms off towards the restroom. He's hot on her heels, begging for forgiveness, and in the chaos, doesn't even glance in Carson and Ally's direction.

Ally catches Carson's eye, and there's a merry twinkle in them. Evidently, he found that little goof funny, and Ally guesses their date doesn't look like such a disaster in comparison.

"Dunno what she's complaining about." Carson drums his fingers on the table. "Malted shakes are awesome."

Ally titters then breaks into a full-on laugh she can't hope to contain. Her chubby cheeks turn bright red, making her freckles show, and there's nothing she can do to stop it. Snorts follow, and soon her embarrassment makes her flush all over again.

"Don't," she wheezes, "don't start with the puns."

"Oh." Carson flashes a smug smirk. "Snort your kinda thing?"

Ally's cheeks blow out like a stuffed hamster in a futile attempt to stifle more laughter. It bursts from her lips with a gush of air as tears form in the corners of her eyes.

"Woo, oh my," she says and wipes a tear. Feeling oddly more at ease and yet also mortified.

"How about I get us some drinks to kick things off." Carson goes to stand, and Ally suddenly finds her hand on his. It surprises them both, the boldness mainly, and he stops.

"Let me," Ally says and doesn't wait for Carson to refuse. She stands up, quickly fixing her yellow dress. "What do you want?"

"Um," Carson's eyes flit to the restrooms, where the milkshake-blasted girl storms out, desperately apologetic boyfriend following on her heels. "Maybe just a Coke?"

Ally nods and heads to the diner bar, feeling Carson's eyes on her as she goes. Of course, they're on you, dummy, she says to herself. How could they not be, with a butt that—stop it! Stop doing that to yourself.

The grumpy teen behind the bar, whose name badge says Alan but whose face says bored as hell, doesn't even acknowledge Ally's presence as she pings the bell. That's nothing out of the norm, it seems, as other patrons line up while he's too busy scrolling through his phone.

"Hey buddy, you mind getting off your phone and doing your job!?" a guy further along the bar yells. "Looking for some Cokes and burgers, pal!"

Without looking up, Alan tosses a pad onto the bar. "Write your order and table number," he drones with no real effort.

"Ain't that your job?"

Alan's eyes rise from his phone, glaring at the customer. "I'm. Busy."

"Jeez," the other guy says and scrawls his order on the pad. "Don't expect a tip, loser."

Alan scoffs and returns his eyes to his phone.

Other customers follow the example. Ally goes last, grateful for the development, quickly scribbling down their order—specifying no ice. It wouldn't be possible for her to make the order face to face the way she is.

Back at the table, Carson nods towards the bar. "Happy-go-lucky kinda guy, ain't he?"

Ally shrugs. "He's obsessed with something on his phone."

"Yeah, wonder what? Maybe he's stalking his ex," Carson suggests with a wicked grin.

"He does give off those kinda vibes."

"So, what kind of vibes do I give off?" Carson catches Ally's eye, and the question stumps her.

"I don't think I should say." Ally blushes.

"Come on. I'll do you if you do me." Carson winks.

"Ohmygod!" Ally buries her face before it turns entirely red. "You did not just say that!"

Carson laughs. "Come on, what's my vibe?"

"Ugh!" Ally raises her head enough to look at him. "You first."

"Okay. You hit like you're the kinda girl who doesn't know how cool she is."

"Oh, that's not me." Ally purses her lips and shakes her head. "I know I'm a big deal, yo!" She holds a cheesy grin for a second, then starts to laugh. "I'm sorry."

"See," Carson smirks. "I was right. Your turn."

Ally squints at him. "I think you're dangerous?"

"What? Like to myself?"

"No. Like a fox. Or a wolf, you're like a handsome wild animal. Beautiful, and I want to pet you, but I know you'll bite my hand."

"Can we rewind to the bit where you said you wanted to pet me?"

"I didn't mean it like that!"

"So...you don't?"

"I didn't say that, either! Oh, God!" Ally slumps back down. "Kill me now, please."

Carson looks away at that, a subtle twitch to his smile. "Anyway, if anyone's a danger here, it's you."

"What do you mean?"

"So far, you've nearly drowned yourself." Carson nods to Ally's soaked dress. "And sabotaged at least one date with a well-timed salt throw."

"God, I'm such a klutz."

"Yep."

"You're not supposed to agree!"

"I like it, though." Carson shrugs. "It's cute."

"How!? How is it cute that I should have a red and white sign wherever I go. Danger: Beware of Ally."

"It makes me want to keep you safe."

An involuntary sigh slips from her lips, and Ally feels her heart skip a beat.

"Just roll you in bubble wrap, and lock you away."

"That was sweet till you went all super creep."

"Maybe that's my true vibe." Carson poses heroically. "Super-Creep!"

Ally laughs again, and a tray of Cokes clatters to the table so violently they almost spill. Ally's eyes flick to the bar, where Alan's still on his phone, then to the waitress, who looks exhausted. It's not just picking up the slack from the lazy colleague, though. Ally can spot the telltale signs of a girl who's been crying—a lot. Red marks where she's been rubbing away the tears, mascara runs that haven't been wiped clean properly—not from laziness, but because more tears are inevitable—because they keep coming no matter what.

The name on her badge reads Molly.

Braden: Man, I could murder a Coke right about now.

A commotion comes from across the diner, and all eyes turn to see the manager yelling at Alan.

It's the perfect distraction.

Ally was wondering how she was going to pull this off. With Carson's eyes on the drama, she reaches into her purse and drops the hidden contents of her closed hand into his Coke.

Alan pulls off his apron, bundles it up, and tosses it in the manager's face, storming off without another word. The manager has a few, though, and yells them to the kid's back.

Carson turns back and takes his drink, surprised to hear something clink inside the dark glass.

"Oh, shoot." Ally slumps. "I forgot you don't like ice."

"It's...cool," Carson winks, and this time Ally rolls her eyes. The same eyes turn to watch Carson down his drink. Eyes that fill with focused intent as she watches him gulp it all down. He guzzles like a man lost in the desert without pausing to sip or taste. It's one of the many things about him she's come to loathe.

"Ah," Carson sighs with relief, then immediately coughs. He's confused; there's something stuck in his throat—this isn't how it's supposed to go. "Did you?" he doesn't finish the question. A gout of blood bursts from his lips, trickling down his chin in quick rivulets. He coughs again, hacking with raw guttural desperation—the blood splattering across Ally's wicked grin.

All around them, the other patrons continue their dates and dinners—eerily paying no attention to the bloody chaos unfolding.

Ally stares, hands on the table, fingers interlocked.

"Why!?" Carson manages to say, choking on a mouthful of blood. He vomits out a glut, and something shiny and sharp follows. As spit and blood trickle between his trembling fingers, Carson holds out a broken shard of mirrored glass.

In Ally's eyes, there's a flash of what came before—she smashes the mirror in the restroom, scaring the life out of the others. She filters through the shards, picks up the sharpest, nastiest piece she can find, and then slips it into her purse. Clacking it closed with a deceptively innocent smile.

"Why, Ally?" Carson manages to say again as more blood pours between his teeth, spilling onto the table like watery drool. It runs to the floor, landing like the pitter-patter of light rain on black and white tiles.

The waitress, Molly, walks past and doesn't even look their way as she takes the tray away with a confused shake of her head.

Carson's head smacks down on the table. Blood still flows from his gaping, slack jaw, reflecting the smiling face of the girl who just murdered him.

Ally pulls her hands from the table as the blood spreads towards her, checking the back of her nails like she's bored. After a minute passes, she seems confused. Almost as though she expected something to happen, and it hasn't.

Kids continue to chat; the jukebox plays tunes, and the distant sound of bowling pins crashing continues. She glances at the donut clock, still ticking away.

Carson sits up with a gasp, filling his lungs with as much air as possible. He slams a fist down on the table, the sound finally drawing some attention from the other patrons but more curiosity than horror. As though they don't see the boy in the leather jacket, covered in blood and fury.

"The hell, Ally!" Carson demands. "Why!?"

She shrugs.

"I'm bored."

We'll Be Right Back After These Messages...

"One year ago tonight," an ominous voice reads over a still black-and-white image of a burned-down farmhouse, "Channel Five reporter Jackie Torrance disappeared during an investigation into one of Clear Lake County's most haunted locations." The image fades to a picture of the missing woman.

"Now, shocking new footage has emerged suggesting Jackie Torrance started the fire that took the lives of the investigators and crew." A grainy, black-and-white video shows a dark-haired woman sabotaging equipment.

The shot freezes, and it's probably just a reflection, but her eyes glow dead white. It switches to a headshot of Jackie and a police sketch of a broad-faced, heavily bearded man in a trucker cap.

"Her whereabouts and the identity of this man are still unknown."

"Kids! Do you wanna have fun!?"

A trio of children stand in front of a rickety water slide. One of them picks his nose.

Behind them, a single rider winds down the tube, looking like he's about to throw up. His float almost squeaks along with a pitiful water flow.

"I said, kids, do you wanna have fun!?"

The trio jump to action as a hand briefly enters the frame, waving them on.

"Yeah!"

"Woo!"

"I want fun," the last boy delivers woodenly.

"The head on over to..."

A purple and blue, spiky text box with the name of the park spins across the screen, coming to a halt across the middle.

"Splash Downs!"

A star-wiping reel of the attractions follows—an arcade, mini-golf, multiple flimsy water slides; a wave pool with off-color water.

"It's just $9 for a whole day!"

A boy playing *Double Dragon* at the arcade leans over his shoulder, declaring, "Trementus—"

"Tremendous," the narrator whispers.

"Tremendous value!"

Another kid stands outside the front gate with an overweight man in poorly fitting shorts and a brown Splash Downs t-shirt. The owner puts his arm around the kid.

The reservation phone number flashes below them along with the location, just off the main highway to Skidd's Bay.

"Indisputably delightful," the kid says in an awful, faux English accent.

"Dude!" the owner adds and holds a shaky thumbs up for way too long.

"Theodore Gorman was a man ahead of his time," a tall man with slicked-back graying hair says as he sits on a folding chair, fingers steepled and legs crossed. Behind him, there's a banner for some horror movie, white background covered in blood splatter. "The man was meta before the concept was ever even dreamed up." The shot cuts to a sepia-toned movie, a stunningly beautiful, tall woman in an elegant dress looking over her shoulder and smiling as she walks through the door of a clearly haunted house. "This Halloween," an announcer declares, "join Channel Five as we present the story of the man behind the terror, an in-depth look at the forgotten maestro of the macabre," a black-and-white image of cheery man in a suit and bow-tie fills the screen, "Theodore Gorman."

We Now Return to The October Society.

Dancing flames gleam in Holly's eyes. She leans forward, as hungry for the story as the Hallow Fire itself.

"Cool." Her cheeks rise, and moving shadows fill the creases.

"What is going on at Dreamland?" Morgan wonders aloud while Gwennie listens in silence.

Chardea feels like she should say something to the girl. Usually, they bicker and peck at each other's stories like sisters, but she seems so far away.

Braden gulps, shifting uncomfortably in his seat.

"What's the matter, Braden." Chardea holds out an innocuous bottle. "Thirsty?"

"No thanks, I'm good."

"Really?" Chardea shakes the bottle, "I thought you said you could...murder a Coke?"

"Yeah! Murder it, not the other way 'round. I mean, why you gotta mess with a dude's loves Char-Char?"

Chardea shrugs, feigning innocence. "Maybe it's because I'm—"

"—bored!?" Carson grips the edges of the table to keep from flipping out. "Bored," he spits out another shard of broken mirror. "Seriously, Ally! Bored!?"

"I'm sick of this. Stuck here, every Friday!" her voice rises. Even with Carson's outburst, only casual glances come their way—more curious about the shaking table and vibrating shards of glass than anything. "It's been a year!"

"So you thought, I'll just cut his throat to ribbons with some broken glass? That'll throw a little razzle-dazzle into date night. Happy anniversary honey; here, have some strychnine." Carson tries to wipe the blood from his chin, leaving crimson smears on his pale skin. "Makes sense to me."

"I just thought if we died, maybe this God-forsaken night would end!"

"Oh, yeah, I see the logic; notice you didn't test that theory on yourself first."

"Stop complaining." Ally groans. "This whole situation is your fault, after all."

"Wait, what!?" Carson stares with head-tilting confusion.

"You did this," Ally says without a doubt.

"I did what now?"

"Obviously, you killed me, us, I dunno." Ally tenses up with frustration, unsure why Carson feels the need to feign ignorance, given their current predicament.

Carson snorts, sits back in his chair, and looks Ally dead in the eye.

"Why do you say that?"

"'Cause, I mean, why else would someone like you ask me out?"

"Excuse me?"

Ally motions to her body, pointing out bulges in her yellow summer dress she wishes weren't there. "Look at me," she gestures to Carson as he leans back on his seat, one arm up, letting his leather jacket sit open atop a muscle-fit, plain-white where it's not blood-splattered, t-shirt. "Look at you."

"What about me?" Carson knows where this is going, but she needs to say the words.

"You're beautiful, and I'm..." The indignant rage and confidence that lit Ally like a bonfire fades, leaving behind shy, insecure embers. "I'm me."

"And?"

Ally looks at the tables, at her fidgeting hands. "Boys like you don't like girls like me." A single crystal tear carves a line over her round cheek, pattering on the back of her hand. She jerks with fright as Carson's hand rests atop hers and she can't bring herself to look up.

"Look at me," Carson says, his voice calm and controlled now. "Please," he adds when Ally still refuses. Eventually, she finds the courage, and her eyes rise slowly over Carson. She meets his gaze and sees in it surprisingly gentle concern, not the wicked contempt she expected.

"You're beautiful," Carson says, and the words crack away at Ally's idea of herself.

"No, I'm not," she and the voice in her head say as one.

"You are." Carson's fingers lock with hers, and Ally finds herself squeezing.

"Bet you say that to all the girls." Ally wipes her eyes with her free hand.

"Just the ones who accuse me of murder," Carson jokes. That gets him a nervous laugh, and Ally grips his hand tighter. "Come on." Carson nods towards the arcade. "I got an idea."

"I don't know what's going on!" a very frustrated teen boy cries out as he forces more coins into the slot for an encased arcade shooter cabinet called Zoozie: Escape from GALEN-9. The outside looks like a retro 1950s-era rocketship with two curtains leading inside, where another kid sits, hands on a plastic raygun and ready to go.

"Come on, man, I wanna blast some ANTZ!" the kid inside whines, frustrated.

"Dude, I've put like five bucks in, and it's still not working!"

"Nuts to this." The second kid slams the blaster back down and storms out.

"Dude, wait!" The first runs after his buddy.

Neither of them notices, even if they could, the spectral form of Carson slipping out of the machine. He parts the curtain for Ally, earning confused glances from nearby patrons who only see the curtain move as though entirely on its own.

Ally takes a seat, lifting one of the plastic rayguns from its cradle as Carson hits the button for two players.

Suddenly there's an explosion on the screen, roaring from speakers by their heads, and a blonde girl with an eye patch and silver spacesuit crashes through the wall of some alien-looking prison.

"There you are!" she says right to the players. "The name's Zoozie, and I'm gonna get you outta here." She tosses two rayguns at the screen as a robotic dog yips at her heels. "Let's go!"

Lights flash across Carson and Ally's delighted faces as they lean this way and that, shooting at giant ant-like creatures that race at the screen.

It's just the kind of silly distraction they both need.

The curtain opens, and one over-excited kid's face turns chalk-white as his eyes land on a pair of plastic rayguns floating in the air, playing the game by themselves. "Mom!" he screams and runs away.

Ally and Carson pay no attention; they're too absorbed in the game. But as they're taken on an action-filled galactic ANT blasting ride on screen, their minds begin to wander.

"Haven't you wondered why, then?" Ally asks, though hesitant to spoil the mood again. She squints at the screen, eyes straining to see what's going on.

"I figure 'cause they're like evil space ants. I don't think this is one of those plot-heavy games, though," Carson teases.

"I mean, why we're stuck here. Who killed us?" Ally blurts out.

"Oh." Carson catches one mean-looking cyborg ant just before it munches on Ally's side of the screen. "No, not really."

"Why not?" Ally forgets to reload and takes a hit for her carelessness.

"I dunno," Carson shrugs, "I guess 'cause it's kinda fun spending every Friday night here with you. Though, yeah, maybe it would be nice to go somewhere else for a change." He smiles at a distant memory. "Just something like a picnic in the park, you know?"

His words stun Ally, she drops her raygun, and the screen flashes red with the words GAME OVER. CONTINUE?, it asks, as numbers count down to zero.

"How can you be this sweet, considering I just tried to murder you?"

Carson hangs up his raygun.

"It's not like you would have done that to me if I wasn't already dead, right?"

Ally hesitates for a little longer than seems right.

"No..."

"So that's how it is, then?" Carson gives Ally a devilish grin as she acts coy. "I don't think I can let that slide."

"Oh, sure, what are you gonna do about it?" she teases.

"This!" Carson jumps at her, hands going to either side of her body as he tickles. Ally squeals and snorts instantly, throwing her head back so hard it bonks on the booth—outside, the sound draws stares from those around the game.

"Not! Fair!" Ally manages to protest between gasps, and as she wrestles with Carson, they become dangerously entangled. Soon his hands aren't at her sides anymore, they're on her back, and his lips aren't curling with glee; they're pressed to hers.

"I can't believe we've been dead this long, and that's the first time you've kissed me," Ally says as they part.

"Yeah, well, trying to murder a guy will do strange things to him." Carson bushes his hair from his face and sits back.

"You're never gonna let me forget about that, are you?"

"Nope." Carson lowers his head as he takes her hand.

"I can't believe it doesn't bother you. Somebody killed us, Carson. Don't you want to know who?"

"No." Carson shakes his head. "Knowing who, it's not gonna help...it can't be undone, and it could make things worse."

"Worse? I don't see how."

"Say we find out who, then what? Not like we can call the cops. Leave a note? And what if...look, if it's that important to you, maybe we can figure it out."

"Yeah?"

Carson feels hope radiate from her. He knows it's a bad idea, but it makes her happy. How can he resist?

"Let's make a list of suspects?"

"Sounds like a plan." Ally smiles, and a voice from outside cuts off what she's about to say.

"Yo! Baby, how's about you bowl me over? Ha-ha!"

"Urgh, that guy!" Ally groans. "Like, who actually says ha-ha?"

"Wanna mess with him first?" Carson offers.

"I love how you think." Ally smiles, crawls across the booth, and kisses him.

A guy with slicked-back hair and a silk bowling shirt blows on his monogrammed ball while whispering sweet nothings to it. "Come on, sweetness, make daddy proud."

He does a funny little dance, skipping and hopping, then releases the ball down the lane.

Carson and Ally stand on either side, about halfway between the bowler and the pins. Invisible to everyone but each other, they watch as the ball rolls close, and as soon as it's in reach, Carson kicks it into the gutter.

"What the hell!?" the bowler yells in disbelief.

"There's the waitress," Carson points out. "The one who brought us the murder Cokes."

Ally sticks her tongue out.

"What about her?"

"Looked like she's been crying a lot. Maybe a guilty conscience?"

"Feels like a long shot." Ally watches the bowler line up another shot. He lets the ball fly; it rolls at speed, only for Ally to stop it dead. She allows it to sit there in the middle of the lane as the bowler stares slack-jawed.

"How's this—No!" he screams as Ally pushes the ball into the gutter with a giggle.

"I was thinking about the guy who got fired." Ally looks back to Carson. "I don't remember him being so miserable back on our first date. You know, the living one."

"Gives us two people to look into, but let's start with Alan," Carson suggests. "Something tells me he's not coming back."

"Good idea." Ally gestures for Carson to take a turn messing with the bowler, and a devilish smile spreads across his face. He follows the ball till it's just about to reach the pins, then kicks it so hard it leaps into the next lane. The ball makes a sharp sideways hop and scores a strike for the player one lane over.

"No!" The silk-shirted bowler drops to his knees, running his hands through his greasy hair as he pleads to the heavens above. "Why do you deny me my perfect game! Why!?"

"Let's go check out Alan." Carson holds his hand for Ally, and she takes it. They leave the bowler behind, crying on the sticky, soda-stained carpet.

Alan sits on a bench in the staff locker room, bent over, weeping into his hands.

It feels immediately wrong for them to be there, even though Alan can't see them.

"That doesn't seem like guilt to me," Carson whispers needlessly. "More like grief."

His phone sits on the bench next to him, screen lit with a photo of a couple—a much happier version of Alan with an equally delighted boy in each other's arms. There's a blue vignette frame around the image. At the top, it reads On This Day and below, One Year Ago.

Ally squeezes her eyes, trying to focus enough to make it out. "It's one of those auto anniversary post things."

"Look at the comments." Carson points to the visible few, and when Ally has trouble, he reads aloud. "Rest in peace; we miss you, Billy." Carson looks at the broken boy on the bench. "He lost someone, and it's just been thrown back in his face. Jeez." Carson reaches out to put a hand on Alan's shoulder, but it goes right through him.

"We should go." Ally suddenly feels very guilty for suspecting this boy. "Let's check out the waitress. This doesn't feel right."

"Yeah," Carson says, and even as they slip through the wall, he feels Alan's suffering stay with him. "Wait, we can't just leave him like this."

Ally turns to Carson. "But what can we do?"

Moments later, they're in the manager's office as he sits at his desk. Ally and Carson stand behind him as the glow from a spreadsheet lights his face.

"Distract him?" Carson asks, and Ally nods. She crosses the room and starts shaking framed photos and certificates on the opposite wall.

"What the heck?" The manager jumps and turns to the noise as folders fall from a shelf all on their own.

Carson leans down to the computer, passing right through the manager, and brings up the same profile Alan had open on his phone and scrolls through Alan's page as the manager cleans up Ally's mess. He quickly skips past the image of a roadside memorial and lands on the auto-generated memory post that's been tormenting Alan just as the manager returns.

"Now, how did..." the manager falls into stunned silence. "Oh..."

The ghosts of Ally and Carson follow him as he goes to the locker room, takes a seat beside Alan, and puts an arm around the boy's shoulder—pulling him in close.

"That was nice of you." Ally takes Carson's hand. "To help him like that."

"Nobody should be alone when they're hurting." Carson squeezes her hand back. "Come on, let's check out the next suspect."

It takes them some time to find her. Carson and Ally search all over Dreamland, but there's no sign of the waitress.

Braden: I bet it was Billy and Annie who did it.
Holly: Who're Billy and Annie?
Braden: The brother and sister who murder folks and make out from Char-Char's last story.
They weren't really—
Morgan: Ew, gross.
I swear to God, Braden, I'm gonna—anyway, Ally and Carson finally find Molly, the waitress, not inside Dreamland, but out. She...

...sits in her car, tears streaming down her face as she reads a book. The cover art shows a cute teenage couple surrounded by a horde of faceless, glowing-eyed shapes reaching for them menacingly.

"She's crying over a book." Carson facepalms.

"Hey." Ally slaps his arm, taking that personally. "I know that one." She notes how close Molly is to the end. "She must have just gotten to the bit where it looks like he had to—"

"Um, spoilers?"

"What? Why are you even? I mean, you don't look like you can read." Ally shoots him a smirk.

"You know, for someone who worries so much about what people think of their appearance, you do an awful lot of judging yourself."

"What do you mean?" Ally asks as they walk along the side of Dreamland.

It begins to rain, beating down on car roofs like thousands of pocket-sized drums, and puddles form in seconds, reflecting wavy stripes of pink and purple neon. It doesn't affect Carson and Ally.

"I miss the rain," Ally says with her hand out, letting it fall through her.

"Don't change the subject. You've made two judgments about who I am from how I look tonight," Carson explains as they watch teens run for shelter, using shirts as hoods and jumping into their cars. "The first was how a guy who looks like me couldn't like a girl who looks like you." He ponders that and adds, "without being some kind of killer."

"Yeah, well, guys who look like they could be shirtless outside an Abercrombie & Fitch don't usually want to date girls who shop at the plus-size store."

"Then it's their loss, 'cause you're awesome." Carson puts his arm around her, and Ally rests her head on his shoulder. "You know what the girls you think I would date say about how I look?"

"Yummy?" Ally looks up with a cheeky smirk.

"They say I'm not boyfriend material. I'm good for a fling, but not someone they want to get close with."

"Oh." Ally feels a pang of guilt. "I sort of get that. I mean, if you weren't dead, I'd be worried about every girl out there stealing you away."

"That's my point." He stops and takes Ally by the hand. "It's like all I am is my looks."

"You're just too pretty," Ally jokes.

"Shut up." Carson laughs. "There's more to me than being really-really-really ridiculously good-looking, you know?"

"Shut up and kiss me, Zoolander."

He does, and it feels like the world slows to a crawl. The rain pauses mid-fall, reflecting the lights from Dreamland like a sea of pink and blue stars.

"We still don't have any clue, though." Ally sighs with a hint of sorrow as the world kicks back into gear.

"How important is this to you?" Carson sighs, and Ally can sense there's something heavy weighing him down.

"You know, don't you?"

Carson slowly nods.

"How—"

"Let me show you." Carson takes her by the hand. He leads her to the far side of the parking lot, away from the heavy bass and neon lights. Toward a dark corner lit only by sealed, electric candles, to a roadside memorial with three framed photos.

Ally squints, focuses her eyes, and when she sees what's there, all she can manage to say is "Oh God..." and her hand flies to her mouth.

The first photo shows the teenager from Alan's memory post. The other two, Carson and Ally.

"It was raining like this..." Carson explains, and suddenly they're back in Ally's car, heading away after their first date.

The rain was so bad she offered Carson a ride home. She didn't bring her glasses, even though she needed them to drive. Too worried about looking like a nerd. Alan's boyfriend, the other driver, was texting. Not paying attention. If he wasn't...if Ally could have seen him coming in time...

Light floods Ally's car, blinding all, and the screech of brakes precedes the crunching of metal and shattering glass.

Carson looks at the third photo. Alan's boyfriend. "He hung on for a few days but, yeah. We died on the spot."

"Why!?" Ally beats Carson's chest to the rhythm of pouring rain. "It was my fault! Why didn't you tell me!?"

Carson catches her arm and pulls her into a hug. She fights, for a second, and then lets his arms wrap around her.

"Why didn't you tell me," Ally sobs.

"Because I was happy," he answers as he strokes her hair.

Ally looks up, eyes blurred with tears. "Happy?"

"Yeah, 'cause there's nowhere else I'd want to spend eternity than Dreamland." Carson smiles. "With you."

"And Date Night comes to an end at Dreamland, as it always should, with a kiss."

"Oh wow." Holly's jaw hangs open as she clutches at her heart. "Right in the feels, girl."

"Yeah, Chardea, I heard your story last year was awesome, but this." Morgan reaches under her mask to wipe away a tear. "Yeah."

"That was surprisingly less evil than your usual stuff, Char-Char." Braden puffs himself up, refusing to cry after the ribbing he took last year.

Chardea glances at Gwennie. "Even ghosts have hearts, and sometimes they deserve a happy ending," she explains and watches as the quiet little witch stands up to leave. "Gwen, I wrote that one for you," Chardea calls after her.

Without turning her back, Gwennie says, "You didn't need to."

"I wanted to." Chardea approaches, reaching out, but Gwennie moves away. "You don't have to be alone."

Gwennie smiles, a sad and weary one that signals a bitter truth. "Sooner or later, we're all alone."

"Gwen, I—"

A violent rustling in The Dark disturbs them; something's coming towards the clearing at speed. Something big.

"What the hell is that?" Braden panics.

"Derek?" Chardea hopes.

A figure breaks from the treeline, stepping into the light—easily taller than the others yet with a sweet boyish face, albeit one covered with sweat, hair plastered to his forehead. He's soaked from head to toe, but that's not what causes the five of them to stare in slack-jawed terror.

It's the small, lifeless shape of a Dachshund cradled in his arms—his little pink tongue hanging to the side.

"Can you help us, please?" the tall English boy asks desperately, "I just found this little guy like this in the forest."

"Rascal!?" Chardea gasps.

Roll credits.

Episode Two

You can sense it, right? There's something amiss, and not just the children's waylaid leader. The leaves that fall from trees this year bring not the smirk of mischief but a sense of dread. Oh, there is a joy to be found as the nights stretch out like gnarled fingers beneath your bed, but it does not belong to you anymore. Something stirs in The Dark, something hungry...

A tiny German Spitz cowers in the corner of its kennel, quivering in gawk-eyed horror at an encroaching, terrible fate. The metal door rattles open, the Spitz's tormentor silhouetted by a harsh strip of fluorescent lights leading down the corridor.

"There you are," the human says, and though the name badge on her fleece reads Rox to the terrified Spitz, it might as well say The Devil.

"It's bath time, little one," Rox says in a sweet voice as she scoops the little dog up. The Spitz knows that the human's kindness is a lie.

Rox sniffs the dog, and her face instantly screws as she gags. "Have you been rolling in poop?"

And what of it, the Spitz thinks with furious indignation, *I've seen you pick your nose, you disgusting human. Now, unhand me or suffer the consequences!*

Rox carries the Spitz along the hall, halting suddenly when she senses one dog staring at her...unnaturally. Glancing to the side, Rox sets eyes on a black, red-eyed Chihuahua sitting upright, staring like she knows the effect she's having.

Why have you halted, human? Do not leave me near the wampir!

"W-what's up?" Rox says to the Chihuahua, who only stares in response. Shaking it off, Rox continues with her work.

Water gushes from the head of a sink shower, pouring over the less than amused Spitz, turning its lustrous floof into sharply pointed, enraged fur spikes. Rox hums along to the radio, unaffected by the Spitz's death glares.

Suddenly the lights and music cut out, making Rox jump and splash herself.

Ha! No more than you deserve!

"Seriously," Rox groans and then puts her face dangerously close to the Spitz. "Don't go anywhere, little one; I'll see what's up."

As soon as Rox disappears, the Spitz clambers out of the sink, shakes as though they'll never be dry again, and begins to tippy-tap their way back to their bed. It comes to a halt as it comes to the kennel corridor, bares its teeth and all that follows is a yelp.

Rox returns to the grooming station moments later, still perplexed, though now the mystery of a vanishing Spitz has been added to her worries.

"Little one!?" Rox calls and shines the light from a flashlight in search. The beam lands on tiny wet paw prints leading to the kennels, and Rox follows them.

As Rox steps into the corridor, something clatters to the floor behind her. She shrieks, turning and sweeping the light beam around erratically. A sigh of relief escapes her lips, and her hand goes to her heart as Rox spots a pet carrier lying on the floor. Something must have knocked it over. Just before Rox can begin to wonder what that something might be, a clattering from the kennels makes her jump again.

This time the light lands on a kennel door, creaking open, and a trail of blood leads within.

"What in the?" Rox races to the door, flush with concern that one of the dogs has injured itself in the dark; only when she comes to the kennel, she doesn't find one dog. She finds four.

The soaking wet Spitz, a Yorkshire Terrier, and a Pug all sit facing the fourth, heads bowed toward the red-eyed Chihuahua. Each of them with seeping puncture marks on their neck.

The Chihuahua's eyes glow, burning in the dark, glinting off her shiny black tag that reads: Carmilla. She shows her fangs, unlike any canine teeth Rox has ever seen. Too big for her little head, the kind you'd expect to see on a large jungle cat. The other three dogs turn baring teeth and put themselves between the human and their new master.

Then, with a low growl from Carmilla, they attack...

"And?" Braden begs for more, literally on the edge of his seat, but Holly freezes up.

"And, I got nothin'." Holly's whole body drops in defeat. "Telling stories is hard!"

"Yeah," Morgan agrees. "I liked where it was going. A vampire Chihuahua." She looks right at Holly. "So cute!"

Leaves crunch as another approaches the Hallow Fire, and the others turn to watch the new boy appear from The Dark, ducking under a branch. Now that he's not drenched in sweat and has his hair brushed back, he looks considerably more presentable but no less awkward.

"Hello." He takes one hand out of his pocket and gives a low-energy wave.

"'Sup, Toby." Braden nods.

"Wait!" Chardea yells from The Dark. "Slow down, or you'll make it worse!"

Rascal barges through the treeline, hobbling with a limp, ears fluttering behind him as the Dachshund races to the clearing.

"Rascallion!" Braden drops to his knees and holds his arms in the air. Rascal hurls himself at him like a furry missile, propelling Braden onto his back with the impact.

"Don't encourage him!" Chardea finally catches up. "He's supposed to be resting."

"Tell him that," Braden protests as he rubs behind the dog's ears.

Suddenly, Racal realizes there's a new person next to Braden and stares at her with a tilted head.

"Heya, little doggie." Holly smiles.

Racal considers the stranger, sniffing the air. He uses Braden's stomach as a trampoline, making the boy oof as the dog hurls himself at the new girl. He covers her exposed face with licks within seconds and Holly giggles.

Seeing the new boy shifting uncomfortably with his hands in his pockets, Chardea goes to him.

"Thank you again, Toby." She casts a glance at the others. Morgan and Braden crowd around Holly as she plays with Rascal. "I don't know what we'd do without him." And the thought of what's become of Derek lingers, unspoken.

"Quite alright. Honestly, I didn't do anything. One second I'm...then there's this wounded little dog. What was I supposed to do?" Toby takes a seat, his knees poking up like spindly mountains.

"How are you dealing with, you know, knowing you're—"

"Dead?" Toby nods and stares into the Hallow Fire. "It's a lot to wrap your head around, isn't it?"

"I'm here; we all are if you need to talk," Chardea offers, and her words trail away as she watches Gwennie approach. "Excuse me," she says and heads to the girl before Toby can react. "Hey, Gwennie, you okay?"

"I'm fine," Gwennie says coldly and heads to her seat.

"You know you don't have to be," Chardea reaches out.

"I'm fine, Chardea," Gwennie insists with an eerie calmness. "I just don't wanna talk, is all. Can't we just do the story and have a good time, like we're supposed to?"

"You don't seem like you're having a good time, Gwen."

"Look, I'm sick of being poor Gwennie. Everyone treats me like I'm made of glass. My boyfriend left. Not the worst thing to happen to me, now, is it?"

But it feels like it is, though, right? Chardea thinks but leaves the words unsaid. There's nothing she can do other than make sure the girl knows she has a friend waiting for her when the time comes.

The five of them take their seats, with Rascal claiming half of Holly's, resting his head on her lap. They all look to Chardea, to the empty throne she stands before.

Chardea looks to The Dark, praying for a sign from Derek.

"Any word from the boss man?" Braden pipes up and forces Chardea to make a decision.

"Yeah," she says under her breath. "Yeah," louder, this time, with forced confidence. "Something came up; he didn't say much but said to go ahead without him for now."

"The boss man?" Toby asks as it occurs to Chardea that neither he nor Holly have met their true leader.

"D-Man, The Derek," Braden explains. "He's cool; you'll like him."

"Any friend of Braden's gotta be cool," Holly adds, and Chardea can't help but notice how she leans towards the boy. She's so complementary to him; does she like him? Chardea doesn't know what's worse. The mental image of those two together, or figuring out why she hates the idea so much. Instead, Chardea puts her focus on trying to fill Derek's absentee chair.

"Welcome, everyone, to The October Society." Chardea takes her seat. "Are you ready, Holly?"

"No!" Holly buries her head in her hands. "I'm so sorry! I've been trying to come up with a story, but all I got is ideas. None of it flows. I thought I did; then you did that killer ghost story last week. I mean, I can't do anything as cool as that."

"It's okay," Chardea reassures her. "Feels like the rules are out the window anyway, so take your time."

"Thanks, Chardea," Holly smiles. "I swear I'll be ready next week."

"Just tell your story. A Holly story. If we all told them the same way, things would get boring pretty fast."

"Gotcha, boss." Holly gives a cheek-straining grin and a thumbs up, but that word fills Chardea with dread.

"Is anyone else ready to—oh no." Chardea's face sinks as Braden's hand shoots up.

"It's cool, Holls; I got ya covered." Braden turns his palm to Holly, who high-fives it without looking. It's so gracefully cute that Chardea wants to throw up.

"I've been dying to hear one of Braden's," Morgan says excitedly, leaning forward. "Dino said they were always full of fart jokes."

Gwennie tenses up at the sound of her ex's name.

Braden wags his fingers like a frustrated teacher trying not to swear. "That's just plain untrue," he says calmly and then turns to Toby. "Tobias, new friend, you may hear some scandalous rumors to the contrary, but despite the lies spread by who I suspect truly began this whole thing." Braden fixes a pretend tie. "I DID NOT START THE FART WAR!"

"Noted." Toby nods.

Rascal harrumphs like he's fed up. Like he has something to hide...

"Truth is a tricky thing," Braden nods to Chardea. She whips the black book to him. Braden catches it and holds it to his chest. "Sometimes, it's obvious. Sometimes you gotta hold on to what you know is true even when the world says it's not. My October dudes and dudettes, it's movie night." The Hallow Fire rages, feeding on Braden's words, "So grab some popcorn, sit your butts down, and behold…"

The Reel Midnight Spookshow

In the middle of the night, rain taps against a small bedroom window like it wants to be let in. Distorted light from a street lamp wavers through a windowpane streaming with water and paints the room in shades of orange and blue. The colors shift over walls covered in posters from animated movies. A haughty cartoon llama struts his stuff on one, while Woody throws bunny ears up behind Buzz Lightyear on another.

Violet couldn't sleep. She's always had trouble sleeping, and while her mom thought it was 'cause she was afraid of the dark—

Chardea: Like Braden—

REALLY it was 'cause she was a night owl like her dad. He was always up all night, in the den, watching things Violet's mom wouldn't let her see...

Violet hurls a glance at her door. Flickering light flashes sporadically in the gap below.

Deciding she's had enough and needs to know the big deal about her dad's movies, Violet throws her sheets down and jumps out of bed. She grabs a bow and quickly ties up her messy hair, not caring that it sits at a weird angle.

Violet edges along a dark hall, heading towards a staircase lit with scattered blasts of light. She moves carefully along the runner, avoiding setting foot on any exposed floor that'll give her away. As she reaches her parents' bedroom, she pauses, then peeks through the cracked door.

Her mother lies on her back, snoring gently, eyes covered with a cooling face mask. The other side of the bed is empty, as if the light and muted sounds from downstairs weren't enough to tell Violet her father was still up.

Violet moves on, and just as she reaches the top of the stairs, she ducks as a woman's scream slices through the midnight silence. She glances back to the bedroom, hoping the sound doesn't wake her mom, as spooky voices laugh over another.

"Shoot!" Violet can hear her father grumble. "Where is it?"

"The ghosts are moving tonight. Restless, hungry..." the disembodied voice of a scared man intones, the volume fading with each syllable.

Violet listens for any sign of her mom stirring, and when nothing happens, she lets herself breathe. She continues, going down three steps, and sits down gently as flickering lights dance through the gaps in the wooden railings.

She presses her face between them and watches as a mustached man with the voice of midnight itself promises there will be "Food and ghosts and murders." A funeral car line snakes around a gloomy, wet road on her dad's widescreen TV.

The angle Violet has isn't the best, but to take another step down would mean risking the creaky board. The one that her dad has promised to fix a gazillion times; one that chooses when it wants to creak, and usually when it's most inconvenient.

She watches for a bit, but eventually, Violet decides to chance a better view.

Dipping one toe on the next step, like testing out a steaming bath, Violet squeezes her eyes and clenches her teeth as...nothing. She puts her whole foot down to silence, save for the thundering of her heart, and the success brings confidence.

Something's happening in the movie; the strangers trapped in the haunted house are in a basement, and Violet's eyes are drawn to it as she stands mid-stride. Her eyes search every gloomy corner, each crooked shadow, until—the gnarled face of a twisted woman lurches from the dark, and Violet screams. Hands fly to her mouth, too late, as the bowl of popcorn on the balding man's lap below flies in the air.

"Violet!?" he hisses, hushed but firm. "It's past your bedtime!"

"I know." Violet glances back at the top of the staircase—nothing. "I just wanna see what you're watching, dad."

Her dad thinks about it for a moment. He picks some popcorn out of his beard and puts it in his mouth. "Did your mom wake up?"

"No," Violet whispers. "I don't think so..."

"Well, get your butt down here before she does."

Giggling, Violet races down the stairs and clambers over the back of the sofa, plopping herself down next to her dad. "What are you watching?"

"It's called *House on Haunted Hill*—"

"Is it about a house?" Violet helps herself to some popcorn, shoving a handful into her mouth, with most of it spilling onto the sofa. "That's haunted? On a hill?"

"You got your mother's attitude, that's for sure," Violet's dad complains and earns himself a funny face in response. "It's about a rich guy who says he'll pay these people fifty-thousand dollars to spend the night in a haunted house."

"Cool," Violet says through vigorous munching. "Would you spend the night in a haunted house for fifty-thousand?"

"Sweetie," Violet's dad says as he scoops up some popcorn, "I'd pay that much to spend the night in a haunted house. If I had it. And if they were real."

Violet throws a handful of popcorn at her dad and then cuddles in. He fixes the bow on her hair, which always makes her smile, then they settle down and watch the rest of the movie together.

It became a tradition for them. Violet and her dad would wait till her mom was asleep, then creep down to the den. Like ninjas. They called it their Midnight Spookshow.

Her dad ran a video rental store, so they had a never-ending source of spooky movies to watch. They'd watch all the great oldies over the years. The Haunting, 13 Ghosts, The Old Dark House, THEM, Invasion of the Body Snatchers. Then, one day, a few years later...

Violet, now around ten years old, rides her bike through the streets of a pretty, postcard-perfect lakeside town. Leaves fall all around, carpeting the road with orange and brown that kicks up in waves as Violet tears through. She whips past a memorial under construction, standing on top of the lake itself, and nearly collides with a portly man in a firmly pressed shirt buttoned to the neck.

"Sorry, Mister Wallace!" Violet waves without slowing down. The gentle, balding man just smiles and waves back.

Her bike skids to a halt outside a video rental store in a strip mall, the wheels still spinning as Violet crashes through the door, desperate to see her dad.

Violet's dad had a lot of friends who hooked him up with cool things. Like studio copies of movies before they were out or bootlegs. He'd told her his contact in Hollywood got him something special, and she couldn't wait to see it.

"Is it here?" Violet yells as she leaps on the desk, suddenly realizing there's no sign of anyone. "Dad?"

Violet hops over into the back and heads for her dad's office. Inside, she finds no one, only an empty projector, repeatedly clicking—blasting a square of grainy light onto the wall.

"Dad!?" Violet calls again, and still nothing but silence.

Violet sat in the store for hours, waiting for her dad, but he never showed up. Eventually, she went home, and her mom called the police. They searched for days, but nobody could find any sign of him. People began to whisper and spread rumors. They said he ran away.

Violet refused to believe that. Something must have happened. She hung onto the love she had for her dad, even when all Violet had to remember him by were the movies they loved and the bow he would always have to fix for her.

Her mom couldn't afford to stay in Cherry Lake, not after the store went under, so they moved to a tiny apartment in Redcastle Heights.

Violet's mom sits at an uneven kitchen table, swamped in papers stamped with bold, angry red words. She sips from a cold mug of coffee and winces, biting down on the cold bitterness rather than wasting what's in the cup.

The apartment door opens and Violet comes through, a few years older but still with the big bow on her head.

"'Sup mom," Violet says, dumping her bag and climbing into a chair opposite her mom. The lack of response makes Violet squint and pluck the bill from her mom's hand.

"Damn it, Vi, you startled me!"

"Seriously, mom, woah." Violet's eyes pop at what she sees on the bill. "That's a lotta cheese."

"Funny." Violet's mom snatches the letter back. "If we don't work something out soon, we'll have to catch and eat those mice."

"Not Edgar and Lenore!" Violet gasps mockingly.

"Quoth this fed-up mother," Violet's mom groans, "nevermore!" And she sends all the bills scattering in a frustrated flurry.

"Yeah, mom! Make it rain!"

"The rain will be coming through the roof soon enough if we don't do something," she says, slumping to the table in a mess of tangled hair. "If only your father left behind something more useful than a movie collection when he ran off—"

"Dad didn't run away," Violet states with absolute confidence.

"Vi—"

"He didn't." Violet holds her ground. "And those movies were his treasures."

"Yeah...speaking of, I saw an ad for a movie memorabilia store—"

"No." Violet does not like where this is going, not one bit. "No."

"We don't even have a projector to watch the damn things, Vi, and we need the money."

"No!" Violet kicks her chair out, jumps down, and runs till she slams her bedroom door closed. She throws herself down on a bed, below a poster of Vincent Price with his arms crossed, the shadow of a bat looming behind, and cries into her pillow.

"Why do you like these movies so much?"

Violet's six years old again, on the sofa with her dad.

A man on the screen puts on strange glasses, and he's shocked to see a ghost through the rectangular lenses.

"Mom says you," Violet searches for the words, "like living in the past, and it's not healthy."

"Yeah, and your mom's favorite movie is *Back to the Future*. Something from the 80s that goes back to the 50s. I like movies from back then 'cause they're just fun. Nothing fancy, just pure spooky delights." Violet's dad hugs her tight. "Anyway, why would I want to live in the past when I got my own little Gremlin right here, in the present?" He kisses her on the forehead and fixes the bow. "Besides, it's not the movies that are special."

"No?"

"No, Sweetie, it's who you watch them with."

Violet sighs.

She clutches a box marked Dad's Stuff on a grimy, slushy street. She tells herself that her mom wouldn't know what half this stuff is worth, and that it's what dad would want. It doesn't make it feel any better.

Violet looks up at the sign, Hardy's Movie Memorabilia. The artwork and design faded, badly needing a touch-up, though the same can be said for the whole neighborhood. She thought their apartment was in a dump, but this part of town makes her feel like she's wandered into a place festering with sorrow.

Taking a deep breath, Violet pushes her way into the store with her butt, a tired bell clanging as the door opens.

"Hello?" Violet's voice carries through an empty storefront. To her right, the wall is covered in framed posters. Old hand-painted ones showing sharp-eyed detectives and beautiful women brush up against ones for movies like *Batman Returns*, covered in silver-scrawled signatures. On the left, there's a glass counter, lit up and displaying all sorts of oddities—from cracked fingerless gloves next to a photo of Bruce Lee to an assortment of different rayguns. The room smells of dust and history, a scent her dad once called the aroma of vintage—whatever that means. One thing's for sure, Violet's dad would have loved this place.

"Hey kid," a tall, too-thin man says as he parts through some beads that lead into the back. There are deep, black shadows under his eyes framed with unwashed hair. He wears a stained t-shirt with a cowboy saying: I'm your Huckleberry.

"Hey, um, the sign out front says you buy movie stuff?" Violet shakes the box. "These were my dad's and...I don't wanna but—"

"I get it," the man says. "More than you know, kid. This is my shop, and I never sell anything. These are like," he gestures to merchandise, "my treasures. But I got a pair of kids myself; daughter's just about your age. I know how it is."

"You're Hardy?" Violet wonders if her dad would have become like this man if he was still around. He seems nice enough, but there's a sadness. Like his collection's trying to fill a gap, and it's only getting wider the more he pours in.

"Yep." He pats the counter. "Let's see what you got."

Violet puts the box down and winces as Hardy starts going through it.

"Can't give you much for these, I'm afraid," he says, stacking a small tower of VHS tapes. "Nobody wants tapes anymore. Maybe give you five bucks each for the bootlegs, though, just for my curiosity." He takes out a stack of 8mm film reels next. "This looks like a home movie."

"Really?" The lowball offer doesn't sting as much as knowing the things her dad cherished amounts to so little.

"Sorry, kiddo, I ain't being stingy, it's just—well now, what's this..." Hardy lifts out a film canister with a handwritten label—The Red Frame.

"What is it?" Violet stands on tiptoes to see.

"No way." Hardy trembles ever so slightly. "Can't be."

"What!?" Violet snaps.

"You ever heard of Theo Gorman, kiddo?" Hardy asks.

"Uh, yeah, I think my dad was trying to get ahold of his movies."

"If your dad did, and this reel is legit, then hoo-boy, is it a find."

"His movies any good?"

"Nobody knows, kiddo." Hardy examines the tape. "He made three movies back in the 40s and 50s, then vanished. The story goes, he murdered the cast and crew of his first movie. *The Red Frame* was his last movie. Some people say it was secretly a dramatized confession."

"Really?" Violet's eyes fill with macabre glee. "Cool."

"Yeah, folks say he put framed photos of all his victims in the background of this one, and that's the real meaning of the title. Though no one knows for sure. His studio went up in flames with him and every original copy of his work inside."

"Awesomesauce!" Violet's almost bouncing now.

"You say you've never seen it?"

"Um, no, that one just arrived before my dad...before he left. We never got the chance."

Hardy sees the sudden gloom spread across Violet's face. Maybe it's the bow on her head making her look younger than she is, or knowing how he'd feel if he missed out on something with his kids, but his heart breaks for her.

"We don't even have a projector anymore, so I can't watch it at home."

"Damn...look, kid, as much as I want this, I can't do that to you."

"But, we need the money..."

"Tell you what, you agree to sell this to me once you've seen it, let's say two hundred—"

"Two hundred!"

"Fine, two-fifty!" Violet almost faints at Hardy's offer. "I'll front you a projector you can use to watch it. Deal?" Hardy holds out a pasty, stick-thin hand that Violet doesn't hesitate to shake for a moment, and even his gross, cold sweat doesn't kill her buzz.

Violet wastes no time hooking up the dusty, chunky projector Hardy gave her when she gets home. She's so excited she doesn't hear her mom come up behind her.

"What is that, Vi?" Violet jumps and yips at the sound of her mom's voice. She notices the box next to Violet. "You said you were going to sell those."

"Yeah, look, mom." Violet holds up the copy of *The Red Frame*. "This is a super-rare old movie, and Mister Hardy says I can watch it before he buys it."

"Really?"

"Yeah, he's gonna give us two-fifty minus the cost of the projector."

"Really? And you don't think this scummy Mister Hardy hasn't just tricked you into buying an old, probably broken machine?"

"That's not—"

"I don't want to hear it, Vi."

"You never listen!" Violet throws the reel down. "About the movies, about what happened to dad, you just made up your mind, and that's it!"

"It's called being an adult, Vi!" Violet's mom glances at her watch. "I'm gonna be late for my shift. Pack all this up, and we'll have words with Mister Hardy in the morning." She storms off, slamming the door as a tear leaks from Violet's eye.

"Way to prove my point," Violet growls and goes about hooking up the machine with furious resentment.

Once it's ready to go and her mom's long gone, Violet reaches for the reels. Instead of putting on *The Red Frame*, though, she loads the one Hardy said looked like a home movie into the projector and puts some Jiffy Pop on the stove.

As images of her mom and dad, much younger than seems possible, fill the screen, Violet finds another tear carving a path down her cheek—one she doesn't bother to wipe away. She laughs at a tiny version of herself, covered in food with a way-too-big bow on her head. Her dad struggles to fix it while baby Violet hurls gloopy baby food at him.

The video then cuts awkwardly, as though someone taped over the original to what looks like a construction site in the woods. Off to one side, a teenage boy, dressed in black, stands beside a punk girl with dyed hair. They watch as another boy, a little chunky, fidgets with something on a table, and then suddenly, the screen's filled with wild red hair and the cockiest grin Violet's ever seen.

"'Sup folks, the name's Caleb, and welcome to The Real World: Cherry Lake edition! We got," he points the camera at the boy by the table, "Mikey making something that'll blow y'all away and," the shot pivots to the other two, "Vinne tryin' his bestest not to fall madly in love with Casey. I give them about a week."

The boy in black turns, curious about something, and his face fills with horror as he realizes they're on camera. He taps the girl beside him, and they both sprint over.

"Caleb, you moron! You can't film this!"

The boy behind the camera snickers. "That's not what your—hey!" They wrestle for the camera, and then it suddenly cuts back to baby Violet flinging food across a kitchen. She has no clue who those other four were, but they seemed like a lot of fun.

"Okay." Violet fishes out *The Red Frame*. "Time for the main attraction," she says with nervous excitement and loads it up. Her Jiffy Pop reaches a crescendo, and she snags it from the stove before it catches fire.

Leaping down onto the sofa with a steaming hot bowl in her lap, she flicks play on the projector, balancing on a stack of angled books behind her. She shoves a thick handful of popcorn into her mouth, most of it spilling back into the bowl as the movie begins, like all the old ones do, with the credits.

She doesn't recognize any of the names besides Theodore Gorman, and that's only because of what Hardy said earlier.

The title card appears, a slanted antique frame with *The Red Frame* written in ornate handwriting.

Violet munches more popcorn as the image fades to a grainy night shot of a Southern Californian mansion sitting on a lonely hill.

"I suppose you can take this as a confession of sorts. In many ways, it is. As a film director, I've killed a lot of people. As a man, even more..."

Spoken by a disembodied voice, those words send a chill down Violet's spine. One that not even piping hot popcorn can combat. It's so creepy, she begins to feel all the warmth sapped from her body; even looking at her arm, she seems to grow paler by the second. Violet watches as both her arms turn pure white, as whatever it is spreads up her body, sucking the color from her clothes.

"I'd like to invite you to come, see the world as I do—picture it through a blood-red frame."

Violet stares at the screen and feels it rush to her. Or she to it, either way, her vision blurs to black and white, then beyond as she's pulled in through the screen.

Moments later, her mom comes back through the door.

"Forgot my purse, gonna be so late. Vi?" Violet's mom halts with confusion at no sign of her daughter. Just an old movie on the TV and a spilled bowl of popcorn on the sofa.

"Vi?" she calls out, checking the apartment with no success. "Vi?" Her voice wavers, fear creeping in.

We'll Be Right Back After These Messages...

"Breaking news in the hunt for missing reporter Jackie Torrance," a news anchor reads as the ticker below repeats the headline. "Shocking footage has emerged from a diner outside Redcastle. Viewer discretion is advised."

The feed cuts to a black-and-white shot of a diner; near the back, a tall, bearded man in a trucker cap sits across from a slight woman with a hood pulled up. Both seem tense.

Two people, with nothing noteworthy about them, approach the pair separately and then fall in synch. One blocks the trucker from view as his arms rise, and the other drags the woman away, kicking.

Once she's out of shot, the other man turns his head for a second, and the trucker decks him, bounding from his table in pursuit.

"We believe this to be missing reporter Jackie Torrance, now wanted for questioning as a suspect in an arson and homicide case." The shot returns to the pair sitting down, and it's put up beside a photo of Jackie and a police sketch of the trucker. "If anyone recognizes this man, please contact the police at the number shown below."

"IT'S KARNAGE!" an exhilarated announcer yells over a still, drawn image of three monstrous animals. "WE GOT RAKOON THE TRASHER!" The shot zooms to a snarling bipedal raccoon ripping a building in half. "CORGO THE DESTROYER!" he screams as the camera pans to a stumpy-legged giant corgi crushing a bus with its fluffy butt. "AND JEFF THE MONGOOSE!" The shot zips to an angry mongoose with an eye patch, speech bubble by its head filled with censored expletives. "AND IT'S SHOWDOWN TIME!"

Cut to: gameplay footage of the three monsters beating up one another and wrecking a 2D city as they go about it.

"SMASH A SKYSCRAPER! CRUSH A CAR! DESTROY DOWNTOWN IN KARNAGE! FROM MONSTERSCOPE GAMES! ONLY IN ARCADES THIS FALL!"

"This week on *Secret Histories*—did man actually meet monster?" a raspy British voice says over dusty bones and an excavation site. "Have we finally found evidence that man and dinosaur existed at the same time?" It appears as though the bones of a raptor are fighting a humanoid shape wielding a curved sword.

"Or is this just an elaborate hoax?" The time and date for the episode stream across the runner at the bottom of the screen. "Tune in and find out, this week, on *Secret Histories*."

We Now Return To The October Society.

"Is this going anywhere, Braden?" Chardea complains.

"It's called setting a mood and establishing characters, Char-Char," Braden snarks back.

"No, it's called spinning your wheels while you make it up on the spot."

"Well, if that's what he's doing, it's kinda impressive, to be honest," Morgan points out.

"Yeah, totally!" Holly agrees.

"I rather like the concept," Toby adds. "I'm to take it Violet's going to be trapped inside a film?"

"Looks that way, don't it?" Braden leans forward. "Question is, who or what is trapped there with her? Violet..."

...opens her eyes to find herself on the floor of a small theater, three sets of comfortable armchairs in rows, rising toward the back of the room, with a glowing white light behind her.

Violet turns to see her apartment on the screen, the only color in the entire room.

"What's going on?" She reaches for home, only for the image to vanish. The room plunges into darkness, lit only by small lights above two sets of steps, and the empty clicking of a projector fills the silence.

She follows the lights and pushes through a heavy door into a lit hallway. Rain rattles against the window to her right. When Violet looks, it seems as though the rain's not falling, but sprayed on the glass from just above. The garden visible beyond looks too flat—like it's all made from painted wood. No colors, just black, white, and every shade of gray.

Heading the only way she can, Violet jumps as she passes a floor-to-ceiling, ornate framed mirror—she doesn't recognize the girl reflected within. It looks like her in the face, and with an even more elaborate bow pinning her hair up, but Violet would never wear a dress. Especially one so cheesy. She looks like a little sailor scout, complete with shiny buckle shoes, making her want to gag. It's enough to distract her from the feeling that she's not the only one looking through that mirror.

Continuing, Violet finds her way to a grand staircase leading down to a pillared stone vestibule, and a sudden infusion of color into this dark world steals her breath. Scattered across the walls are framed portraits, none the same size, and each hung in a red frame. The color is so vibrant against the grayscale it seems to pulse, and they only get more disturbing as Violet investigates.

Each portrait is of a different person—men in slick suits, coats, tails, and hats—women in gowns, dresses, and finery. Faces scored out in each of them, torn and slashed angrily with something sharp. Some of them are signed, names like Sylvester Jackson and Temperance Calloway—people she's never heard of but sound like old movie stars.

The final red-framed portrait unsettles Violet the most. Hanging at the bottom of the stairs, it's the only one not ravaged by a blade. Instead, it's too blurry to make out. Like an underdeveloped photo, but even so, the stupid dress the girl's wearing in it is very familiar.

She's still reeling from that weirdness when Violet passes another still face, though this one's neither framed in red nor crossed out. This one blinks.

Violet jumps back so far that she falls over the arm of a leather sofa, landing on firm cushions that have never been worn in—like the rest of the house, it looks old, yet it all feels hollow. The cobwebs on the chandelier above are so thick and heavy, yet there's no sign of dust or neglect elsewhere—it's all for effect. Antique by design.

As Violet recovers, she realizes it wasn't a picture that blinked—whatever it is she doesn't want to call alive, but it's moving from the shadows, stepping into the light. It moves with rasping breaths and an unblinking ravenous glare. Eyes like black, sunken hollows with thin strands of scraggly hair atop a wrinkled dome.

"S-sorry."

Violet scrambles and puts a tall-backed armchair between her and the strange hunch-backed man shuffling toward her.

"I didn't mean to break into your house or nothin', Mister."

The creature groans, its mouth a crooked gap of rotten teeth and blackened gums that a spider crawls from, skittering over its face.

Violet gags and tries to stop herself from dry-heaving. She hates spiders; her dad used to tease her by pretending to eat them, and it's like this thing knows. This house knows. She can feel eyes on her, as though there's a silent audience watching on the edge of their seats.

"*Jeepers*!" Violet blurts. She turns and runs for it.

The creature gawks as though this shouldn't happen. As though it expected the girl to stay there, screaming till it reached her and put its pallid hands around her throat. A sudden compulsion, a command to chase, takes over, and the creature obeys.

Violet pounds through a long, twisting corridor, tearing past mounted busts that seem to turn and follow.

The hideous caricature of a man, the sunken-eyed mockery of a human being, lurches after her with a lumbering gait. It reaches out to her, almost as though pleading for Violet to stop.

There's no way she's going to listen to this thing, and instead bashes through the closest door, quickly wedging a chair against it to keep the creature out. It bangs, rattles the handle, and roars something that sounds like "No!" but in an indecipherable, inhuman gargle.

With a moment to catch her breath, Violet notices two things. The first is that this room's almost pitch-dark, save for a feeble lamp that barely punctures the gloom, and the second—she's not alone.

Someone is sitting in a chair in the middle of the room.

As Violet creeps closer and the creature's assault on the door intensifies, she realizes this person is tied to their chair. Was the monster beyond the door saving them for later?

"Hey, you okay?" Violet asks with no response besides a desperate struggle. "Don't worry; I got you." She runs over as the monster roars and begins working at the prisoner's bonds. They're so tall that Violet only comes up to their chest, so she starts at their feet, pulling on bow-like knots till they give. Then its arms—Violet frees one, and as soon as the second comes undone, the prisoner rises with such suddenness she's thrown back into a nearby table. The lamp falls to the floor, shining like a spotlight on the prisoner as they rise to their feet.

"What in the *jeepers*!?"

From its feet up, it appears as a tall, thin man in a work shirt with a pocketed vest stuffed with all sorts of lenses and gadgets, but where his head should be, there's just a chunky, gray camera. Machine and flesh stitched together painfully. A single, long flashlight-shaped lens moves and twists on its own, bringing Violet's cowering form into focus. It flickers to life, sputtering a beam of light that holds steady after a moment, and the reels spin. The Cameraman records Violet as she crawls away, looming over her with its elongated, skeletal frame, zooming in with its single-lens eye.

A voice comes from everywhere and nowhere, all at once. "Die for me."

"*Jeepers*!" Violet kicks the Cameraman in its knee—it feels more like booting a metal frame than flesh and bone, but the thing's at least part human. It can't cry out in pain, but it still goes down. Violet takes the opportunity to scramble past it, gets to her feet, and books it to an adjacent door.

Crashing into another hall, Violet runs past more mirrors, feeling the eyes of the imaginary audience upon her grow hungry—like dogs drooling over some raw meat. Only the reappearance of the hollow-eyed creature takes that chill away.

"Darn it!" Violet skids to a halt, quickly turning and doubling back to find the Cameraman in her path. "'Course, Vi, you've only gone and made a rookie horror movie mistake." She berates herself as both monsters close in. "'Least you didn't hide in the bathroom." Though she'd take that, there aren't any doors between her and either of the approaching nightmares. Just a small wooden panel on one wall.

Nothing else for it; Violet chances it and yanks open the panel.

"Yes!"

She hits the lowest of three buttons next to the dumbwaiter and climbs in as it begins to descend. Just before the hallway slips from view, the Cameraman reaches the hole and watches—eye-lens twisting to focus.

"The heck is going on in this place." Violet tries to wrap her head around what she's seen. Before any ideas can begin to form, she hears a metallic twang from above—almost as though on cue. "*Jeepers*," she quips as a second twang echoes through the shaft, and then the wooden box rockets down, untethered and unstoppable.

Violet crashes hard and crumples out the portal in a flurry of shattered wood, colliding with heavy hessian sacks that both break her fall and tumble on top of her, pinning one leg as she lands on a hard stone floor. She tries pulling herself free, and another sack falling over stops that, knocking Violet out cold. Bits of broken wood patter down on her head.

A hand gently taps on little Violet's forehead as she dozes back in the den with her father, the black-and-white horror on a screen where it belongs.
"Wakey-wakey, sleepyhead."
"I'm not asleep!" Violet jerks awake, dazed and confused.
A man stares in horror at two versions of his reflection on the screen—one normal, the other slightly twisted and deformed.
"Sure you weren't," her dad teases, then yawns himself. "Yeah, maybe you got a point."
"This one's kinda boring, dad," Violet admits. "Sorry."
"Not your fault, Sweetie. The Hays Code really did a number on this one."
"Wassat?"
"Just a set of boring rules movies had to follow for a while. No naughty stuff, no swearing, no fun."
"Sounds like mom was in charge," Violet pouts.
Violet's dad chokes up, trying to stifle a laugh. He casts a wary eye up the stairs.
"Yeah, your mom—I mean the Hays Code was a total buzzkill. Even a swear word could shut down production."
"Oh." Violet flashes a wicked grin. "You mean like da—"

"Darn it!" Violet curses as she pushes against the sack pinning her leg.

Giant oak casks surround her, dripping a thick, dark liquid that Violet can tell is blood despite the lack of color. Or, at least, it's meant to look like it.

One wall is entirely occupied by dusty wine bottles, though there's no dust anywhere else.

"It's all fake!" Violet finally realizes and feels like a moron for not getting that earlier. When she was upstairs, she was running around like a stupid brat in a horror movie, and that's not her. She's seen too many of them to act like some silly final girl.

The door at the top of the stairs creaks open; a hunched silhouette stands in the light.

"*Jeep*—wait. Why am I saying that?" Violet groans and tries to free herself, but she can't.

The hollow-eyed creature slinks down the stairs, almost falling in its desperate lack of grace.

"Come on!" Violet grits her teeth and puts all her strength into it—still nothing.

The creature hobbles across the stone floor, closing in, and all Violet can do is close her eyes, shield her face, and wait for the inevitable.

She feels the weight lifted from her leg first, as when she dares to open one eye, Violet sees the creature worrying over her bruised leg with some pained, twisted form of concern painted across its face.

"You're not gonna hurt me?"

The creature shakes its head, smacking dry lips like it's trying to remember how to talk. It reaches up and straightens the bow on her head as it finally manages to form a single word, pushed through lips unused for anything other than malice for nearly a decade.

"Vi-o-let."

Speaking that word brings some humanity back to the creature, and Violet watches as its corrupted features soften just enough for her to see through, to see the person beneath.

"Dad?"

The hollow-eyed creature nods as a tear leaks, racing down its sagging cheek.

It doesn't make any sense, but in her heart, she knows this thing is her dad, no matter what's happened to turn him into such a monster. Violet throws herself into his arms, and they hug on the cold stone floor of a haunted house like it was the sofa back home, with the scaries on a screen instead of above their heads.

"I missed you so much, dad!"

"Missed you. Vi-o-let," he groans back.

Coughing as though forcing more of his old self to return, Violet's dad shakes his head and slaps his cheeks. "We don't ha-ve long. Direct-or not in cont-rol down in prop ro-om."

Violet looks around, her dad's words helping her truly see what's there. Boxes of rubber swords and coat racks full of costumes.

"How did I not—"

"You…playing a part," her dad explains painfully. "His victim." He touches her shoulder. "His monster." He places a hand on his chest.

"*Jeep*—damn, why do I keep saying that!?"

"Character playing. Hays Code. No swearing."

"Well, we have to stop him, this Director."

"Impossible," her dad shakes his head. "Already dead. Long time. Only escape."

"What, like out the front door? No, that wouldn't work in a movie, so it's not gonna work here. Think,

Violet, think." She paces the floor as her dad watches, love in his eyes. "What do all these old haunted house movies have in common? There's gonna be a secret room somewhere; that's where the Director will be. He seems all gimmicky, definitely a William Castle type." Violet realizes her dad's staring, awestruck. "What?"

"So grown up," he smiles.

"Whatever, oh! They remade *House on Haunted Hill*!"

"Any good?" her dad asks distrustfully.

"Eh." Violet waves her hand. "It's cool, but you can't beat Vincent Price." She picks up a silver-plated lighter from a dressing table. It doesn't look like a prop. There's weight to it, and it's engraved with a rose. It's an odd thing to find, Violent notes, given the abundance of signs warning about how flammable celluloid is.

"No. You can't," Violet's dad agrees as his daughter tests the lighter.

"So what's the movie's gimmick? Gotta be those red frames, right? This guy, Hardy, told me the real dude who made this movie hid, like, a confession in it, but that can't be it. Too meta for the time. It's gotta be more literal. Red frames, frame—oh! The giant framed mirror upstairs!" Violet pockets the lighter. "Betcha anything that's where this creep's hiding."

"Upstairs." He taps his chest. "Monster again."

"No." Violet crosses the basement and hugs him again. "No matter what, you'll always be my dad." As they part, she looks him in his sunken eyes. "All the same, I think I'll take a head start."

As soon as Violet makes it to the main hall, she's greeted by the Cameraman. Even though it squats, leering forward, it still towers over her. Violet's not afraid anymore. She knows what this thing is, just a tool used to record this horror show; it won't harm her. All the same, it's in her way, and she needs it to move.

"Hey, does this bother your Hays Code-behind?" she asks and flips it off.

The Cameraman panics, turning away quickly, and Violet bolts for the stairs.

Her dad groans as he reaches the hall, becoming the Director's monster again, and the Cameraman skits around to follow the action.

Violet doesn't stop until she reaches the big, framed mirror and then kicks it as hard as possible. Nothing, not even a crack. Every instinct she has tells her to run, find somewhere to hide, and be a victim!

"*Jeepers*, you know what, f—" Violet curses, loud and brash, so jarringly, everything shakes. The silver-screen magic wavers and Violet throws her whole body through the mirror.

She lands on the other side, on a dark soundstage. Behind her, the mansion she ran through, is no more than several separate three-walled sets.

Blinding stage lights blast to life, one by one, forcing Violet to shield her eyes. A slow clapping fills the room, echoing through the darkness.

"Bravo, my child, bravo," a voice as cold as death pours forth as the Director steps from the dark. His hair is jet-black, slicked and combed to a perfect sheen, and his brow arcs like he's perpetually composing some dastardly scheme. A thin mustache twitches above sneering lips, below lifeless eyes, which are the only part of his face the light seems to hit—no matter how he moves. He somehow makes a bowtie menacing.

"A rather vulgar display, yet your grasp of cinematic laws shines through. Rather than becoming my next victim, perhaps you'd like to join my crew?" The Director gestures to a fixed camera that turns at his command.

"What's this? You shooting some behind-the-scenes for the DVD release?"

"Oh, what I could achieve with the technology you have today, my child. Allow me to introduce myself; I'm—"

"Yeah, I know who you are, and you're dead."

"As long as my films live, so shall I," the Director scoffs.

"So you're what? Just an after-image left behind on a B-movie nobody knows about?"

She edges away towards a mounted camera pointing at the set.

"How dare you! My work is art!"

"Dude, William Castle's more beloved than you are these days."

"That Barnumesque hack!"

Violet steps closer to the camera.

"Yeah, you wanna know what happened to the real deal?" Violet takes the lighter out of her pocket. "He burned out." She tears open the gate, flicks a flame to life, and brings it toward the reel.

"No!" the Director screams, his head and hands bursting into ribbons of black film reels—flickering and fluttering as they race towards Violet. They wrap around her wrists and ankles like sentient vines, causing her to drop the lighter. It slides across the ground, disappearing into the shadows.

"You will not ruin my film!" His voice comes from everywhere at once.

Violet's lifted into the air as the Director holds her like a star, arms and legs outstretched to breaking point. He pulls her towards his fluttering body made of living film stock.

"You're going to find out precisely what happens to unruly children on the backlot—"

"NO!"

Violet's dad erupts from the set, wrapping his rotten arms around the Director's shifting form.

"Dad!"

"Let. Her. Go!"

"Or what!? You're MY actor, you buffoon, and an easily replaced one at that. Now do as you're told and—"

Violet's dad silences the Director as he flicks the lighter to life. Holding it inches from the fluttering celluloid, he repeats, "Let. Her. Go."

"You wouldn't. I can't be killed; all you'll do is destroy this footage. Yourself included. As long as a single copy of my masterpiece remains, I am eternal!"

"Let. Her. Go!" Her dad moves the flame closer.

"Fine!"

Violet falls to the floor, landing with a thud.

Across the soundstage, a screen lights up to show Violet's apartment.

"Leave now, child, lest I cut you from existence and my film."

"Dad?" Violet looks at him, and through his monstrous visage, she sees the man, the kind one who loves her. Who stayed up all night watching scary movies with her. Who showed her a whole world she couldn't imagine not being a part of.

"I love you." He smiles with the last vestige of humanity left within. "Go!" He brings the lighter up.

"No!" the Director screams in utter agony as the flames whoosh across his body.

"Dad!"

All around, the set bursts into flames instantly; they race to envelop everything within seconds.

"Go!"

The Director's wails merge with the crinkling of plastic, with the clanking of heated metal, and Violet has no choice but to run as the raging inferno consumes everything.

Tears stream down her face as smoke fills her lungs, and Violet propels herself through the screen.

Violet's mom is just about to dial 911 as Violet hurtles through the screen, hitting the sofa so hard she flips it over, rolling onto the floor on the other side.

"Holy! Vi!" Her mom slams the phone down and races to her daughter. "Where the, how the!?"

"Dad!"

Violet jumps to her feet and turns back to the TV. The monster that her father had become smiles at the screen, holding back the Director as the flames consume them both.

"Dad," Violet's heart breaks as the image burns to nothing, and tiny wisps of smoke rise from the projector.

"Oh, Lord!" Violet's mom rushes to her daughter, the air filling with the smell of burning plastic. "What just happened?" she demands as she waves away acrid smoke.

"Dad," Violet cries and runs to her mom. "Dad saved me." And though it makes no sense, Violet's mom finally believes her.

The next day, Violet heads inside Hardy's Movie Memorabilia.

"Hey, kiddo, how was it?" Hardy asks, desperate to hear firsthand from someone who's actually seen one of Theo Gorman's cursed movies.

"It sucked." Violet dumps the burned, melted tape on the counter.

"What did you do!?"

"Same thing I'm gonna do to every copy of this damn movie," Violet snarls, "and you're gonna help me track them down."

"Woah! Go, Violet!" Holly's so close to the edge of her seat she's practically falling off. "That was such a cool story, Braden, so many layers."

"Yep," Braden declares proudly. "I'm basically an onion."

"So that's what the smell is," Chardea teases.

"Rather twisted and delightful," Toby adds. "What a frightening power, to twist reality with your imagination. Tell me, is this Gorman a real filmmaker?"

"I dunno." Braden shrugs. "The name just came to me. Maybe I picked it up somewhere. See, ideas are like fleas. They jump on you from all over, and it doesn't really matter at that point. They're part of you."

The rest begin scratching, even Rascal, who naps by Chardea's feet.

"Gross! Why do you have to ruin every half-decent thing you do with some moronic comment like that?" Chardea grumbles.

"I'm special like that." Braden puffs his chest like a smug pigeon.

"What did you think of the story?" Toby leans toward Gwennie, smiling gently.

"I liked the ending. It's honest."

"Oh? I guess it was a bit of a downer, though."

"How am I supposed to follow that!?" Holly grabs the side of her head. "I've gotta go after you two?!"

"Don't think like that," Chardea says. "Believe me. Braden's told some lousy ones."

"I heard he told one about magic skates?" Morgan joins in on the ribbing.

"Laugh all you want; I'll just put you in my own movie..."

Holly, Morgan, and Chardea look at one another, and as one say, "Gross."

"Not like that!" Braden slumps. "Seriously, you guys."

"I guess that's it till next time." Chardea feels the worry sneak back in. Damn it, Derek, don't make me do this without you.

"Will Derek be back next week?" Morgan asks, almost as though she can read Chardea's mind.

"Maybe, we'll see." She hefts Rascal up, and the Dachshund puts up no resistance. He curls up against her chest, flicking his little pink tongue against the pointed chin of her devil mask. "I guess I'm on dog-sitting duty till he comes back, though."

"Thank you, all." Toby nods politely around the Hallow Fire and then heads into The Dark.

Gwennie follows silently, then Morgan with a wave. Braden waits by the edge, looking at Holly.

"I'll catch up." She shakes her head. "I think. I gotta ask Chardea something first."

"Okay...sure, no problemo," Braden says, then awkwardly heads away.

"You need some help with your story?" Chardea asks as she runs a finger across Rascal's nose, comforting him till he falls asleep.

"Like you would not believe," Holly giggles. "But I was wondering. Where do we go?"

"Huh?"

"Between these meetings. I can't seem to remember anything but them." Holly scratches her head. "And also, like, it doesn't feel like a week's gone by since, you know."

Chardea holds her hand to the flames. "Time doesn't work like you expect here. It's always Halloween for us."

"Huh?"

"What year was it for you?"

"Um, 2002..."

"I died in 2017." Chardea smiles. "And I've been here longer than Gwennie. She died like a hundred years before I was born, I think."

"That's just...Woah, I mean, what about where we go then? Please make that make sense for me?"

"Some of us haunt where we came from. I think Morgan visits her sister. Others, like Braden and Dino, made little worlds for themselves. Carved from their memories and imaginations. Braden calls it the In-

Between. For Gwennie and Dino it was The Crossroads."

"Woah, okay, so, like, can we visit these places?"

"Sure, it'll make more sense once you make your pact with the Hallow Fire."

"Cool," Holly nods. "Cool-cool-cool. 'Cause, see, I sorta have a crush on someone here, and I don't wanna ask them on a date if, like, there's nowhere to go. Being dead is weird."

"Yeah." Chardea's heart pounds, and she lets out a nervous laugh. "So weird."

Roll credits.

Episode Three

So, can you smell it in the air? It's celebration and chaos; it's wickedness and wonderment—the scent of Halloween. It smells like caramel and spun sugar, doesn't it? Like fire and bottle rockets.

The night's approaching fast, perhaps too fast. You feel that dread, yes, but it's laced with something foul. Like tainted candy. There's something wrong with this Halloween; it's...off. A pumpkin carved far too soon, collapsing under the weight of damp, rotting flesh.

They feel it, too, The October Society. Oh, how they hide it, Braden with his brash jokes, Holly with her wide-eyed excitement. Morgan with her grace, Gwennie with silence, and, worst of all, Chardea with her lies. They're chewing her up inside, and she doesn't know what's worse. The ones she tells the others, or the ones she tells herself...

"Still no D-man?" Braden asks as Chardea comes to the Hallow Fire. Rascal trots beside her, a tiny yet fancy little scarf tied around his neck. He shakes his head as though purposefully trying to draw attention to his new accessory.

Chardea looks at the flames and lets them caress her fingers. On the other side, Gwennie and Toby sit together, whispering.

It warms her heart to see the girl engage again, but it worries her too. None of them truly know Toby yet, and it won't end well if Gwennie's only turning to him as a Dino substitute. It's a silly thought, but the boy does have similar qualities to the girl's departed boyfriend.

"Yo? Char-Char?"

"No." Chardea closes her eyes as she prepares another lie. "I mean, he can't make it. Again, that is."

"Seriously?" Braden gets to his feet and joins her by the fire. "I mean, like, is the dude okay? Can we help or something?"

"It's—"

"Ohmygodhe'swearingascarf!" Holly squeals as her eyes land on the now fashion-forward Rascal. He preens, smug though slightly annoyed it took someone so long to appreciate his magnificence. Holly drops her bag and almost skids into the dirt as she races to meet the dog. He jumps on her lap, paddle-paws on her chest, and holds himself up for Holly to bask in his eminent glory.

"Where did he get a scarf from!?" Holly's about ready to cry.

"Who has a—ohmygodhehasascarf!" Morgan mirrors Holly's reaction, and soon she's on the ground, also admiring Rascal.

"I put it on him as a joke," Chardea explains, quietly thankful she can use this to escape the conversation with Braden, "and he refused to let me take it off."

"And why would he?" Holly blows kisses at the smug Dachshund. "He's so handsome."

Although he knows this to be true, Rascal still turns his head for Morgan to confirm his handsomeness.

"Handsomest boy there is!" Morgan agrees.

"It's just a scarf," Braden pouts.

"Is somebody jealous?" Holly looks at Morgan, and they giggle.

"Just sayin'." Braden kicks a rock and acts like he doesn't care.

Much to Rascal's dismay, both Holly and Morgan abandon their fawning and go to Braden, quickly attacking him with tickles from both sides.

"He is! Poor Braden," Morgan teases.

"Stop!" Braden tries to protest, but his words turn to hysterical grunts, both girls making him twitch and swat at their hands like he's being stung by dozens of electric bees. "I'm gonna pee!"

Holly and Morgan stop at that instant, look at each other, shrug, and resume their assault.

"Are they usually this rambunctious?" Toby asks Gwennie.

"Braden is," she answers with a hint of disappointment. "Holly and Morgan are new."

"Really? Braden makes friends fast, doesn't he?"

"Forgets them even quicker," Gwennie hisses.

"Children, behave," Chardea tuts.

Morgan ceases her tickling, but Holly does not.

"That's—that's, woo!" Braden collapses with Holly to the ground.

"Whatcha saying? Huh? Mr. Handsome?" She keeps going.

"That's what," Braden breaks free, "they say when we're together!" He skitters a few inches from Holly.

"Huh?"

"Children behave," he sings, "that's what they say when we're together."

Holly facepalms and then climbs to her feet. She dusts herself off and then offers Braden her hand. "Let's go, Mr. Handsome."

Chardea watches as Braden takes her hand, and Holly pulls him up—the two colliding in not quite, but almost, an embrace. They stand like that, a little too close, for a little too long.

"Holl—" Chardea's voice cracks unexpectedly. "Holly, are you ready?"

"Yeah!" Holly pumps her fist and bounces on the spot. "Do I need the, yeah?" she asks as Chardea takes the black book from her bag. It's been challenging not to look through it, go back before her time, and see what she can learn about Derek. See if there are any clues as to why he's gone.

Holly takes the book and then brings it to her seat, sitting down with it flush to her chest. She feels the eyes of everyone on her and caves to it.

"Oh man, the pressure!"

"Relax," Chardea says as she takes her seat. "I know it can be embarrassing the first time, but remember, it's what we're all here for."

"I think my mom said that to the guy who mowed our lawn," Braden says without a clue.

"Okay, y'all." Holly shoots a short, sharp breath. "Here goes."

Toby's fingers rest on his chin as he considers it'll be his turn soon. Gwennie folds her legs into a cross and gets comfortable while Braden nods to Holly, encouraging her.

"I haven't seen beneath your masks. I can only see what you let me see, the faces the Hallow Fire chose for you, but I feel like I've known y'all since forever already. Maybe that's the magic of this place, or I dunno; I'm just being weird, but it got me thinking about how you can look right at someone, see the smile on their face or the sadness in their eyes, and never truly know if that's real or just a different kind of mask." Holly's eyes flit from mask to mask, landing on Toby's exposed face last. "And what secrets they might hide."

Toby smiles at the premise, a glint of anticipation in his eyes as Morgan leans on her knuckle, half hiding behind it.

"My October Fellows, let's listen and hear…"

The Song of Sorrow

The boy with a bloody nose squints at the sun through blurry eyes; the refracted rays dance like a glowing fairy begging for attention.

"Hey, listen," the light chimes. "You'll be okay," it promises as the contents of his backpack are shaken out. Even if he wasn't so dizzy and had the will to resist, he couldn't. Firm hands hold him in place from behind.

"See if he's got any money on him."

The words feel so far away. The bloodied boy barely hears them as rough hands rummage through his pockets.

"Nothin', Noah."

He's shoved to the ground, landing against a low wall with a wince. Three silhouettes, black shapes against the midday sun, tower over him.

"Yeah, it doesn't surprise me Peter Poorer doesn't have any green," the one in the middle snorts.

"Peter Poorer! Classic," the one on the right laughs.

"Yeah," the last one kicks Pete's foot. "Were you bitten by a radioactive hobo or something?"

"Hey, don't make fun of the homeless. That's not cool. Can't compare them to this trash."

"Sorry, Noah."

Noah, in the middle, leans down, face blocking the sun. As Pete's eyes adjust, he sees soft, gentle features that hide heartless cruelty.

"You should have stayed where you belonged," he sneers, and as Pete attempts to move, Noah brings a knee to his head. Pete's skull cracks against the wall, and he blanks for a few seconds. He hears laughter. It could be three people, could be a hundred. The real world seems so very far away now.

"Hey, listen," the voice in Pete's head says as Noah and his buddies head off, leaving Pete curled up on the pavement next to his backpack. "You'll be..." but the voice rings hollow. Pete wants to shut his eyes and go away, but he picks himself up and limps on, even if he doesn't know why.

Life sucked for Pete, and that's not even half of it. He was a talented kid who could draw like you wouldn't believe, and that's how he earned a full ride at the Niles Institute—a prestigious art academy.

The problem was, Pete was from the wrong side of town; his mom and pops worked five jobs between them to make ends meet. Kids like him weren't supposed to go to the pretty, perfect tree-lined campus of the Niles Institute. Not when everyone else's parents had to pay through the nose, and especially not when they got better grades than all the rich kids with their private tutors.

It would have been fine if he were from the "right" neighborhood, but Pete wasn't, and it was embarrassing. And it wasn't just the students of the N.I. who thought so...

"You're late," the principal states with no concern for the dried blood on Pete's shirt or the bruises on either side of his head. He checks his watch. "A full half-hour. You'll sit here and think about how you're wasting an opportunity I, frankly, don't believe you deserve."

"I—"

"We can't keep having you come into lessons halfway through, disrupting the process. This institute's students have real potential for the future; you know. And what have you done to your shirt?" The principal finally notices how beaten up Pete is, though the way his face screws up betrays more disgust than concern.

"I got jumped," Pete says, looking at the floor and picking at the crusted blood.

"You'll get that everywhere," the principal groans and gets to his feet. He leans out his office door and calls, "Can you bring me some paper towels. Wet a few of them, would you?" Turning back to Pete, he continues, "Now tell me what happened."

"It was," Pete bites down as his eyes land on one of many framed photos on a Wall of Achievement—a clipping from a local newspaper showing Noah and the principal on stage at some award show. The headline reads "Superstar Freshman Wins National Prize," and it shows the principal and Noah holding a trophy aloft together. "I didn't see them," Pete gulps. "They jumped me from behind."

"Really." The principal shakes his head. "Things have truly gone to seed across town, haven't they?"

"Yeah." Pete stares down at his shoes. There's a knock at the door, but Pete doesn't look. The principal opens it and, a second later, hands Pete some paper towels.

"Clean yourself up; you can at least be presentable for your next class."

"Yes, sir," Pete says and winces as he dabs at his nose.

"I grant you being assaulted excuses being so late," the principal says, checking a file, "but your record is far from spotless on other occasions, young man." He tuts. "Seventeen tardies this semester alone."

"But—" Pete lets that slip out and immediately regrets it. He knows better than to speak up.

"But what, young man."

"It's just," too late now, Pete, just say it, "coming all the way from Southside and—"

"Your problem," the principal slams the file closed, making Pete jump. "You chose to come to this school, young man, when frankly, I believe you'd be better suited to a mainstream school in Southside, where you belong."

Pete doesn't say anything; he knows it won't do any good.

"If this keeps up, I will be looking at having your scholarship revoked. We simply cannot allow you to keep jeopardizing the future and safety of the students who belong here."

"Sorry, sir." Pete says what he knows the principal wants to hear. "I'll do better."

"See that you do." The principal waves him off. "You can wait outside for your next class. I have work to do."

Pete kept his head down for the rest of the day, hanging back till everyone left so he could walk home without being harassed. He passed a thrift store, one he usually hits up for books and games, and his eyes filled with something they so rarely reflect—hope.

A video game cartridge sits on a shelf alongside some worn books and a crumpled jigsaw puzzle box. There is no packaging, just the rounded, rectangular gray slab with a printed label—*The Mask of Heroes: Song of Sorrow*.

Pete presses his face up against the glass till it fogs over.

The one true escape Pete had from his miserable life was video games, but his family was poor and couldn't afford to buy them often. He was still playing on an old Nintendo 64 when every other kid in school had a PlayStation 2—so finding a new game, one he might never have heard of before, in a thrift store was a win he sure needed.

Pete quickly shuffles off his backpack and checks that no one's looking. Sure he's safe; he opens a hidden section at the bottom and takes out a small wallet. He quickly counts the money, heart beating faster and faster, suddenly glad for all the lunches he skipped to save up, grateful that Noah and his buddies were too cocky to think of checking thoroughly. They don't need Pete's money; they'd have just emptied it down a sewer for the laughs.

"Yes!" Pete fist pumps as he confirms he has enough cash on him. He heads inside the store, and a moment later, a hand lifts the cartridge from the shelf.

Pete rushes home, barely stopping to say hi to his parents, and quickly slams the cartridge into his N64. A smile runs from ear to ear as light from the screen gleams in his eyes, and he presses start.

The following morning, Pete's mother opens the door to her son's room, finding nothing but a controller on the floor and the game playing on the TV. It's odd, but she assumes he must have left for school already and forgotten to shut it off. She hits the power button and then shivers—it's freezing.

Badly pinned posters rustle and curtains billow, drawing her attention to an open window. She heads over to shut it, and her eyes catch sight of a crowd forming in the street below. When she realizes what they're staring at, Pete's mother screams.

One Year Later:
Noah sits with his friends in the Niles Institute auditorium, somewhere close to the back. He yawns as the principal drones on, standing before a massive monochrome projection of Pete's face.

"Thank you all for coming to today's memorial."

"Like we had a choice," Noah snorts, and his squad does their best to suppress their laughter.

A few rows behind them, close enough to hear, another kid glares at Noah. "I'm gonna say something," he says, only for his friend to put her hand on his.

"Robin, don't. You know it won't do any good."

"Peter Williamson was a rising star here at the Niles Institute," the principal continues as the slide changes to display the boy's artwork. "Beautiful images of a fantasy world, drawn from a magnificent imagination. Peter's struggles were his own, and perhaps if he shared them with us, he would still be with us today." The principal bows his head, leaving a moment of silence. "Let's hope he's in a better place, like one of these fantastic worlds he designed."

"Technically, anywhere's better than Southside, even if he's in Hell," Noah snickers.

"Hey, shut up, Noah!" Robin snaps.

Noah turns, and when his pretty blue eyes land on Robin, he winks.

"Now, if anyone needs to talk, please make an appointment with the counselor," the principal concludes as a black-and-white portrait of Pete's smiling face fills the screen with the inscription "Rest in Peace."

Kids filter out of the auditorium, some respecting the solemnity of the memorial, but they're in the minority.

"Look, all I'm saying is I appreciate trash that takes itself out." Noah forces an innocent grin that causes his followers to crack up.

"I can't believe you just said that," one of them manages to say through redfaced gut laughter.

"Noah!" Robin yells, coming out the doors with his friend, trying to keep up. "The hell!?"

"It's called a joke," Noah sneers. "I mean, I'd figure you'd know what one is." That doesn't get a response from his followers, so Noah gratingly explains. "'Cause you are one." That does the trick and the rest of the gaggle chuckle.

"It's not cool to pick on a dead kid." Robin gets in Noah's face.

"Mona, you might want to put a leash on your boyfriend here," Noah says without flinching. "He's about to get himself hurt."

"Always someone else's fault, right Noah?" Robin's eyes narrow.

"Don't act like you're better than me." Noah looks Robin up and down. "You know you're not."

Robin pulls a fist, his knuckles turn white, and just as he goes to raise it—

"Is there a problem here, gentlemen?" the principal interrupts.

"No, sir." Noah casually brushes Robin aside. "Robin and I were just talking about how much we miss Peter."

"Yes, well, perhaps these things are best discussed with the counselor?"

"Absolutely, sir," Noah says and walks off, his friends following.

Robin remains tense and ready to pop even after the principal and the others disappear into the crowd of kids and staff making their way to their next class.

Robin jumps as Mona puts her hand on his shoulder.

"Woah, Robin, what's gotten into you?" She backs away, almost hiding behind her low black fringe. Robin doesn't answer; he just walks on without saying a word. Mona looks the other way, toward the direction of their next class. "Hey! Where are you going?"

Robin turns, holding his arms out. "Going to see the counselor."

There's already someone in the office, and though the door's closed, the girl on the other side's so loud, Robin can't help but hear her warbling sobs.

"I-I-I didn't know Peter or, like, had any classes with him." Robin can hear her blow her nose. "But I'm still, like, so sad. Living with that trauma, you know? It's been like a year, and I still can't believe someone in my school did that to themselves."

Robin recognizes her voice. She's in the same homeroom as him. The same one Pete was in last year, too. It burns him that she probably sat in the same class as the kid every day for a year and didn't even know he was there.

"I think about him every day."

Robin recalls her and a few other girls picking on the chubby goth girl who sat at the back of their homeroom class just this morning. She didn't seem to have Pete on her mind then. He picks at his hands in frustration, cracking his knuckles till the door opens and the girl leaves, dabbing at her eyes.

"Come on in." The counselor smiles gently. "Take a seat."

Robin does as she says and then immediately changes his mind. "This is stupid; I'm gonna go."

"Of course, you don't have to be here, but would you mind telling me why it's so stupid?" She takes a seat calmly, unfazed by Robin's rejection.

Without realizing it, Robin begins to talk. "Everyone's making this whole thing about them; nobody here cared about Pete when he was alive."

"Oh, what makes you say that?"

"For starters, you all keep calling him Peter; he hated his full name. He was Pete."

"It sounds like someone here knew him well, at least."

"I, no." Robin shakes his head and pushes down the bad thoughts. "I wasn't his friend; I barely knew anything about him. I just can't stand the posers making his death all about themselves or the jerks who think it's funny to rib a dead kid."

"You barely knew Pete, yet you're feeling something for his loss. Could it be that the others feel something too?"

Robin thinks of Noah's smug grin.

"No. If anyone had given a crap about Pete, they would have said something at the time." He spits his words, full of venom and disgust. "Spoken up when it could have made a difference."

"Perhaps others are going through something similar to Pete? Having dark thoughts and the anniversary of his passing brought them to the surface. Who's to say their feelings aren't valid. Are you having dark thoughts?"

"What!? No! I'm not gonna do what Pete did."

"What happened to Pete was a tragedy—"

"No, see, that's where you're wrong. It was cruelty, plain and simple." Robin stands up, flustered. "I can't do this. I'm out."

"We can't change the past," the counselor calls after him, causing Robin to halt by the door. "We can only learn from it. Try to do better, and save others from the same fate."

"Some people don't deserve to be saved." Robin slams the door behind him.

Robin took a long walk after school, hoping to shrug off his mood, and it didn't work. He arrived home to the smell of baking and laughter.

"Robin, dear!" his grandma calls from the kitchen as soon as he's in the door.

"Hey, Gams," Robin says as he takes his shoes off. He pads across a brand-new plush carpet that looks like a shaggy dog's coat.

He knew she was visiting the second he smelled the baking; every time his grandma came by, she insisted on taking over the kitchen. Not that he ever complained. She made wicked cookies.

Braden: I could sure go for some cookies right about now.

Rascal: Bark-bark!

"Come here and give your Gam-Gam a hug." She holds sticky hands up and lets Robin in.

"Your grandma has a surprise for you," Robin's mom points out, knowing the older woman would forget.

"That's right! I almost forgot! It's in a bag on your bed. Why don't you go see?"

"Sure thing," Robin smiles ever so slightly—the promise of a gift and cookies raising his mood slightly.

He finds a plastic bag on his bed, below a poster for *Devil May Cry* ripped carelessly from an issue of *PlayStation Magazine*. Robin looks inside to see a tangle of wire and plastic. It smells of stale Doritos, Mountain Dew, and dust. He empties it on his bed, and it all comes out as a clump. Robin's so focused on unfurling it that he doesn't hear his mother approach.

"I know you just got that new station-thingie, but let her see you play it."

Robin lays out a dusty, secondhand Nintendo 64 console on his bed. There's only one game with the cartridge already jammed into the machine.

"No, mom, this is cool." Robin takes the trident controller in hand. It's not an official one, some third-party cheaper version, and the thumbsticks are too loose. "I love retro games."

"Did it come with any?"

"Yeah." Robin looks at the cartridge, and without even reading it, he knows the title. As a PlayStation gamer, he knew of this series but never played it. The idea of doing so feels a little dirty. Like he's cheating on his PlayStation.

"*Mask of Heroes*..."

"Is that a good one?"

"I think so." Robin tugs at the cartridge, but it remains fixed.

"Well, plug it in," Robin's grandma says, joining in at the door. "I saw it at a yard sale. Hope it still works."

Robin quickly unfurls the cables and plugs the console into his TV, resting it on the floor for now. He switches it on, and nothing happens, so he hits the reset button a few times.

"Is it broken?" his grandma asks, concerned.

"I dunno," Robin rechecks the wires, that everything's correct, and confident it is, he tries again. Still nothing. "Maybe," he sulks.

"I'll take it back and have words with that—"

"It's cool, Gams. It might just be the wire. I'll see if I can fix it or get another one at G-Force." Robin sniffs the air, then leans down to do the same at the console. "You smell that?" he says, getting a nose full of dust.

"What?" his mother asks.

"Burning."

"My cookies!" his grandma yells and races downstairs.

It's sometime after midnight, as Robin twists and turns in his restless dreams, that the console turns itself on. The room fills with light and the sad, somber piano music of the game's main menu screen. It feels more like the Hero is searching for something they've lost rather than preparing for a grand adventure.

The sound of a horse galloping, metal sword and shield clanking on the rider's back, stirs Robin from his sleep. He cracks a strained eye against the surprising brightness.

"What's going on," he mumbles as he climbs out of bed, rubbing his eyes. "Huh?" He jerks, fully awake, as he realizes the N64 is on. The words **"PRESS START"** flicker gently on the main screen as a young knight rides into a starry night on horseback.

Robin scoops the controller up and sits cross-legged on the floor. He presses start, and he's taken to a save select screen.

"No way." His throat goes dry, and his hands shake as he reads the name on the top save file: Pete. "No freakin' way."

A part of him wants to open the save file, as though he can somehow use the save data to confirm this console and cartridge really did belong to Pete, but as he hovers over it, he feels wrong—like that would be digging up the kid's grave or something. So Robin selects a blank data slot, and the screen turns black.

What is your name...

An onscreen keyboard appears, and Robin moves the cursor around, spelling out "Hero." He hits enter, and the screen shakes. The bar empties, and the prompt appears again.

What is your name...

"The hell." Robin tries another word, smirking as he spells out "Fartman."

Again the screen shakes, the input deletes itself, and it asks:

What is your name...

Robin types in his own name this time. Instead of shaking, a glowing ball of light with wings darts across the screen.

Hello Robin.

The words appear across the bottom of the screen.

It's nice to meet you.

"This is so weird."

Are you ready to go on an adventure?

Two words appear on the screen:

Yes - No.

Robin picks yes, and—

—suddenly, the room is filled with bright morning light. A bird lands on Robin's window ledge, little feathered chest puffed as it tweets, but there's no sound. Nothing but melancholic accordion music, building incrementally in pace.

Robin stares at the screen, slightly swaying to the laconic lullaby. The door behind him opens, making no sound. His mom enters the room in total silence, and though her hands move and her mouth opens, it's to no effect.

"I said, Robin!" Her shout cuts through the song.

Robin jumps, dropping the controller. He looks around, bags under his eyes, as though just realizing it's now morning.

"Have you been up all night playing that game?"

"No?" Robin answers, though he genuinely doesn't know. Technically it's not a lie because it feels like just ten minutes ago he crawled out of bed, called by the siren song of the game's menu music.

"What time is it?"

"It's half past eight." His mom shakes her head. "I shouted twenty minutes ago."

"Crap!" Robin slaps his face.

"Language, young man!"

"I'm gonna be late for school!"

Robin hits the power button on the N64, and though the red light instantly goes out, the image of the game's Hero, his sad eyes staring through an emotionless mask, lingers on the screen for a few moments. It fades to black—the screen reflecting Robin's tired face in place of the Hero's.

We'll Be Right Back After These Messages...

The Channel Five News logo flashes.

"Good evening, folks. This is a Channel Five News Update. Missing reporter and alleged arson suspect Jackie Torrance has been arrested."

The feed cuts to a live newscast from what looks to be an abandoned shack. Spotlights dance from helicopters, and the lights from multiple cars cross the building. Armed police march a woman out, moving her towards the nearest car.

"Our source with local PD has informed us that she'll be held, without bail, with a trial due to start in the coming months. There are no leads on the identity of the mysterious bearded man."

"It's alive!" a man in a very cheap wig declares, jumping erratically. He prances through a garage made up to look like a laboratory.

"It's alive!" He stops before a sheet covering a car—fake thunder rumbles.

"It's alive!" he declares again, wig falling askew to reveal his own hair as he whips the sheet away. Below, there's a car with a large banner across the windshield that reads HALLOWEEN SPOOKTACULAR SALE.

"It's alive!" he yells into the camera. "Bert's Automobile's Spooktacular Sale's alive!"

Another voice quickly reads out the various locations of the dealerships while they flash on the screen, and the actor struggles to hold his pose.

[Static]
What absolute dreck.
[Static]

"Bonkin's Bonanza," an announcer, deliberately and dramatically oozing menace, states as a still image of an abandoned carnival, brightly colored cobblestones faded and cracked with weeds, appears. "Once the site of a drug-induced tragedy, now haunted?" The image fades to black-and-white as a clown cackles.

"Summerland." A second announcer takes over, far less sensational than the first, and yet she's just as unnerving as an image of an empty amusement park appears. "A haunted visage of faded joy?" The sound of a roller coaster and disembodied screams accompanies the image as it fades.

"Marybell, Kansas." The shot changes to an old photo of a quaint, small town from sometime in the 1980s. Then to the remains of a long-abandoned carnival in a field. "A town whose fortune changed for good after the carnival came rolling in."

Three people step out of the shadows, two men and one woman, looking as serious as possible.

"This Halloween, *Haunted Hunters* takes you to three of the scariest fun grounds in America and invites you along for the ride."

We Now Return to The October Society.

"You look like you've been up all night," Mona half-mumbles with a Snickers bar in her mouth as she sits across from Robin. "Want some?" She bites off a chunk and offers the rest to him.

"Nah, I'm good." He waves the offer off and puts his head down on the table. The cafeteria's buzzing with laughter and jeers; you'd never know less than a day ago they mourned the death of a former student.

"Yeah, you totally look it." Mona wraps the back of Robin's head with her knuckles. "Did Wittle Wobin have bwad dweams?"

"Quit it!" Robin bats at her hands but doesn't have enough energy to keep up with Mona's taunts. Eventually, he caves. Sitting up, Robin takes the remaining Snickers bar and begins to explain. "I started up this new game, well, an old one. My Gams found an old N64 at a yard sale or something—"

"Oh, no way! What games? *Jet Force Gemini*?" Mona crosses her fingers on both hands, holding them high. "Please-please-please, that game is ridonkulously Rare," she snorts. "Rare. Get it? 'Cause they made it? No? Sorry, continue."

"Thank you." Robin rolls his eyes. "It only had one game, jammed so hard into the machine I can't get it out. *The Mask of Heroes: Song of Sorrow*, heard of it?"

Mona chokes on her soda and a stream of purple gushes out her nose. "Chyeah! That's even harder to find than *Jet Force Gemini*."

"I can see why; I don't know anybody who'd wanna play it—"

"Fifty bucks!" Mona slams her hand down on the table. "I NEED it for my collection."

"Yeah, sure," Robin agrees, and Mona dances in her seat. "Weirdest damn game ever. Like, you play this kid with a talking mask. Makes no sense why the kid couldn't just talk instead."

"It's because you're supposed to see the Hero as yourself. Imagine it's you behind the mask. It's a long-running series, dude. Been out since the old NES days."

"Anyway, the mask's creepy, but the game is what's messed up. Like, you get to this town, only it's like everyone there's all depressed. There's a store, but they don't have anything for sale, and the big guy running it just cries about how his wife is gone. Then there's this other guy with a music box that doesn't work, but he just keeps turning the handle—"

"Dude. That's not *Song of Sorrow*."

"Huh?"

"I've seen it in magazines, and it doesn't sound like what you played at all. It's like, super colorful and joyful, and you've got to stop some Big Bad taking it all away with the Song of Sorrow."

"Maybe you're thinking of a different game 'cause this one was beyond depressing."

"Dude, I know what I'm talking 'bout." Mona points both hands to her chest. "They don't call me Super Mona Drive for nothin'."

"Nobody calls you that." Robin slumps again, and then something catches his eye, someone at another table.

"Come over after school; I swear I have it in a magazine somewhere."

"Yeah, sure, no worries." Robin's attention wanders. He catches sight of someone familiar sitting at a table across the hall, glimpsing them through students horsing around and eating their lunches—a small kid with dark hair in a cheap cut with a bloody nose and lips.

"Pete?"

Robin rises, deaf to whatever Mona's saying, as the same sorrowful lullaby from the game fills the hall. He pushes between friends, barging past others. A bunch of kids dressed in band uniforms flows past, and Robin has to wait before he can continue.

He takes two steps and stops, staring with utter confusion at the table.

"What you lookin' at, Boy Blunder," Noah sneers, and his followers titter to one another.

"N-nothin'." Robin shakes his head.

He shakes it again in Mona's room.

"That's not the same game." He looks at a two-page spread in a back-issue *Nintendo Power* magazine sitting just on top of a mylar pocket.

The town looks like the one from the game, but it's more vibrant and full of life. The NPCs all look like they're having a jolly time—the music box man's caught mid-jig, surrounded by clapping village children, and even a cute dog standing on two legs. The image of the dog's collar, snapped and abandoned, flashes inside his head.

"Maybe what I saw is what happens if you lose?"

"Nah, see," Mona points to a page that shows a black screen with a broken sword on the ground. "That's the GAME OVER screen."

Robin reaches out to touch the page, and Mona slaps the back of his hand without hesitation.

"Ouch!" He pulls his hand back and shoots an accusing glare at her. "Why!?"

"The oils on your skin will ruin the pages, duh." Mona rolls her eyes like Robin should know that.

"Are these collectible or something?"

"They will be, one day." Mona takes a pen and uses the top end to point to the game's title. "See, *Song of Sorrow*."

"So weird." Robin spots the merchant from his version of the game. Only this man has a round, happy woman by his side; the two look inseparable.

"Mona!" a woman yells from the hall, pushing open the door. "Keep this door open when you have a boy in your room!" She smiles at their guest. "Hello, Robin."

"Hi, Mrs. Smalls."

Her smile vanishes when she turns back to her daughter. "Behave," she warns with a pointed finger.

Once she's gone, Robin looks Mona in the eye and asks, "Your parents still don't know you're into girls?"

"I mean." Mona holds her hands up in a who knows way, drawing attention to the posters around her room.

Lara Croft grins over a pair of aviators; Jill Valentine has her back to a wall, knee up, while zombies close in; Rikku, Yuna, and Lulu stand together on a beach; Nina Williams kicks high.

"I'm not exactly subtle here."

"You could always, you know, talk about it with them."

"Ew, gross."

"Okay, them, I get." Robin points to the posters "Though Ada Wong's way cuter than Jill."

"Fight me."

"But her." Robin points to a poster of Princess Peach.

"Her…" Mona sighs. "She's my princess in another castle."

"We need to find you a real girl."

"Eww. Real people are overrated."

"Hey!"

"And what we need to do is find out what's up with your game, 'cause I assure you it's not *Song of Sorrow*."

"Then what is it, oh mighty Games Master."

Mona screws up her face as she thinks it over. "It could be a bootleg. A fan game, or maybe a cracked copy."

"You think someone messed with the code?"

"Could be, but all I know for sure is I gotsta see it!"

"Welp, that was disappointing," Mona groans as she stands over Robin. He smashes the power button on the

N64 in his bedroom. Mona snorts. "Bet I'm not the first girl to say that in here."

"I swear it worked fine last night." Robin's too focused on the console to pay attention to Mona losing it.

"Maybe it's the console?" Mona suggests. "Gimme the cart, and I'll check it out on mine."

"Can't." Robin tries to pull the game out. "It's stuck."

"Hmm, maybe it's a modded console too?"

"Is there a way to check?"

"I dunno, but maybe we can take it to G-Force tomorrow and see what Barry thinks?"

"Yeah," Robin agrees. "Maybe he'll want to buy it if it really is a cracked bootleg."

"Aw, you don't wanna hang out with your creepy, crying villagers anymore," Mona teases, and the very thought sends a chill down Robin's spine. He's silently grateful the console wouldn't start. If he never sees those dead-eyed NPCs again, he'll consider it a win.

It's just after midnight when the N64 turns on again, and Robin's bedroom fills with that haunting lullaby.

He stirs from his bed, slipping from the sheets like a sleepwalker, and sits on the floor—a dark silhouette against a glowing screen.

```
WELCOME    BACK,    ROBIN.
LET'S GO ON AN ADVENTURE.
```

His fingers flick the controls without conscious thought, and Robin guides the game's Hero across a vast open field with flat walls made to look like mountains. The skybox above swirls with pixelated shades of gray, from dull to nearly black, as the Hero journeys toward a distant temple looming on the horizon.

I'M SO GLAD YOU'RE HERE, ROBIN. IT'S SCARY TO GO ALONE...

The Hero comes across a ranch, and a piercing wail shakes the screen. Though Robin knows he needs to get the Hero to the temple, he decides to take a detour to investigate.

Inside the ranch, he finds the NPC of a small girl sobbing over two rectangular mounds of earth.

"Papa and Mama wouldn't listen to me. And now they're dead. They're all dead," the girl's speech box reads. The camera shows a pen filled with dead polygon cows with their feet in the air. It should feel silly, but Robin's stomach twists like he's looking at the site of actual mass slaughter.

The girl NPC slowly looks at the Hero and repeats, "They're all dead."

"I swear, they were all dead!" Robin insists before Mona and a big man with a scruffy beard that sticks out in every direction. Both of them stare at Robin in disbelief.

All around them are shelves packed with recent and retro video games. A mount above the counter holds a replica of Squall Leonheart's Gunblade from *Final Fantasy VIII*, and a TV runs a demo reel for the new Xbox console showcasing *HALO: Combat Evolved* and *Dead or Alive 3*.

"Sure they were, kid," the big man says.

"Why would I lie, Barry?" Robin throws his arms up. "What do I have to gain other than making the two of you think I'm crazy—"

"—ier," Mona butts in. "I don't think he's making it up, though, Barry. Since it seems to only turn on after midnight, maybe someone messed with the internal clock or something?"

Barry, and his chair, groan as he gets up and heads into the backroom. He comes back a moment later with a set of tools.

"Lemme see it." He says and takes a thin screwdriver between his teeth, clearing his counter.

Robin exchanges a glance with Mona, then shrugs his backpack off. Unzipping it, he takes the N64 out and places it down.

Barry takes a shot at pulling the cartridge, then shoots Robin a glare. "Did you glue this in?"

Robin's face screws up, even more so when he turns to see Mona with an accusatory raised eyebrow.

"You guys really think I'd go this far for a prank!?"

"Could have been an accident," Mona shrugs as Barry works at unscrewing the console.

"How did I accidentally glue a game into my N64?"

"I dunno, you're the dummy with the stuck game."

"Well, the console's fine," Barry interrupts. "Looks good to me, and since I had to break the seal to open it, I'm 100% sure nobody's tampered with the machine."

"So it's gotta be a cracked game, right!?" Mona goes on her tiptoes to peer inside the machine, watching as Barry puts the case back in place.

"Or it's cursed," Barry says with such nonchalance that it makes the kids turn to one another, silently asking if they heard that.

Mona snorts. "There's no such thing as a cursed game."

"Au contraire, mon ami!" Barry flips the N64 upright. "Ever heard of a game called *Berzerk*?"

"Um—"

"T'was the glorious 1980s! A time of mullets and shoulder pads! Hair metal and spandex! And, somewhere in Illinois..."

A kid decked out in denim cut-offs and a Van Halen t-shirt strides into a neon-lit arcade flooded with screaming kids. He walks up to a red and blue cabinet, BERZERK flashing on the screen, and drops a quarter.

The kid puts on a pair of over-ear headphones, hits play on his Walkman, and smirks as he hits start.

Blue and red lights flash across his face as he kicks it, rocking along to his mixtape, and as his score climbs, an audience gathers. They watch in awe as the kid edges closer and closer to the high score.

Eventually, when the kill screen flashes, the kid nods along to cheers as it tells him to enter his name on the leaderboard—his score 16,660. As soon as he enters his initials, the kid begins to feel funny. He clutches at his chest as his face turns pale.

The audience steps back, hands cover mouths and eyes, and the high-score kid collapses, face twisted and frozen in agony.

"The same thing happened a year later," Barry continues, turning from Robin to Mona. "When another kid hit a high score with the number 666 in it...the number of the beast..." Barry makes devil horns with his hands, sticks his tongue out, and headbangs.

"That's just, like, an urban legend, though. Right?" Robin asks with genuine worry.

"Maybe." Barry shrugs. "But lemme tell you about something similar. Something that happened to a buddy of mine..."

Inside a dark, dusty attic, a TV sits atop an upturned milk crate. The only other object is a PlayStation 2, standing upright beside it.

"See, this guy said he wasn't scared of nothin' when it came to horror games, so he bet he could play *Silent Hill 2* from start to finish, alone in the attic of an abandoned house."

A skinny guy climbs into the attic and takes a copy of the game from his backpack. He settles down on the floor and starts the game. Now and then, his eyes shift, looking to the dark corners of the attic, and each time they do, he tenses up a little more.

Onscreen, he guides the character through a dark apartment complex. Strange mannequin-like creatures attack him as he explores.

"He'd never played it before, so he didn't know what was coming..."

As the guy reads a note inside one of the apartments, a ghostly, disembodied voice whispers all around him—coming from the darkness in the attic. The controller flies in the air and barely hits the floor as the guy clambers back down the ladders.

"See," Barry laughs, "it wasn't an abandoned house. Another buddy was fixin' it up, and we hooked up some speakers. Hid them good. He didn't know that there's a spooky whisper easter egg if you hang about in one of the rooms." Barry almost loses it. "Scared the hell out of him."

"Honestly," Mona points out, "that game's scary enough. You could have given him a heart attack."

"I know." Barry wipes a proud tear. "So I'm thinking maybe you've come across a rigged prank game."

"It doesn't feel like a prank to me," Robin says.

"Sure, but does it ever to the prankee?"

"You've got a point," Robin concedes.

"Tell ya what, leave it with me for the night." Barry writes a receipt. "I wanna check out this spooky midnight mystery for myself. If it's for real, I'll buy it from you. Hundred sound good?"

"I don't care about—"

"Deal!" Mona snatches the receipt.

"Come back tomorrow; we'll see what's what."

The next day Robin and Mona stand outside a dark, closed video game store. Mona leans against the shutters and peers into the gloom.

"There's nobody in," Mona confirms.

"Maybe he's just sick or something. Or had a family thing," Robin says, ready to just walk away and leave it.

"Or, maybe the cursed game got him..." Mona goes slack and silent.

"Shut up, that's not funny, Mona." Robin grows wary when she doesn't respond and stands there, perfectly still. "Mona?"

The girl slowly turns, slouched over so her hair covers her face while a raspy groan escapes her lips.

"So not funny, Mona. You know I hate that movie." Robin backs away as she raises a shaky hand to him.

"You...cursed...me...Robin..." Mona croaks, taking lumbering steps towards him. She staggers at him with a sudden burst of energy, making the boy shriek.

"Not cool!" Robin shields himself as Mona playfully claws at him.

"Lighten up, dingbat. I'm just kidding."

"Look, I really think there's something up with that game." Robin rubs his arm as they walk. "I didn't tell you before. I dunno why, but there was already a save file." He stops walking. "The name on it was Pete."

"So." Mona shrugs. "Lots of kids called Pete. Doesn't mean anything."

"I saw him too."

That makes Mona stop in her tracks and turn to Robin without an ounce of snark. "What?"

"In the cafeteria the other day." Robin gulps. "I saw Pete. Only when I went to him, it was Noah..."

Mona puts a hand on each of Robin's shoulders. "I'm worried about you," she says, suddenly sincere.

"I'm worried too. This game—"

"Not the game! You! Robin, you can't keep doing this to yourself. It's been a year, and, look, did you see him before or after you played the game?"

"After."

"So you saw him after the memorial and after seeing a Pete's, not necessarily THE Pete's, save file." Robin looks away, but Mona turns his face, forcing him to look at her. She meets his eyes and sees the pain buried deep within. "I think you should talk to the counselor. For real." She taps on his head. "'Cause this save data's corrupt, my friend, you need to defrag it."

"Maybe you're right."

"Well, duh, it's me we're talking about."

"Okay," Robin agrees. "Tomorrow, I'll see the counselor after school."

"Good," Mona nods. "Then we can get our hundred bucks from Barry."

"Yeah." Robin's smile grows and stops as he realizes what she said. "What do you mean *our* hundred?"

"Is that you, Robin?" his mom calls as he comes through the front door.

"Yeah, mom," he heads for the stairs. "Been a long day; think I'm just gonna head to bed if that's okay."

"You okay, honey?" His mom appears from the lounge and looks at her son with concern. Reaching for his forehead, she asks, "Do you have a temperature?"

"Yeah, I mean, no, mom. It's just all this Pete stuff..."

"Oh...do you want to talk about it?"

"No, I just, I'm just tired."

"Okay, but come down and get something to eat if you're hungry." She hovers over, wanting to hug him, but he seems so fragile she worries it'll do more damage. She watches as Robin climbs the stairs, and just before he reaches the top, she calls out, "You're not alone. You know that, right honey?"

"Yeah, mom." Robin nods back. "I know," and he heads off to his room.

He's only a few steps through the door when his eyes land on it, and his blood runs cold.

The N64 sits on the floor, right where it was two nights ago. *Song of Sorrow* sticks out of the console, the controller resting next to it, waiting for Robin to pick up and play.

"No…" Robin shakes his head, insisting it can't be true.

Anger rises, his knuckles turn white, and before Robin knows what he's doing, the machine's in his hands. He rips it free from the wires and storms over to his window.

The console hurtles through the night air a second later, crossing half of Robin's backyard before landing in a clatter of shattering plastic.

Shaking, Robin lies down on his bed and covers his eyes with his hands. His heart beats so fast that he doesn't think he'll ever get to sleep, but he does. The next thing he knows, it's sometime after midnight, and the room fills with light accompanied by that familiar haunting lullaby.

Robin gets up and crosses his room to the reappeared console in a second. "You want me to play!? Fine." He snatches the controller. "Let's play."

Robin's throat dries up at the menu screen. There's now a third save file, this one called: Barry. Like the Pete one, the life bar next to the name is empty. Looking at the one by his own name, Robin gulps to see it at one-quarter full.

```
HELLO    ROBIN.   ARE   YOU
READY    TO    GO    ON    AN
ADVENTURE?
```

"I'm gonna finish your stupid adventure," Robin growls and picks up where he left off.

```
THE   SONG   OF   SORROW   HAS
BEEN   SUNG.   ONLY   YOU   CAN
MAKE IT END.
```

Ignoring all distractions this time, Robin heads straight to the looming temple, the skybox darkening as he gets closer and closer. As soon as he makes the

Hero step inside, the words Temple of Truths fill the screen, and Robin pushes on.

Minutes then hours pass as he fights through the cold, mausoleum-like dungeon. Each monster he slays seems somehow grateful to meet its end.

Just before dawn, Robin's Hero stands before an oversized door, a skull with a gaping mouth for a keyhole. He smashes the pots next to it, filling up on arrows and life energy.

"Alright." Robin cracks his neck. "Boss time."

He goes through the door, and it slams closed behind him. Heavy bars slide across it, blocking any thought of escape.

The chamber is impossibly tall, with windows too high for anyone to reach. Robin guides the Hero towards a pedestal in the middle, and as he makes it to the center, the meager light fades, plunging the room into near darkness.

Suddenly, three tall hooded figures float in, surrounding the Hero, and the boss' name fills the screen.

THE LORDS OF SORROW.

Though Robin's ready for a fight, his character isn't. The Hero drops his sword and shield, falling to his knees.

"What are you doing? Come on!" Robin mashes the controller, but nothing happens.

The three shadowy, hooded figures close in, surrounding the Hero, and start kicking him.

Robin bashes the controller harder.

"Fight back, damn it!"

The Hero screams so loud that the bosses throw their heads back, unfurling their hoods.

"No..." Robin drops the controller as he recognizes the person below the hood. Mapped into rough, angular polygons, it's blurry with jittery animations but unmistakably Noah's smug, cruel face.

"It's not possible."

The second boss's face comes into the light—Mona.

"Please," Robin begs, but he knows who it is under that third hood.

His own polygon face stares down at the sobbing Hero. Desperate gasps of pain punctuate the humming Song of Sorrow.

"This isn't real," Robin insists as the three video game versions of them kick the Hero repeatedly, without remorse, till his mask cracks.

"Pete..."

The image of Pete, the real one, lying on the ground as the three of them tower over him flashes in Robin's mind. He can see his own jeering face as though through Pete's eyes.

Robin stares at the terrified, polygon face of the boy he bullied to death and feels the weight of his guilt crush him.

DO YOU WANT THE SONG OF SORROW TO END?

"Yes." Tears stream down Robin's face. "Pete, I'm so sorry, I didn't; I've no excuse. I'm sorry."

ONLY YOU CAN MAKE IT END, ROBIN...

A new source of light fills Robin's room, and when he turns to it, he sees a door, just like the one to the boss's room where his window used to be.

MAKE IT END...

Robin hears Pete's pleas for mercy, not from the game but the glowing door.

SAVE HIM...

Robin nods, biting down on the overwhelming regret coursing through him. The guilt, the sorrow, all of it. He just wants it to end. He puts the controller down and heads to the door—the three on the screen watch with static, emotionless smiles.

SAVE YOURSELF...

Robin hears the words as though they're typed inside his head, and stops.

"No," he clenches his fists the same way he did on that day a year ago. "Some people don't deserve to be saved!"

He turns back to the game, anger rising once again.

HE'S ALONE. I'M ALONE. IT'S SCARY TO GO ALONE...

"Life is scary!" Robin yells. "It's full of monsters like me. But I'm done hiding from what I am. Done blaming others. Noah started it, but I took part. I'm just as guilty."

ROBIN...

"I'm done playing games!" He grabs the cartridge with both hands, pins the console to the floor with his foot, and pulls.

DON'T YOU WANT TO GO ON AN ADVENTURE?

"No!" Robin growls. "It's time I lived in the real world!"

DON'T YOU WANT THE SONG OF SORROW TO END?

"Yes! But that doesn't mean it should!"

The game comes free, as though it was never stuck, and Robin watches with bulging eyes and gritted teeth as the three polygon bullies fade to black. Before the screen goes completely, Robin sees Pete's face, the real one. He closes his eyes. A sad smile spreads across his face, and he nods.

Robin drops to his knees, sobbing.

"Robin!" His mom hurries into the room in a dressing gown. "Robin, what's wrong?" She kneels and pulls her son into her arms as he breaks down.

"I bullied Pete Kinney," Robin admits aloud for the first time. "I'm the reason he—"

"Shh, honey, no." His mom takes him in her arms. "No, what happened wasn't your fault. It—"

"Yes, it was, mom," he cries into her arms and stares at the discarded cartridge. "And I need to find a way to live with that."

"Later, when Robin and Mona checked, the save files were gone. If Pete truly was trapped in that game, his soul was now free. Robin's, however, had a ways to go before it could be. He saw the counselor a lot after that night; accepting he needed help wasn't the hardest part—"

The rest of The October Society waits, on edge, as Holly finishes.

"—convincing himself that he deserved it was. He started by owning it and accepting his mistakes. He had to. Otherwise, the guilt would have kept growing till it consumed him. Just like Pete's pain did to him."

Holly looks to the Hallow Fire, through the dancing flames, to Toby and Gwennie on the other side.

"The truth is, we're all heroes of our own stories, and sometimes we're villains in someone else's." She closes her eyes and listens to a wall of silence from the rest of The October Society. "I'm sorry if that wasn't very fun or the right kind of story for this thing." A tear races down her cheek. "The thing is, I've been where Pete was, and—"

Chardea goes to the girl and pulls her into a hug.

"When my house was burning, and I knew I was gonna, I didn't fight it." Holly sobs. "I didn't want to. I hated my life. School. I was ready to go. Wanted it."

Braden joins Chardea, putting his arms around both girls.

"I'm sorry, I'm so sorry." Holly loses her voice. "I—"

"Shh," Morgan says, kneeling by Holly's side, placing a hand on her knee. "You're safe now."

Rascal clambers up to her lap, desperately trying to lick the sadness from Holly's face.

"Thank you all so much." Holly squeezes Chardea's and Braden's arms tight. "I don't think anyone's ever been as nice to me as you guys."

"You're gonna make me cry now," Braden jokes.

"Please don't," Chardea sniffs. "You always fart when you cry."

That causes a nervous titter to spread through the group, one that cascades into laughter, then hysterics. It's what they need, and soon they feel their spirits rise, like the Hallow Fire itself.

"So what now," Holly asks. "I mean, I'm cool with an all-night group hug session, but I think our friend's trying to say something," she nods to the fire.

"Time to see if the Hallow Fire's embraced you," Chardea says as they disentangle. "Though I think it's pretty clear you belong here."

"Yeah," Braden agrees. "If it doesn't pick you, I'll resign in protest."

"Please," Chardea half-heartedly jokes with crossed fingers.

"Wait," Morgan says, "what happened to Barry? Did the game make him…"

"When Mona and Robin checked on him, it turned out he fell down the stairs. Broke both ankles."

"Did the game make that happen?" Morgan asks.

Holly shrugs, "Maybe. Maybe the game didn't do anything, and it was all just Robin's guilt manifesting."

"Oh." Morgan looks to the ground. "I don't know what's scarier."

"Okay, Holly." Chardea stands close to the Hallow Fire; it rages higher than all of them except Toby. "You need to reach in. Don't worry—"

Holly shoves her hand into the flames and giggles as they tickle her arm. "Oh, wow, that's amazing. There's something there."

"Take it," Chardea says, feeling the same pride Derek once felt saying that to her. "It's yours."

Holly pulls something green and spiky from the flames. It's round in shape, coming to a point with a snout covered in scales. "It's a dragon?"

"Yeah." Chardea puts a hand on Holly's shoulder. "That makes sense to me."

"I don't get it." Holly runs her hand over the rough mask.

"I do," Chardea nods. "You've beaten the biggest, baddest dragon there is, Holly. It only makes sense you'd wear the mask of one."

"Holly, the dragon slayer!" Braden cheers as she joins the two of them. The rest follow in and stand around Holly as she holds the mask to her face. "Welcome to The October Society. Officially, that is."

Holly smiles as a single tear of joy leaks from her eye and drips onto the mask.

"Thanks," she says to the others. "Thank you," she nods to the Hallow Fire and then the rest of them again. "Thank you all so much," and as she slips on the mask, she hears the Song of Sorrow in her own heart fade.

Roll credits.

Episode Four

How quickly it's approaching, that sacred night—the eve of mischief and mirth. The things that once were, and shall be again, stir from The Dark as closet doors refuse to close and shadows beneath beds grow longer.

And yet it is not these things sitting upon the hearts of children everywhere—like a dread weight upon them. All the Children of October, the current, the soon-to-be, and the once-were, sense it.

They feel it in their hearts, yet there's not one among them celebrating. Their missing leader weighs heavy on their souls, and though most have swallowed the Devil's lies, it's a jagged, broken candy—stuck in their throats. Of course, they joke and play, but beneath the laughter lies something else—fear.

Braden snorts as he bawls, barely able to keep upright in his seat.

"I-I can't," his voice reaches a near ear-splitting high. He turns his head and covers his eyes, but that doesn't help.

"Don't you vant a taste of ze apple?" Holly uses a gruff, cracked voice and cackles as she guides Rascal's paw to Braden's knee. "Come, child, he-he-he-he!"

"Stop!" Braden protests, but he can't help himself. He slowly lifts his hand from his eyes, turns slightly, and loses himself in hysterics again. "I can't!"

Rascal stands upright, on two legs, supported by Holly. His fancy little scarf is tied over his head like a bonnet, giving him an uncanny likeness to a woodland crone. Big, round eyes both plead for Braden to make it stop and also want to know if he has any biscuits.

"Come, child." Holly makes Rascal point his chunky little paws while hiding behind the dog, doing the evil witch's voice. "Don't you vant—"

"An apple?" Morgan swoops in behind Braden and holds a shiny, red apple in front of him. "It's like, totally not poisoned or nothing."

"I dunno," Chardea teases, though her heart's not in it. She stands close to the Hallow Fire, staring into the flames and a million miles away at the same time. "I think anything other than junk food's deadly to Braden."

"That probably explains the legendary Fart War I keep hearing about." Holly lowers Rascal back to all fours, and the Dachshund shakes off the scarf, only to paw at it and look at Holly expectantly.

"I'm not even going to dignify these scandalous accusations anymore." Braden crosses his arms and goes in a huff.

Holly fixes Rascal's scarf around his neck, where it belongs, and the dog trots around, reminding everyone how handsome he is.

"Holly." Morgan looks at the girl in the dragon mask. "I think we upset little Braden."

"Less of the little," he pouts.

"Aw, didums!" Holly giggles as Morgan stands beside her; the dragon and the fox laugh as one at the sulking pumpkin's expense.

Rascal paws at Chardea's legs, and she scoops him up in her arms. He rests against her chest, quietly licking her.

"I wish you could tell us what happened, little one," she whispers and then leans in, nuzzling the dog close. Rascal groans in response, sharing Chardea's concern for their absent friend.

Her eyes wander to Braden with the girls, and her heart skips a beat as Holly playfully shoves the boy, goading him into accepting a truce. Chardea pushes that feeling down hard. She doesn't have time for whatever it is.

As Holly and Morgan teasingly apologize to Braden, Gwennie and Toby emerge from The Dark together on the far side of the circle.

They strike an unusual duo. Exact opposites, a boy taller than most adults and a girl so slight that Chardea once joked she could get swept away with a strong enough breeze.

Once again, Chardea tells herself it's a good thing Gwennie's made a new connection, yet she can't help but worry. It feels like they're fracturing. Braden, Holly, and Morgan are on one side. Gwennie and Toby, on the other, while she's somewhere in the middle, pretending she's in control.

"Fine!" Braden dramatically accepts Holly's apology and unfurls his arms as the girl holds out her fist.

Gwennie watches it from across the circle. Her gut twists as she sees Braden fist-bump Holly. An image flashes before her eyes—Braden and Dino doing the same thing countless other times.

"Really!" Gwennie snaps.

None of them have ever heard her so loud, so forceful before, that it takes a second for their minds to accept this came from Gwennie.

"Don't think you're special," Gwennie continues, getting up in Holly's face. "Once you're gone, he'll just replace you too."

"Exsqueeze me!" Holly gets defensive.

"Took no time to forget Dino, didn't it?" Gwennie says around the girl, pointing to Braden.

"Gwen, why would you—"

"Back off." Holly blocks Gwennie and sizes her up. "Witch."

That word ushers in heavy silence like the eye of a hurricane.

"I'm not bein' funny." Gwennie steps up to Holly. "But are you his bodyguard or his girlfriend?"

"That's a bit rich." Holly nods to Toby. "You seem awfully cozy with Skeletor over there."

"Pardon?" Toby protests.

"That is enough!" Chardea steps in between them. "Holly, you're new, so I'll let that slide as long as Toby's okay with it."

"I suppose," Toby shrugs.

"Oh, of course!" Gwennie throws her arms in the air. "Holly-Holly-Holly! Break the rules for Holly! Let's all coddle Holly, make her feel special. Like she belongs. Like she's one of us!"

"She is!" Chardea shouts. "The Hallow Fire chose her—"

"It chose Dino too—"

"And it was his time, Gwennie." Chardea lowers her voice. "He was ready to go. You have to accept that."

Gwennie clutches her bag.

"I miss him too." Chardea offers Gwennie a hug, but the girl steps back.

"No, you don't." Gwennie looks to Braden sitting, uncharacteristically quiet, with Morgan by his side and Holly standing guard. She takes another step back. "None of you do." She turns and runs, bashing aside Toby as she flees into The Dark.

"Gwennie! Come back," Chardea yells, but it's no good. She's gone.

"Well, that was something," Toby mutters with a dry laugh. "You suppose I should go after her?"

"No," Chardea shakes her head. "It's getting on, and you have to tell your story." Chardea turns to the Hallow Fire. She never knew flames could look ill, but that's the only way she can describe it. Everything that's going on, the disharmony in The October Society, it's poisoning them and the fire. They're halfway to Halloween, and if things don't change, if she doesn't find a way to bring them together, Chardea doubts they'll make it to the final night.

"We just going to go on without her?" Morgan asks while Holly takes her seat beside Braden, putting her arm around him. "Doesn't feel right."

"No, it doesn't, but it's not like we have a choice. Gwennie will come back when she's ready," Chardea says with far more confidence than she feels. "Okay, everyone, it's time for Toby's initiation tale." She turns to him. "Are you ready?"

"As I'll ever be, I suppose," Toby shrugs.

The rest of them take their seats as Chardea fetches the black book. She hands it to Toby. "Hold this to your chest."

"Of course," he says and hesitates for a second before taking it. "Well, tonight's been somewhat eventful." Toby's face screws up as he scratches his arm. "And, well, I'm sorry," he puts the book down. An angry red rash spreads across his arms. He grunts as he scratches.

"Dude, you okay?" Braden worries.

"Are you allergic or something?" Morgan adds.

"Well, yes, I mean I was. Before all this," Toby stammers, "to leather, but I never imagined it would affect me here."

"I dunno," Chardea weighs in, "I mean, Braden's farts still work, so I guess it makes sense?"

"One of these days," Braden grumbles.

"So how can I? Don't I need to hold the book?" Toby looks to Chardea for answers she doesn't have.

"Maybe you can just rest it on your lap?" she offers.

Toby does that and still tenses up even at the proximity.

"You don't look very comfortable," Morgan points out.

"I'm fine, really," Toby insists, but he clearly isn't.

"There's gotta be a way we can do this without melting Toby." Braden looks around for suggestions. "Maybe one of us can hold it for him?"

"Worth a shot," Morgan agrees.

"That's...oddly sensible, Braden," Chardea forces herself to admit and then rises from her seat. She sits next to Toby and takes the book from him. "Let's see if it works." She nods for him to go ahead.

Gwennie listens from The Dark, her back braced against a gnarled, twisted tree, holding her bag tight to her chest.

"Well, the story I've concocted for you all is rather pointed, given tonight's events. It's about the assumptions we make," Toby begins.

Gwennie reaches into her bag, takes out Dino's old werewolf mask, and holds it on her face, breathing in the scent of rubber and the boy she misses so dearly.

Toby looks around the circle. "And how dangerous they might be."

Chardea opens the book and watches as words inscribe themselves on the yellowed page. She looks at Toby, nodding for him to continue.

"My October Fellows, allow me to tell you about..."

The Unkindness of Ravens

Electricity crackles as lightning cracks the midnight sky above a Manhattan skyscraper—the flash of light that follows brings into brief focus two bound prisoners. One a bruised, beaten yet impeccably dressed man, and the other a woman ready for bed. Both are gagged and struggle against ropes that hold them aloft between stone pillars, arms and legs spread like stars.

A mad cackle proceeds the roll of thunder, coming from a man cloaked in robes so black that his movements flow like a cloud against a midnight sky. He turns from them and beckons to the night.

"Haha! Their time is almost upon us!" His pointed beard cuts like a dagger below a crooked, bird-like nose. "And there's nothing anyone can do to stop me!"

"Think again, Draven!"

The robed man turns, and his cheek meets a fist that sends him spiraling to the ground. Draven spits blood, and when he sees jet-black ichor instead of red, a wicked smirk cracks across his crooked face.

"You're too late, Knight. The change has already begun!" Draven rises and holds his palm to the other man, showing him the wet, black smear. "Soon, I will be as a God!"

Knight rips away the rest of his torn khaki shirt, revealing a scarred chest packed with toned muscles.

"Always wanted to punch a God." Knight puts his dukes up.

"Fool!" Draven points to the largest scar on the other man's chest. "Don't you remember what happened last time we fought?"

"Sure I do; this time's different."

"Oh? How so, Mr. Detective?"

"This time, I got help." Knight whistles and a sleek shape pounces from the dark, colliding with Draven and pinning the madman to the ground.

"What in the name of G'rlock!" Draven struggles as a hulking, blue, almost black jungle cat with gleaming gold eyes pins him to the ground. It bares its teeth in warning.

"How! I killed that wretched beast in the ruins of Mu!"

"That's a good girl Neesha." Knight jogs over and rubs the panther behind her ears affectionately. "If he moves, bite his head off."

"You can't stop this, Knight," Draven threatens, a tremor of panic slipping into his voice. "The Old Ones are already here. Look!" Draven uses a finger to point up. Knight follows with his eyes as another spear of lightning rips across the sky—in the brief moment of illumination, things move within the clouds. Giant things, impossible in scale and scope. Ill-defined as though formed by mist but becoming more solid with each passing second.

"See! It's not too late, Knight. Bow to them, kneel, and deliver the sacrifices." Draven nods to the prisoners. "And the Old Ones shall bestow their power on you too!"

"I got all the power I need right here, chump." Knight raises his fists for emphasis and then heads to the captive woman. He begins tearing at her ropes with his bare hands, sandy hair falling over his eyes as he pulls on an intricate knot.

Draven begins to cackle, defying Neesha's low growls and narrow-eyed stare.

"What's so funny." Knight frees one of the woman's hands, and it shoots to her mouth, pulling on a gag.

"You're not the only one with friends," Draven laughs.

"Huh?"

"Look out!" the woman screams too late.

A wall of fluttering darkness collides with Knight, sending him crashing to the ground. Shapes roughly in the form of purple-black birds with glowing red eyes peck and caw at him, covering Knight in feather and shadow.

Just as the world disappears behind vaporous wings, Knight hears Neesha roar, leaping into action. She charges into the flock, and soon they're swarming the mystical jungle cat instead.

"Neesha!"

The beast swats at the flock, slashing with mighty claws and lunging with crushing jaws.

"Watch out!" Knight yells too late.

The phantom birds torment the cat, confuse and fluster her, so she doesn't notice how close she is to the roof's edge. Neesha leaps and disappears, falling to the sleeping city below.

"No!" Knight's heart goes with the cat. "Neesha," he laments, and drops to his knees.

"You could have been a God." Draven stands above him, brandishing a strange, pronged dagger with a curved handle inlaid with carved tentacles. "You could have joined me." He raises the blade. "And ruled this world together, under the blessing of the Old Ones. Now, you'll be but one more offering—what's wrong with your nose?"

"Oh, this?" Knight tugs on and pulls away a fake nose, then more prosthetics, revealing himself to be the double of the man tied up behind them.

"You're not Dirk Knight! You're his blasted cabby! So where—"

"Right here, Draven!" the real Dirk Knight announces as he jumps down, ripping free of his bonds with inhuman might. The fake cabby driver pulls prosthetics from his own face, revealing the true Dirk Knight.

"Blast your pathetic disguises, Knight!" Draven raves with a raised fist.

A rocket blasts somewhere below the building, and a dark shape soars through the air. Neesha lands beside Knight, jet boosters clicking back into place, the robotic jaguar resuming its convincing animal form.

"Double-blast your incessant robotics too!"

"It's over, Draven." Knight cracks his knuckles as Neesha bares her teeth.

Another bolt of lightning cracks the sky, framing Knight and—

A sudden blast of light fills a bedroom, like full-on high beams, making a mousy girl sitting in bed shield her eyes and drop her book—*Dirk Knight: Curse of the Obsidian Dagger*—just as it was getting good.

"Ouch," she complains, and drops the beaten, old paperback to the floor. She gets out of bed and makes her way to the window. The light vanishes, and before her eyes can adjust to the sudden darkness, she stubs her toe. "Gosh-darnit!" She hops around, clutching her injured foot as another beam of light bursts through her window, blinding her again. This time she falls on her butt with a thud.

Footsteps race through the hall outside, and the bedroom door flies open a second later.

"Evie, what's going on?" Her mother flows into the room and shields her eyes. "My word, what is that?"

"Stubbed my toe, mom. I'm okay," Evie grumbles and blinks till she can see again. They move to Evie's window and bend the shades, peering as a heavy truck rumbles through a quiet neighborhood lined with orange poplar trees. "That's weird," Evie says. "Is somebody moving in?"

"That...shouldn't be happening," Evie's mother says.

"Yeah, who moves into a new house in the middle of the night?"

"Yeah," Evie's mother adds, "that's what I meant."

"What are you two nosy-birds up to," a tall man in pajamas says from the door. He takes two steps into the room when another searing light blares through the window, making him screw up his face and bang his toe too. He hops around, cradling it as Evie did moments ago.

"It would appear that we have a new neighbor," Evie's mother says, though it sounds oddly like a question.

"That doesn't make any sense." Evie's father hobbles over to the window. "How could they—" Evie's mother coughs, cutting him off.

"Move at night?" she quickly adds.

"Yeah," Evie's father says meekly. "Yeah," this time with confidence. "That's what I meant."

Evie's too fascinated with what's going on to pay much attention to her parents. Or even the three massive moving trucks, blasting their high beams into the night.

It's the sleek, dark old-fashioned car following them that catches her eye. The kind of car with a long hood and swooping wheel covers on the front makes her think of rolling waves and a prominent grille up front that roars like there's a monster caged within.

"Woah," Evie gasps. "That's a car."

"A 1940s Bentley, if I'm not mistaken," her father adds as he pushes his glasses up.

"What's an old English car doing here?" her mother wonders out loud.

The Bentley pulls up in front of the only house on the street that shows no sign of life: a three-story brick estate house covered in twisting vines that crawl up the walls and a side tower that rises into the night.

"Is someone moving into the old Welles house, mom?" Evie asks.

"They shouldn't be," she answers and shares a silent look with her husband.

The Bentley comes to a rest, and the lights go out. A moment later, a tall man unfolds himself from the driver's seat, dressed in a sleek suit. He places a matching hat on his head and leans on a cane that seems fancy, but Evie can't make out much from across the street.

The man dusts himself off, and just before he turns to head to the house, his cold, emotionless eyes lock with Evie's. She gasps as he waves and remains frozen as her parents return the gesture cautiously.

"We'll have to have a meeting about this," Evie's mother says.

"I'll arrange it in the morning. Best not wake—" Somewhere in the house, a phone rings. Then another. "Too late," he smiles and then heads off to answer.

Evie doesn't pay attention to any of that. All she has eyes for is the old pulp paperback dime novel on her bedroom floor. The book with the mad warlock Draven on the cover. The villain with the same cold, dead eyes as the man across the street. She takes the book to the window, holding it tight as she watches the slender figure duck his head and enter the house.

Evie closes her front door and sits on the front steps, pulling on a pair of rollerblades. She's so focused on the house across the street that she doesn't realize she's trying to force her left foot into her right skate.

A pudgy boy with a backward cap and a lollipop in his mouth weaves down the street on a skateboard with an absent-minded grace.

"Hey, Rob," Evie nods, then screws up her face as she keeps unwittingly forcing the wrong skate to go on her foot.

"'Sup Evie." He hops off his skateboard, lets it glide solo for a few seconds, and then kicks it up. "You know you got the wrong foot?"

"Huh?" Evie realizes her mistake, then groans. She switches feet, grumbling.

"What's biting you?" Rob asks and follows as Evie nods to the house across the street.

"Someone moved in last night. Real creepazoid."

"Yeah, heard my folks talkin' about it this morning." Rob pops the lollipop out and offers it to Evie. "Sour apple?"

"Ew, gross!"

Rob shrugs. He pops the lollipop back in and continues to look at the house.

"My mom was more miffed than when we made a death ring in Layton's yard."

"Our folks weren't mad about the ring," Evie corrects as she pulls on her other skate. "It was the fire damage, mostly."

"Oh yeah." Rob giggles and leans his skateboard against the side of the house. "Not like we meant to burn down his mom's greenhouse." He reaches into the front pocket of his hoodie and holds something out—a pair of steel cylinders. "Check it."

"Are those—"

"Oh yeah." Rob swipes them away, stashing them in his pocket as Evie reaches.

"And Layton's cool with this?"

"Cool with what," a bookish boy in a tucked-up button-down shirt calls as he skids his bike to a halt. Evie and Rob flash him a grin. "Guys?" he asks with a smile that begins to turn along with his stomach. "Guys..."

"GUYS!" Layton screams through bared teeth, his cheeks warbling as his bike rockets down the street.

Evie and Rob hold onto lines tied around the saddle of Layton's bike—Rob on his board, Evie in her skates, faces alive with wild joy.

"GUYS, THIS IS CRAZY!" Layton yells with nothing but laughter in response. The two steel cylinders spurt narrow, fierce blue flames from either side of Layton's rear wheel, effectively turning the BMX into a rocket bike. They whine like a blowtorch and then flare out in three flickering spurts.

Layton already has his brakes half-squeezed, so the deceleration is almost instant to him. Not so much for Evie and Rob, who slingshot past him on both sides.

Rob weaves from side to side on his board, gradually using the curves to slow down. Evie, however, loses control. She presses down on her stoppers, only to hear a whine and smell burning rubber. A neighbor in jogging gear, walking a Bullmastiff almost the same size as her, crosses the street.

"Out of the way, Mrs. Howard!" Evie yells.

The woman's reaction time is too slow, but the dog's more on the ball, and it pulls the woman to safety like it's trained for it.

"Sorry!" Evie yells back and turns just in time to see the rapidly approaching Bentley. Nothing she can do but close her eyes, shield her face, and brace for impact.

It never comes.

Suddenly Evie feels light as a feather. She's airborne and spinning around. Landing on her feet, shaking, she opens her eyes to see the tall stranger from last night before her. His white, almost dead eyes stare into her soul.

"You could have hurt yourself, dear." His voice sounds like one of those creepy old guys from those British horror movies Rob loves. "Are you all right?"

"Um." Evie feels faint. "Dizzy," is all she says.

The boys catch up, then immediately skid to a halt a safe distance away.

"You ought to be more careful." The tall man with a long, crooked nose pats her shoulder. "Would be a terrible shame if you were to come to harm."

"Yeah, um, yeah." She's still too dazed to think, to wonder if that's a threat or a promise. Her brain must be scrambled because she can't tell if his suit is dark blue, purple, or plain black. Something catches her eye, glinting on one of the eerily long fingers resting on her shoulder—a black ring shaped like a bird's beak that extends to a sharp point.

"What's your name, dear?" the tall man asks.

"Evie," she gulps. "Evie Marsh."

"Marsh?" The tall man smiles, so wide Evie's sure he'd have no trouble swallowing her whole. "I knew a Marsh once. My name's Corvus, Obediah Corvus. It's a pleasure to meet you, Miss Marsh." Corvus offers her his hand. Evie stares, then eventually, she takes it, his hand dwarfing hers. It feels like she's touching Death itself.

"Thanks." Evie nods. "Thanks for saving me, Mister Corvus."

"Oh please, not necessary." Corvus lets go, then uses his hand to make a show of shielding his mouth as though imparting a secret. "Besides, I was just saving the Bentley." He shoots her a wink that hits like a knife to the spine and then strides towards his house, waving politely to the gawking boys.

"I gots to get me some of those mini-rockets," Braden quips, rubbing his hands gleefully as Toby pauses in his story. He takes a deep breath "'Cause I feel the need…the need for speed!" The others only stare in silence. "You guys need to start watching good movies."

"I'm with you, Braden," Chardea says. "Though would two be enough to send him into space? Better make it three, just to be safe."

"Char-Char, I don't need to leave this planet to see the stars." Braden places one hand on his heart and gestures to Chardea with the other. "You're my sun and my moon."

A moment of silence follows. The Hallow Fire crackles, then Rascal groans, burying his head. Chardea snorts, then laughs, and the others join in one by one.

In The Dark, just beyond the reach of the Hallow Fire's glow, Gwennie hugs her ex-boyfriend's mask tight and tries to push down the anger rising within. How dare they laugh.

Chardea rises, her knees clicking.

"Ouch, you okay, grandma?" Braden jokes and then yelps as Chardea hurls the black book at him.

"Your turn, rocket boy," she grumbles and stretches her legs on the way to her seat.

"I got ya, T-1000," Braden jokes as he sits down next to Toby, nodding for him to continue.

"Well, Evie couldn't shake the feeling that this Corvus fellow and the chap from her book were one and the same..."

"I swear," Evie insists as the boys follow her to her room. "It's the same guy." She quickly grabs the old dime novel from her bedside table and shoves it in their faces. "See!"

"Um, what am I supposed to see?" Rob looks from her to Layton.

"This!" Evie taps the cloaked warlock on the book's cover. "Count Draven, sworn enemy of Dirk Knight."

"Right. Like that explains anything. And the old guy with the sweet car wrote this book or something?"

"No, dummy, look!" Evie shoves it in Rob's face. "It's the same dude!"

"Okay, first, why do old books gotta smell so bad." Rob pulls a face like his parents are boiling cabbage.

"That's the smell of knowledge," Evie snaps back. "Not that you'd know."

"Second, and I'm choosing to ignore that insult for now, how is the creepy D&D dude from your old book somehow real and living across the street?"

"The guy who wrote these old pulps said he based them on true stories—"

"Here we go." Rob rolls his eyes.

"Zachariah Smythe worked closely with a top-secret organization formed to monitor paranormal threats in post-war Europe and America. He based the character Dirk Knight on the brave men and women of that group and villains like the evil Count Draven on those who would seek to do society harm through nefarious means. He was a celebrated socialite and close friends with other noted creatives of his era, such as infamous film director Theodore Gorman."

"That proves nothing." Rob throws his hands up. "Anyone can make up garbage on a blurb." He coughs, "Rob Waylan Thurston is the most handsome author of his generation, celebrated far and wide for—ouch!" Evie smacks him with the book.

"Quit it!"

"You're not buying this, are you?" Rob turns to Layton and eyes the suspiciously quiet boy. "Dude, no, you can't!?"

"It's just," Layton sighs, "he was very fast for such an old man. You saw how quickly he snatched up Evie."

"Pfft, big deal." Rob taps his chest. "I coulda been that quick if I wanted to."

"Like the time you got knocked out by Trish Harrigan's fastball?" Evie smirks.

"That was a foul ball!" Rob protests. "And I wasn't ready!"

"Not to mention how strong he was," Layton continues. "He swooped Evie up like she was made of air."

"Hmm," Rob rubs his chin. "It's true, Evie's packed on the pounds lately, maybe you—Hey!" Rob swats at Evie's hands as she pinches his belly roll.

Layton wanders to the window, leaving them tickle-slap fighting.

"Can you imagine living across the street from some kind of supervillain?" Layton pushes his glasses up his nose, both lenses reflecting the decaying house across the street.

"Why would a supervillain move into Raven's Court?" Rob pushes away from Evie. "The most boring neighborhood in the world, where nothing remotely interesting happens. Ever."

"It's the kind of place an evil mastermind would lay low?" Layton suggests.

"See!" Evie sticks her tongue out at Rob. "Not so crazy."

"Do you have any more of those books with Count Draven on them?" Layton asks.

"Sure, my dad collects them. They're in the library downstairs; let's go."

Moments later, the three of them are in a large two-story balconied room, three walls across both floors packed with books while light streams in through a grand bay window. It lands on plush leather couches and a reading chair recliner.

"They're over here." Evie leads Layton to the rest of the vintage pulp dime novels while Rob throws himself onto one of the couches.

"You know, your dad might have questionable taste in books, but the man knows how to pick a couch." Rob wiggles his butt into a groove, and the other two ignore him. Instead, they take creased, worn books from a carefully organized shelf and check the covers. One shows the shirt-ripping hero, Dirk Knight, in the grip of vines, seemingly controlled by a beautiful woman wrapped in leaves. Another shows a scrawny scientist wearing elaborate armor, firing a blast of light at a beaten-down Knight from robotic gauntlets.

"Oh, oh," Evie says as she reads the back of one. "This one has the origin story of Count Draven." Both boys look at her, waiting for more. "Before he joined the Cult of G'rlock, and became its high-priest," Evie gulps. "Obediah Corvus was…"

"Pfft," Rob waves it off. "A coincidence."

"Maybe," Layton says as he looks at the next cover. "Maybe not."

"I knew it!" Evie makes excited fists as she looks at it too.

"What've you dorks found?" Rob asks, unwilling to get up and look.

Evie and Layton turn to him, presenting the cover of another Dirk Knight novel with the same Bentley their new neighbor drives on the front, Count Draven behind the wheel as it races towards a tied-up Dirk Knight.

"Okay, I'll admit, that's a bit creepy," Rob relents.

"You thinking what I'm thinking?" Evie says to the boys.

"Stakeout." Layton nods.

"Pizza," Rob says. "Um, I mean takeout. Steak. Steakout! What?" He holds his belly. "I'm hungry!"

Later that night, the adults of Raven's Court organized an impromptu Homeowners Association meeting at Evie's to discuss the new resident in their neighborhood. The gathering provided the perfect cover and excuse for the trio to reconvene in Evie's room after dark and without suspicion.

A telescope pokes through the shutters at Evie's window, wired to a tablet she sets down on the floor between the three of them, next to an open box from Zahn's Pizza. The image shows the house across the street, the waxing moon almost in line with the tower.

"Borrowed it from dad," Evie explains. "This way, there's no chance of him seeing us like some dumb kids in an old movie. And we can do this," she says, tapping on the screen. It zooms in.

"Nice." Rob burps. "Can I borrow this next week?"

Evie and Layton shoot each other a look like they're going to regret asking. "Why?"

"Zenna Henderson's gonna be back from college, so—"

"Ew!" Evie almost retches and throws a slice of pizza at Rob in disgust. "Bad Rob, bad!"

"Woah, check it out." Layton leans over toward the tablet and points to Corvus as he comes down the steps, looks around suspiciously, and climbs into his Bentley. The roar of its engine reaches them through the open window, and the trio watches as it drives off.

"Well, there goes that stakeout," Rob groans. "Instead of probably nothing happening, now it's absolutely nothing."

"Damn it." Evie crushes a corner of the pizza box with her fist. "I'm going over there."

"Wait, what!?" Both boys gawp at her. Layton's thick, almost singular brow furrows.

"I'm gonna go see what I can find," she says as she rummages in a drawer. "You two keep a lookout."

"Evie, you can't," Layton warns as she turns around with a pair of walkie-talkies.

"Sure I can," she insists.

"No, I mean, it's your house. What if your parents come upstairs? Won't they find it weird there's just us two here?"

"Nah," Rob waves the idea off. "They'll just assume you're going through her underwear drawer."

"Ew! Rob!" Evie snaps. "You got a point, though."

"Yeah, Layton's a weirdo. Oh, you mean the first part?" Rob stands up and rubs two hands covered in pizza grease on his jeans. "I'll do it," he says, snatching one of the radios. "One of you keep an eye on the tablet and the other on our folks. I'll go see what kind of stuff the old creep's into."

Their parents are all gathered in the library, in the middle of a heated debate.

"I dinna see how," a voice Evie recognizes as Layton's mother complains. "Were there no bylaws for this type of situation?"

"Technically, yes," Evie's father explains.

"You and your damn technically, Dwight," Mr. Howard from down the street complains.

Evie nods for Rob to go, and he creeps past the open door, keeping low.

"I'm confused," Rob's father says. "It shouldn't matter how rich someone is. If they're not one of us—"

"I think," Evie can hear her mother say. "Technically..."

With Rob safely to the other side, she hurries back to her room, giving Layton the thumbs-up as he watches Rob come into view.

"How's he doing?" Evie asks, eyes flicking from Layton to the other end of the hall.

"Moronically," Layton explains as, on the tablet, Rob rolls from bush to bush, jumping into piles of leaves and army crawling across the lawn. He eventually makes it across the street and pauses to give a thumbs-up as he heads around the side of the house.

"Red Falcon to Brown Trout," Rob calls over the radio. "I repeat, Red Falcon to Brown Trout, over?"

"Don't call me that," Layton complains.

"That's a negative there, Brown Trout, over."

"Just play along," Evie hisses. "We don't have all night."

"Fine," Layton groans. "This is Brown Trout; come in, Red Falcon."

"That's a ten-four there, BT. Found a possible entry point."

"Huh?" Layton looks at Evie, and she shrugs. "Say again, Red Falcon."

"Dude left his basement window open; I'm going in!"

"Rob! Don't!" Layton shouts into the radio and immediately hunches up as Evie urges him to be quiet. "Rob, that's against the law! Don't!"

"Too late, dude." Rob's voice cracks over the radio. "You should see this place. It's...wild, like...spooky as sh—"

"Rob? Red Falcon? Come in," Layton begs into the radio. "Rob, stop kidding around."

"Oh no." Evie points across the room to the tablet as the Bentley returns.

Evie and Layton look at one another, their faces turning pale as Corvus steps from his car, a bag in hand, and heads to his front door. Their throats run dry and their hearts race against their chests as Corvus opens the door and steps inside.

"What do we do?" Layton turns to Evie, and the only answer that follows is silence.

We'll Be Right Back After These Messages...

Cicadas sing into the night, a lullaby for a sleepy southern town, for a beautiful house sitting in the dark.

Cut: inside, a man wakes, getting out of bed without disturbing his sleeping wife. He pads down a long hallway, blue light filtered through wooden shades, running a hand through tousled hair.

"Mary-Lee?" the man calls as he pushes the door open. It creaks an inch—

Flash-cut: a long-shot of a dilapidated well, somewhere in the swamp.

"Honey?" The door opens wider—

Flash-cut: a mid-shot of the well. Is that a hand in the rim?

"Mary..." The door opens fully, revealing a child's bedroom. Bed empty, window open wide, curtain fluttering in the breeze.

Flash-cut: long, inhuman fingers uncoil and slide down into the well to the accompaniment of hair-raising string music. "Mary-Lee!" the man's voice echoes with pain as though bouncing off the walls of the well.

"A missing child," a dramatic narrator announces.

Cut to: fires burning outside an isolated house, a dark-skinned boy and pale girl within, alight with flame and terror.

"A town soaked in evil," the narrator continues.

Cut to: a tall, muscular man pouring startlingly blue river water over his scarred back.

"A man drowning in mystery... This Halloween, NBC presents *Mississippi Blue*, starring David

Duchovny, Sherlyn Fenn, and Brandy Norwood. Friday nights at ten."

A pale man with shiny, slicked back hair and oversized fangs rises from a coffin with his arms crossed over his chest. He licks his lips and yawns, glancing at an ornate grandfather clock. Cracking his back, he heads to a window and pulls back thick, velvet curtains.

Brilliant, bright sunlight streams through the window, making the vampire squeal and leap back as smoke hisses from his flesh. He scrambles for a pair of antique glasses and squints at the clock, unable to make out the time.

"Bah!" He tosses the glasses away.

"Don't let out of prescription glasses ruin your night," a voice-over states.

Cut to: a modern optician's office as the vampire floats to the counter.

"Come on down to Tully's Opticians, where we pride ourselves on the friendliest service," the voice-over continues. "We don't bite."

"Mr.," the receptionist checks a form, "Impaler, the doctor will see you now."

"Please, call me Vlad," the vampire winks at the screen.

"Promise," the voice-over adds.

We Now Return To The October Society.

"Oh man." Braden rubs his hands together. "Rob's in for it."

"You're a strange, little boy, aren't you," Chardea snipes.

"Wonder if Corvus is gonna sacrifice Rob." Holly bounces with macabre glee.

"Funny." Toby flashes a sinister smile. "That's exactly what Evie and Layton were arguing over..."

"He's gonna use Rob's blood to open the door to the Old Ones for sure." Evie paces back and forth; hair pulled up into spikes as she runs her hands through it.

"What do our grandparents have to do with this?" Layton's confused.

"Not oldies." Evie snatches up the Dirk Knight book from her bed and taps the misty, tentacled shapes in the clouds behind Draven. "Old Ones, you know, the nasty old wriggly crab-things from another dimension. Ancient before man was born. Duh."

"Must have missed that history lesson," Layton mutters. He scrunches his face up like something's stuck in his teeth.

Evie goes to the window and pulls down the shades.

"Be careful. Bad enough Rob's in for it. We don't want to end up like him."

"What? Awesome?"

Evie and Layton jump and see Rob standing in the doorway with one hand behind his back, and the smuggest grin spread across his face.

"Rob!" Evie gasps. "We thought you were a goner."

"Puh-lease," he waves off their concerns. "I'm basically a ninja."

"You were basically dead if Corvus caught you," Evie growls, and her eyes narrow. "What's behind your back?"

"Something," Rob teases. "Something pretty wicked."

"Oh no," Layton sighs.

"What did you take, Rob."

Evie's face drops as Rob brings his other arm around and reveals a dagger. Jet-black pronged blade so clean it's like a dark mirror, the curved handle inlaid with twisting, tentacle-like designs.

"It looks just like the one described in the book. The Blade of G'rlock."

"The blade of what-what?" Layton asks, stepping around to examine the strange weapon.

"G'rlock," Evie repeats. "Used to summon the Old Ones."

"It doesn't look man-made," Layton observes. "Almost like it's forged from polished coral or something."

"It's going on my wall, is what it is." Rob pulls it away as both Evie and Layton reach out to take it.

"It's going back!" Evie growls. "Hopefully, before Draven—"

"Corvus," Layton corrects.

"Corvus," Evie nods a thank-you, "notices it's gone."

"No fair," Rob whines. "Finders keepers."

"Only if you find it on the street." Evie grabs the dagger. "Otherwise, it's just burglary, you moron!" She wrestles the blade from Rob, and the world goes quiet for a second. There's only a hum, more like a distant buzz so loud she can still feel the vibrations from a world away. The longer she listens, the more distinct the sound becomes. The closer it gets to something resembling a voice.

"**EEEEEEVVVIEEE**." Her name's formed by something vast and ancient, the sounds made without a mouth or tongue. "**C'TARL EVIE C'TARL C'TARL...**"

"Huh!?" Evie drops the dagger onto her bed.

"I said, Evie, you alright?" Layton shakes her shoulder. "You wigged out there for like five minutes."

"Yeah." Evie shakes her head. "Yeah, I'm good." She grabs a t-shirt from her laundry hamper and wraps the dagger in it, careful not to touch it.

"What's the plan?" Layton asks.

"Need me to," Rob strikes a ninja pose, "sneak back in?"

"No." Evie shakes her head. "You're not going anywhere near that house again. You're on lookout duty."

"Aw, but I wanna—"

"You'll stay here and keep out of trouble," Evie warns him.

"Jeez." Rob kicks the air. "You sound like my mom." A smirk appears on his face. "You won't know where to sneak back in without me."

"If you found an open window so—"

"I closed it, but the lock's busted," Rob proudly states. "And I dunno if I can remember where." He whistles badly.

"Ohmygod." Evie slaps her forehead. "Fine, you come with me, but you're staying outside."

"Aye, aye, Captain!" Rob salutes.

"I'll watch your backs," Layton reassures.

"I know," Evie nods, and minutes later, she and Rob scamper across the street. They stick to the shadows provided by rows of poplar trees that filter the orange glow of street lamps, then follow the side of the house around to the backyard.

"Okay, tell me exactly where you found this," Evie shoves the t-shirt-wrapped dagger into her belt.

"It's better if I show—"

"No, no way." Evie holds a finger in Rob's face. "Tell."

"Fine." Rob crosses his arms in a huff. "Go up the stairs from the basement and first door across the hall. It's like a big old lounge. There's a bunch of moving boxes; it goes in one of them. Got its own special case."

"And you didn't think he'd notice that was missing?" Evie shakes her head.

"He's got loads of them!" Rob shrugs. "Figured he wouldn't miss one." He avoids Evie's stare for as long as possible before eventually meeting her eyes and pointing to one of the ground-level windows. "That one."

Evie pushes it open with a grunt and slowly lowers herself inside. The basement's empty except for a strange row of generators, all brand-new with not a speck of dust on them. Evie figures they could put out a tremendous amount of power from the size and how advanced they look, but currently, they're as silent as the rest of the house. So silent, she worries that each creak of the stairs will bring Corvus running.

Her focus is entirely on what's ahead; a tumbling, clattering from behind makes her jump. She turns to see Rob forcing his way through the window.

"What are you doing!" Evie hisses, frightening Rob—he falls the rest of the way, landing hard on the table below.

"I'm good," Rob insists, and the table cracks like thunder in the empty basement.

Evie tenses up, shoulders hunched as she slowly turns toward the door at the top of the stairs. Any second now, she expects to see the dark shape of shoes in the lit-up space between floor and wood. Seconds tick past, and nobody comes. Evie allows herself to unclench her teeth.

"Don't help me up or nothin'. I'm good," Rob grumbles.

"What part of wait outside didn't you understand!"

"Figured you might need backup." Rob shrugs. "Anyway, it's too late now—"

"Yeah, and you broke our way out!"

"Well, if you didn't yell at me, it wouldn't have happened."

"Don't you dare blame me for this," Evie snarls.

"Kinda is if you think about it." Rob smiles smugly. "You're the one who insisted this dude was some supervillain cultist."

"Forget where it came from; I know exactly where I wanna shove this dagger!" Evie grabs the wrapped blade stuck through her belt.

"Evelyn, are we going to stand around jawing all night or do this?"

Evie's ready to smack him. Her whole body trembles, but she keeps her cool. "Fine." She grabs Rob and pushes him up the stairs. "Lead on."

They emerge into a large hall, dominated by a single wide staircase covered with a dusty red runner. It's as dark as the basement but not so silent. From somewhere upstairs, soft music plays—old-time stuff that neither of them would recognize, even if it were more than a barely audible mumble.

Rob points to a room across the hall, and they both creep their way to it. Their eyes never leave the staircase till they're through the door.

A grand fireplace dominates one wall, with all the furniture covered in dusty sheets. Bookcases stuffed with dusty tomes line the walls, including the curved section where the tower encroaches on the room. Rob's description of the boxes turns out to be lacking; they're more like black, carbon, almost military-style crates.

"Which one?" Evie asks, and Rob points.

Clean, white halogen light fills the room as Evie cracks the case open.

"Woah," her jaw drops.

"I know, right?" Rob smirks.

The inside is lined with padded grooves, all but one filled. One clear box contains a gold signet ring, a figure of eight on top that seems to flow constantly, and in another, a beetle-like device with five extending wires, each ending in a finger-sized hoop. One more contains a simple rope, coiled like a sleeping snake, yet it's the most secure case in the box. In the space between them is an empty container with a depression in the exact shape of the pronged dagger.

Evie takes the blade from her belt, careful to keep her t-shirt between it and her skin, and she puts it back where it belongs.

"That's that then," Rob complains, his eyes wandering to the other wonders in the crate.

"Don't even—"

A tremendous thud from upstairs cuts Evie off, and she and Rob look at one another. The sound of footsteps pace across the ceiling above, heading toward the hall.

"Book it!" Rob yells, and, for once, Evie sees no reason to argue.

The two of them race for the front door, hearts pounding, and they're through it before the house's occupant reaches the stairs. They're safe across the street before he gets to the hall and bends to scoop up the t-shirt so hastily forgotten in their hurry to escape.

Evie and Rob burst into her bedroom, panting and celebrating equally.

"Layton! You're not gonna...Layton?"

The room's empty.

"Did he have to go?" Rob wonders.

"He wouldn't have left without saying something," Evie says as she picks up the other radio from the bed.

Curtains flutter with the night's breeze.

"Was that window always open?" Rob asks.

"No." Evie's throat dries up. She walks over to the window and looks through. There is still no sign of Layton—just a single, long black feather sitting on the window ledge.

The following morning...

Evie presses a doorbell outside a house covered in greenery. The yard's packed with strange and exotic flowers, and the only visible parts of the actual building are planter-lined windows. Vines snake around the pillars, while walls of roses grow in every available space.

She presses the bell again, and Layton's mother comes to the door, barely cracking it open, dressed in gardening overalls, her face smeared with mud.

"Um, hi Mrs. Dahlia, is Layton home?"

"Oh, Evie." She looks over her shoulder as though checking with someone. "Layton and his father have gone on a wee boy's trip."

"Really?" Evie doesn't buy it.

"Mhmm, camping up north."

"He didn't say anything about that last night."

"It was a last-minute thing. You know how it is."

Evie does not. "But—"

"Must go. The ghost orchids need me!" She slams the door on Evie, the suddenness only adding to her suspicion that something's wrong.

It plays on her mind as she walks past two more pretty suburban houses. Several black, raven-like birds stand on power lines and tree branches, watching her go. Evie barely notices them; she's too lost in thought. She turns up the walk on the third house and raps on the door.

"Something weird's going on at Layton's," Evie states as she pushes inside and continues before Rob can close the door. "I went to see him, and his mom came to the door."

"Nice." Rob smiles. "What was she wearing?"

"Dude, no." Evie grabs his shoulders. "This is serious!"

"So is Miss Dahlia's hotness," Rob points out.

"I think something's happened to Layton, and Corvus has put, like, a spell on his mom."

"She put a spell on me, that's for—"

"Rob!" Evie shakes him. "Layton's gone."

"What do you mean gone?"

"His mom says on a camping trip with his dad, but you know..."

Rob shakes his head. "That doesn't sound like Layton at all. Or his pops. But this ain't one of your dumb books, Evie. Corvus is just some old dude. A creepy one with a house full of weird stuff, but still."

"Just keep your head down." Evie looks through the curtains down the street to Corvus' house. "We don't want Corvus coming after us."

"I guess," Rob half-agrees, and Evie leaves him, confused and staring after her.

Although wracked with concern for her missing friend, Evie kept her head down and tried to keep a low profile for the next few days. Each night, strange lights from Corvus' house would flash, with no specific pattern or reason. When Evie brought it up, nobody seemed to know what she was talking about—nor were they concerned about Layton and his father, who had still to return to the neighborhood.

As the residents of Raven's Court strung up spooky lights and put candles inside carved pumpkins—

Evie skates along the street, weaving between piles of fallen, raked leaves. She pretends she's just out for fun, but her route takes her around Corvus' house several times.

Evie observed.

Red-eyed ravens perch on the branches of shedding trees and watch Evie. Their heads turn as one, following her wherever she goes.

Unbeknownst to her, she wasn't the only one.

A flash of light dances across Evie's bedroom, and even if she were asleep, it would have woken her. She grabs her tablet and quickly checks the feed. Though it's the black and green of night vision, Evie can see the bursting glow emanating from the basement windows across the street.

She throws her bedsheets off, already dressed, and slips on her sneakers. Snatching a high-tech camera stolen from her father, she races out into the night—avoiding all the patches of dried, fallen leaves that might give away her approach, sticking in the shadows as much as she can with clear skies and a waning moon high above.

Evie had been waiting for Corvus to slip up, do something she could use to prove he was dangerous—that he had done something to Layton.

Chardea: Clever girl.

Well, so she thought...

Evie readies her camera and sneaks up to one of the windows as another flash comes.

"Let's see what you're up to," Evie whispers as she checks the recording to see it's just the basement light flaring up as the generators whir. He must be pumping more power through the house's wiring than it can handle. Hardly the evidence she needs to prove that Corvus isn't who he claims to be.

"No, please, no!" a voice yells from up high—from the top of the cylindrical parapet above the house. "What's happening? I don't wanna—"

"Layton." Evie recognizes the voice right away—and he's in trouble.

"Please!"

Evie looks to the vines snaking their way up the tower. She doesn't know if they can take her weight, but her friend is up there, and he needs her. Tucking the camera into her pocket, she tugs on the closest vine, and when it stays fixed to the wall, she begins the climb.

"What's happening!" Layton cries, full of anguish. Evie can hear raw, guttural fear in his voice, spurring her on. She climbs faster, not even stopping to test the strength of the vines anymore as she races to the top.

Near the lone window, Evie wraps one arm around a vine to secure herself and then takes the camera out. She uses her nose to start the recording just as Layton screams again, but before she can point it to the window, something comes at her from the night—a flurry of wings with a razor-sharp beak.

"Go away!" Evie swishes at the raven with the camera, and it dodges her effortlessly. "Move it—oh, crap!" The vine comes free, dislodged with the exertion, and Evie grabs hold as she drops down almost an entire floor before the vine snaps taut.

"Phew," Evie breathes a sigh of premature relief. "Oh, no," she gulps as the raven finds purchase on the wall and begins to peck at the vine. "Nice raven, good raven, please stop..."

The raven caws then continues pecking.

"This is gonna suck." Evie braces herself for the fall, and she rappels at speed a moment later.

She hits the ground hard, not enough to break anything, but enough to make it feel like she has. Still, Evie gets to her feet and scampers away before anyone can come to investigate the noise.

Moments later, she's back in her room, with the lights off. The only sound is the tap-tap-tapping of her heart against her chest. As she catches her breath, she realizes that the sound isn't coming from her but the other side of the room.

Carefully, Evie approaches the window, the sound growing louder with each step. She reaches the wall beside it and sides up to it, readying herself for quick action. Snatching the curtains, Evie yanks them open and spins around with a fist held high—she freezes at the sight of a raven tapping on her window. It taps once more for emphasis, then flies off—leaving something behind.

Evie waits till it's long gone, then cracks the window. She reaches out and picks up the raven's gift—almost dropping it the second she recognizes her t-shirt. Her knuckles turn white, clutching the t-shirt, and Evie looks to the window atop Corvus' house. At the silhouette of a tall man just standing there, watching.

"He's got Layton," Evie barks before she's even inside Rob's house.

"Huh," Rob grumbles, still half asleep.

"I've been up all night, couldn't sleep. Corvus has Layton, and he knows I know. I think he has these birds spying for him."

"Whazzat?"

"Corvus." Evie grabs Rob's shoulder and shakes him. "Has Layton!"

"Evie." Rob shakes her back. "You're crazy!"

"Crazy, huh?" Evie pulls out the camera. "Listen to this." She hits play, and though the recording only shows the exterior of Corvus' house, they can hear Layton calling for help.

"No way." Rob's face turns white. He stumbles back until he finds a seat.

"Told you," Evie points out.

"What are we gonna do? Should we tell our folks?"

"No." Evie thinks of how strange Layton's mother was acting. "Who's to say he hasn't gotten to some of them too?"

"It's hopeless then."

"No." Evie sits down beside Rob and puts her hand on his shoulder. "I've got a plan."

"Yeah?"

"Yeah." Evie nods. "Tomorrow night, Halloween, we're getting our friend back."

"Hey, mom?"

Evie's parents flutter around, getting the house ready for their big Halloween party.

"Yes, dear," Evie's mother says, dressed as a primal witch with blood-red markings across her face.

"I was thinking…maybe you should invite Mr. Corvus from across the street to the party."

"Watch out, pumpkin." Evie's father dances around her, carrying a tray of baked snacks. He titters at the pun—Evie's dressed in a giant, puffy pumpkin costume that's far too big for her.

"There's an idea, honey," Evie's mother says to her father, dressed in a mad scientist costume complete with a wild-haired wig. "Evie thinks we should invite the new neighbor to the party?"

Her father scratches his nose. "Would give us a chance to find out about—" he shuts up as Evie's mother elbows him. "Want me to go invite?"

"No." Evie's mother brings out her phone. "I'll ask Delilah."

"Good idea. She can make any man," he catches her glare, "be a loyal and faithful husband and nothing more."

"I'm just gonna go trick-or-treating with Rob, okay?"

"Sure thing, dear," her mother says, already typing the message and thinking of ways to grill Mr. Corvus.

Evie leaves through the front door, making a big show of it, and quickly glances around. The sun's low, casting long shadows and a red glow through the neighborhood. Kids run wild, screaming with bags already sagging with candy as rolls of toilet paper sail through the branches of orange poplar trees. She doesn't react to the fact that at least a dozen ravens watch and acts cool as she pulls her costume mask over her head.

She heads around to the shed out back, two ravens leaving their perches to follow. As soon as she's inside, Evie picks up speed.

"Quick," she hisses as she pulls the costume off and hands it to Rob, who sits on the ground in Evie's rollerblades. "Get this on and get out there before Corvus gets suspicious."

"Got it." He takes the discarded pumpkin costume from her and suits up.

"Make sure you don't take the mask off; the suit's so big that he can't tell the difference unless he sees your face."

"I'm not, despite what you might think, an idiot," Rob insists.

Evie takes out a duffel bag she placed there earlier and begins pulling on a second costume.

"What's that one?" Rob asks as he pulls the mask down over his face.

"I'm," Evie spins around, cloaked in black, her eyes showing through a small rectangular gap, "a ninja!" She strikes a pose.

Moments later, the ravens spying on the shed flutter to life, hurrying to keep up with the pumpkin on skates. Evie watches from the shadows as they follow and, sure none of them remain, she creeps along the side of her house.

She watches from the corner as Mrs. Dahlia stands in front of Mr. Corvus' front door in an off-the-shoulder little dress that makes her look like an exotic flower. She takes Corvus' hand, tilting her head towards Evie's house. Though the man shows some resistance, he eventually caves—emerging from his home a moment later with a bird-like face mask and tophat, letting Mrs. Dahlia take him by the arm and escort him to the party.

"Gotcha, you bird-nosed freak," Evie smirks and slinks towards the now empty house across the street.

The window 'round back, though flush-tight, still hasn't been fixed, and with minimal force, Evie pushes it open and slips inside. She doesn't mess around and breaks for the second floor without worrying about getting caught.

Given what she saw the night she climbed the tower, Corvus had to have stashed Layton there. There didn't seem to be an entrance on the first floor, so it must be on the second.

Evie finds just a rounded brick wall where the tower pushes up against the rest of the house.

"Hmm." She taps on the bricks, testing them, but they're solid. That only leaves the lounge, where a curved bookcase covers the rounded wall instead of bricks. Evie's read enough comics and old pulp mystery novels to know that has to be it. She could test every book to see which one opens the secret door, but she doesn't have time for that and looks for the newest book instead.

Near the right side, the third shelf from the bottom, she spots a nondescript black book with a groove smeared in the dust.

"Gotcha." Evie pulls on it and steps back as the curved door clunks open on heavy, ancient cogs. One thing's for sure, Corvus didn't build this place, which begs the question—did he choose this house precisely because of this secret area? And how did he know?

Those thoughts are blasted away by blinding halogen lights as soon as the door comes to rest. Those lights bolted crudely to the ancient brickwork are definitely new. Evie shields her eyes against the searing white glare and squints through the gap in her fingers.

Above her, a wrought iron staircase spirals up the tower. "I'm coming, Layton," she whispers between quick breaths. Evie's pounding footsteps ring and echo as she races to the top.

"Woah," her jaw drops inside her mask when she reaches Corvus' lair. It's not a sinister arcane chamber filled with black magic as she expected but a pristine, high-tech laboratory. A wall of monitors covers much of the available space, with a sleek control console below them. "What the..."

Each monitor shows a different view of the neighborhood, from high angles and through windows. Several of them follow a chunky, rollerblading pumpkin as it loops around the area. The decoy's still working, at least.

Caw!

Evie jumps at the sound and turns around.

Caw!

She approaches a workstation, pulling her mask off in disbelief, and misses as the shot of her house shows Corvus heading through the front door, waving off requests for him to stay.

A raven lies on its back below a work lamp, wings spread wide and its chest wide open.

Caw!

Instead of blood and guts, the creature's filled with wires and plastic components.

"They're robots," Evie says as she turns to the monitors again. "Spy drones."

Ca-a-a-w... the robotic raven's red eyes fade, and it stops twitching.

"So weird, but where the heck is Layton—"

"Layton. Dahlia. Whereabouts unknown. Do you wish to see the last known location?" A soulless, formless female voice asks, and Evie yips.

"It's an A.I.," she thinks to herself. "Yes," she says out loud, "show me Layton Dahlia's last location, um, please, and thank you."

A single feed takes over all the monitors, spread across them. It shows a view of Evie's room through one of her windows, Layton standing in the middle holding the tablet. The date at the bottom confirms Evie's suspicion; this was the night he went missing.

Layton puts the tablet down and walks to the window, scratching his arm like an allergy's flaring up. His lip twitches like his gums are itchy.

"What's happening," Layton says and stumbles, holding onto the window frame for balance. "No, please, no," he begs as his face tenses up. His jaw opens wide, locks, and then stretches even further. "Mom! Dad! Help!" His eyes change color, turning yellow, and an annotation appears onscreen, drawing a line to a white glint caught in the boy's glasses. It reads: waxing moon triggering change, subject confirmed lycanthrope (no evidence of druidic powers yet).

"No way..." Evie stares at the screen as Layton drops to all fours, growling, and his parents race into the room. A tab at the bottom catches her eye, labeled Subject X. "Open the file on Subject X," Evie says and almost faints as every screen fills with different annotated still images of her.

"Playing most recent notes," the disembodied voice says.

"Subject X," a rough, male New Yorker voice takes over. "Evelyn Marsh displays no signs, as yet, of either Eldritch or Technomancy powers. Perhaps she was spared Draven's influence? I'll continue to monitor—"

"No." Evie backs away from the screen.

"Such a combination of powers would make for the most dangerous—"

She backs right up into Corvus, standing watching her. "Uh-oh."

Long, cold hands land on both shoulders as Evie gulps.

"I must admit, Miss Marsh. I'm rather impressed you gave me the slip. A simple trick, but effective nevertheless."

"Does that mean you'll let me go?" Evie pulls a butter wouldn't melt smile.

"No, child, I'm afraid not." She feels his grip tighten.

"Thought so." Evie stomps on his foot, making him release his grip. She elbows him in the stomach, and when he doubles over, she whacks his nose with the back of her head. Free from his grasp, Evie bolts for the stairs.

"Wait!" Corvus yells, only it doesn't sound like him. His accent is more Brooklyn than Buckingham now. "Kid, you gotta listen to me. Your folks ain't whatcha think."

Evie turns at the top of the stairs and watches as Corvus pulls free his long, crooked nose—strands of latex snapping as it comes away. He yanks back a wig, sleek gray-black hair replaced by white, sandy blonde.

"I know you," Evie says but can't place him.

"My name is—"

"We know who you are!" a woman's voice booms up the spiral staircase, and both the older man and young girl watch as Mrs. Dahlia rises, lifted by twisting vines that carry her with the grace of an acrobat.

"Couldn't just leave us alone, could you." Evie hears her mother's voice before she appears from a purple portal that rips through the air and vanishes behind her as she steps through.

"I'm coming," Evie's father calls from below, desperately out of breath.

Vines shoot from Mrs. Dahlia and pin the stranger to the wall; he groans through gritted teeth.

"These stairs, woo!" Evie's father reaches the top, dripping with sweat.

"That's what you get when you keep using jet boots to get to work, darling," Evie's mother tuts.

"Says you," He heaves. "Using magic, oh my stars, portals to go shopping in Milan."

Evie's mother shrugs. "It was fashion week."

"Villians!" The man clenches his fists. "All of you! Your kind will never—"

"Oh, shut up!"

Evie's mother waves her hand, and the man's mouth seals closed. He mumbles, the whites of his eyes showing, but his lips won't part, no matter how hard he tries.

"Honestly, you and your kind still think we're in the days of capes and tiny little face masks. Standing on giant robots and declaring your intention to destroy the world is, well, it's rather gauche."

Evie's mother walks up to the man and rips his shirt, revealing a massive scar down his chest.

"Dirk Knight. You might have been a match for our parents, but these days we rule the world with our phones from coffee shops while we enjoy a nice pumpkin spice latte. Honestly, do you think we're still in the so-called Golden Age?"

Evie's mother crosses the room and puts an arm around her daughter.

Evie's hands glow purple, like her mother's, and her eyes emit a blue vapor.

"Mom? Dad? What's happening to me?"

The broken robot raven flutters to life and flies to Evie's shoulder as her father comes to stand beside her.

"You're growing up, kiddo." His right arm comes apart in a cloud of blue steam, mechanical parts reconfiguring themselves into a glowing cannon pointed right at Knight. He takes a side glance at his daughter and beams with pride.

"No," Knight protests. "Kid, it ain't too late for you! You don't have to be one of them."

"How dare you!" Evie's mother's eyes and hands glow. "She's our daughter, and we love her. Cherish her! How many orphan sidekicks have you gotten killed in your righteous crusade!?"

"Evie, honey, go wait downstairs till mummy and daddy take care of this." Her father's arm cannon whines as it charges.

"*Chan eil fàilte oirbh an seo.*" Mrs. Dahlia's vines snap like angry piranhas as her voice becomes inhumanly deep.

Evie looks through her father's eyes and sees strings of code. She feels how she could so easily alter it with her mother's hand.

"Mr. Knight?" Evie focuses on the old hero. "Did you kill my grandpa like in the book?"

"He was a monster, would've killed millions. Turned the Earth over to things—"

"But he was my grandpa." Evie clenches her fist and holds her ground.

Her parents look at one another, eyes welling with pride.

"That's our girl," they say before Knight's screams fill the tower and ring out into the night above an otherwise idyllic suburban neighborhood.

"Knight was stuck in the past, and refused to move with the times. Locked in his old-fashioned ways, he couldn't see how easily he was outmatched by the children and grandchildren of those he swore to defeat. And that, unfortunately, was his undoing."

The Hallow Fire crackles as Toby awaits the response.

"Bam!" Braden yells, jumping to his feet and dropping the black book in the dirt. He holds one arm out like a cannon. "Bam! Bam! Bam! I want me some energy blaster arms."

"I'll take the ability to shut people up with the flick of my hand, thank you very much," Chardea says with a wayward glance.

"So, were Evie's parents trying to make a super-supervillain, or were they just like a real mom and dad?" Morgan asks.

"Kind of sad if it was just for the powers," Holly agrees, "but they seemed to love her. All the parents did."

"Wait, was Layton a werewolf?" Braden asks, and the others all roll their eyes.

"Well, what did you all think?" Toby asks nervously. "I hope—"

"It was AWESOME," Braden yells. "Like a neighborhood full of supervillains and robo-ravens, that was cool."

"I think, for once, I have to agree with Braden," Chardea says and then shudders. "I need a shower."

"Yeah, cool story, bro," Morgan nods.

"Yeah-huh," Holly agrees.

"Well then." Toby looks at the flames. "Do I?"

"Reach in." Chardea nods, and Toby unfurls his long legs, rising to his feet. He steps to the Hallow Fire, towering over it, and the shadows twist across his face.

Toby puts his hands into the flames; they seem to recoil at first, as though unsure of him, but then wrap around his arms as they should. Concern spreads across Toby's face as he roots around, not finding anything.

"What's going on?" Braden looks at Chardea. "Has it done that before?"

"Once, yeah," she says with dry lips. "It rejected a kid, but—"

"Ah!" Toby sighs with relief. "There it is." He pulls a chalk-white mask from the flames with no detail, just a cold, expressionless sculpted face. "Phew."

"Dude, that is the creepiest mask I've ever seen," Braden gulps.

"Um, thank you, I suppose." Toby stares at the pale mask.

"It's like a No-Face or something," Holly notes.

"I don't get it." Braden pulls his cap off and scratches his messy hair.

"Sometimes, the meaning of the mask isn't clear right away," Chardea explains. "But the Hallow Fire's chosen it for a reason, and it'll make sense. Eventually."

Toby puts the mask on, and the effect is unsettling. Toby's long, slender form becomes more imposing beneath the expressionless mask without his soft, polite features.

"Welcome to The October Society," Chardea almost stammers, and the others all take a turn welcoming him though they cannot hide how much the mask unsettles them.

Braden leaves with Holly and Morgan, the trio joking into The Dark, while Chardea scoops up a sleepy Rascal.

"Sorry things are kinda weird," Chardea says.

"It's quite alright," Toby nods. "Till next time?"

"Yeah." Chardea kisses Rascal's little head. "See ya." She heads into The Dark, feeling somewhat guilty about how relieved she is to be away from that mask.

As Toby heads off alone, he stops just beyond the light of the Hallow Fire. Without turning, he speaks. "Do you want to talk?"

Gwennie slips from the shadows, her mask resting on her head, eyes puffy and red. She clutches Dino's werewolf mask against her chest and only nods her answer.

"Come on then." Toby holds a hand for her, and she takes it. The pair of them slip off into The Dark together.

Roll credits.

Episode Five

Did you know, before the days of candy corn and midnight movie marathons, your kind dressed in animal skins and wore their skulls? They frolicked around open fires, invoking evil spirits to push back against the rising of The Dark. Foolish, yes? But is it any different from your store-bought costumes? Your hayrides and haunts?

Is something wrong? Does the mention of those things not fill you with excitement? That autumnal thrill of sugar-coated danger that comes with the lengthening of the night? Don't you want to play tricks for your treats or bob for apples with blindfolded eyes? Don't you want to embrace the wonder of Halloween?

"I want to talk about my behavior last week." Gwennie stands before the rest of The October Society, all eyes upon her. "I've been a brat, and I think you all know for why." She takes a deep breath.

It pains them, Braden and Chardea especially, to see her suffering, yet they know they must listen. As uncomfortable as it makes each of them feel, they know it's worse for Gwennie, and the foul air between them has tainted the season.

"I've pushed away folks who just want to be my friend," Gwennie says as her eyes meet Chardea's—the devil nods to the witch. "Made new ones feel unwelcome," she glances at Holly, eyes watering behind her dragon mask. "And forgotten the old,"

Gwennie drops her head in Braden's direction. "I've just been a right fool, so I have."

Gwennie glances down to see Chardea taking her hand. Her tanned fingers lock with Gwennie's porcelain ones. Chardea nods, silently encouraging the little witch to continue.

"I'm not being funny; I wouldn't blame any of you if you didn't want to be around me anymore," her voice wavers. "Truth is, I don't want to be around me."

Gwennie takes her mask off with the other hand, letting the others see her face for the first time since Dino left. Her cheeks have hollowed, her eyes sunken and raw, and the shortness of her hair only brings the complete absence of softness into sharp focus. Those who knew her before see a flash of a sparkly-eyed girl—wispy hair caught in her lips as she laughed till bursting. The dead can't age, and yet she seems so much older.

"Dino was, well, he was my bridge to the rest of you. Not being funny, but sometimes I don't have a clue what you all talk about—like a Nintendo? What is that? I died nearly a hundred years before any of you were even born, and Dino was like the halfway point." Gwennie smiles wistfully. "He used to explain things, as best he could, after the meetings, so he did. I'm lost without him, and I don't want to be like this anymore." Her fingers tighten around Chardea's, around the mask. "Sad. Weak. It's pathetic—"

"Gwen, no—" Chardea tries to interrupt.

"No, please, let me finish! I tried not to be. I thought cutting my hair was something brave and more grown-up," Gwennie snorts, "but I was just being a silly little girl." She looks at Toby, eerily stoic in his emotionless white mask, and smiles. "So I'm going to do something about it, for real."

Gwennie drops Chardea's hand and approaches Holly. "I've been awful to you."

Holly, arms folded, meets Gwennie's eyes.

"I've seen you and Braden; the two of you have this connection. Like Dino and I used to. I was jealous."

"Uh," Braden goes to cut in, but Holly shakes her head, silencing him.

All the while, Chardea thinks back to what Holly said to her on the second night. About crushing on someone. She worried that a new romance would break Gwennie, but she already knew. Of course, Chardea thinks, if it's clear to someone who's never been in love, then it must be blinding to someone who's just lost it. That should grant her some relief, but why does the looming announcement stick in her throat like a lump?

"I'm sorry I've been so mean to you, Holly; you don't deserve it, you don't." Gwennie holds out her hand. "Can we start over?"

Holly chews on it for a second, then jumps to her feet. She's only slightly taller than Gwennie, so their eyes line up almost perfectly.

The air around the Hallow Fire is so tense not even the flames dare crackle.

"C'mere!" Holly throws her arms around Gwennie and pulls her into a hug. Gwennie, once the shock passes, puts her arms around Holly too. "I never met Dino, but from how y'all talk about him, he must have been somethin'."

"Um, may I?" Morgan appears beside them. "Dino was the one who found me in The Dark. I'd be lost without him. I mean, I'm still not giggin', but I guess I wanna say, like, I feel it that he's gone, Gwennie, so I can't even imagine. That's all." Morgan glances at Holly, then returns to her seat.

"Thank you." Gwennie wipes away a tear. "It should have been on me to help you figure this out."

"It's on all of us," Chardea adds. "Something's just off this year."

"It's the D-Man taking an extended vacation or whatever he's doing," Braden quips. "We need those shirts that say: in my defense, I was left unsupervised."

"You don't have to keep joking." Gwennie goes to him. "I don't deserve it. Out of everyone, I've been the worst to you."

"Nah, it's cool—"

"No." Gwennie kneels and takes Braden's hands. "I know you two were like brothers, best friends—"

"My only friend." Braden tears up, a raw surge of emotion crashing through his goofy barrier. "I didn't have any before I died. Before Dino, all of you. I know I say stupid stuff all the time; I can't help it. I just want people to like me."

"And we do." Gwennie leans over and pulls him into a hug.

"Yeah," Holly adds, "you're awesome, dude."

Morgan nods, and Rascal yips a yes from his spot by the Hallow Fire.

"An absolute delight," Toby chimes.

Silence follows. All eyes turn to Chardea.

"Urgh! Fine!" she uncrosses her legs and pouts. "Braden's not bad, I suppose."

"I love you too, Char-Char," Braden jokes as he wipes his eyes.

Those words give her the strangest fluttering sensation in the pit of her stomach.

"I hope you can forgive me." Gwennie stands and looks at Toby. He nods ever so slightly, and the hint of a smile twitches on Gwennie's lips.

The other four look to one another, then almost as one:

"It's cool."

"Nothin' to—"

"Fasho—"

"Of course." Chardea takes the black book from her bag. "So, who's up tonight?" Her eyes dart between Morgan and Gwennie.

"I'll go," Morgan pipes up. "If that's cool with you, Gwennie?"

"Uh-huh." Gwennie takes her seat next to Toby.

"Well done," he whispers as Chardea passes the book.

"This sorta links to the story I got." Morgan holds the book to her chest. "Emotions are like a bottle of soda, you shake them up enough, and the lid's gonna blow. Same's true for a lotta things. Sometimes you might do something stupid, something you think's a goof. Something you didn't even mean to, and before you know it, you've let something out you can't put back, no matter what."

The Hallow Fire surges, flames waving around and almost framing Morgan's sly kitsune mask.

"My October Fellows, we all got skeletons in our closets, and if you listen carefully, maybe you'll hear the rattling of…"

Those Quiet Bones

A hazy sun rises over Beacon Beach, a pretty little town hugging the hills of the Bay Area coast. It burns last night's rainfall into a fine mist that rises from the picturesque coastal highway and drifts between houses built on slats up the forested hill to the old military overlook.

As though lost in the mist, voices float in the air.

"Welcome," says a boy trying so hard to sound menacing it's adorable, "truth-seekers, to another episode of *Laughing at the Dark* where we poke fun at all things creepy and kooky—"

"Should we be laughing at kooky people?" asks a girl who sounds intentionally disinterested. "I mean, what if they're born that way?"

Their voices drift through a scenic lookout point with a World War II memorial wrapped in folds of fog. Words engraved at the base read: In Remembrance of Lives Lost for Liberty Beyond This Shore.

Waves lap, somewhere unseen below, slapping against the rocky shore like distant gunfire.

"It's just an expression, you know? Like 'under the weather' doesn't mean you're physically under the weather."

"But you are physically under the weather when it rains."

There's a moment of dead air and a heavy sigh as their voices bring us to a shimmering silver diner, lit up marquee reading Coast to Roast gleaming through the morning fog. Inside, two kids sit at a booth with a phone between them.

"Anyway, we are your hosts, Henry Kaneda—"

A boy's eyes narrow, pulling his lips into a smirk, like a puppy trying to look fierce.

"And Poppy Dewit."

A girl leans back, one arm over the back of her seat. She acts like she doesn't care, even though she bites nervously on her fingernails as they listen intently to the podcast.

"And we ask all the questions everyone else is afraid to."

"Yeah, like if Henry's girlfriend is real, why hasn't anyone ever seen her?"

"I have photos!"

"Please, they're more fake than the photos of the Morgawr you showed me last week."

"Anyway! This is the paranormal podcast where we talk about all the scariest things in life—"

"Like Henry's report card—"

"And laugh at them! Mwahahaha!"

"Bwahahaha!"

"Ny-ahahaha!"

"Ah—" the girl on the podcast coughs, then chokes till she spits. "Sorry, Skittle got caught in my throat."

"If you kids are gonna listen to that crap," a gruff voice cuts in as a thick shadow falls upon them, "use a damn pair of headphones!"

It's only then that the kids notice other patrons staring at them like it's way too early in the morning for this.

"Sorry, Mr. Powers," Henry cringes as he looks around the diner. "Sorry, everybody!"

"You two goofballs still doing that creepy podcast thingie?" a smart, older version of Henry with his long black hair slicked back says as he comes over, a steaming to-go cup of coffee in his hand.

"None of your business, butt munch," Henry snorts.

"Yup." Poppy gives a dreamy, toothy smile. "We just uploaded our eleventh episode!" She's eager to impress.

"Uh-huh, and what's this one? Space ants from Mars?"

Poppy snorts. "Right! Who'd believe in bunk like that."

Henry gives her a look that says: you.

"This episode was about the Kentucky Goblins, Brendan."

Brendan stares at them like those two perfectly recognizable English words were spoken in some ancient alien language indecipherable by modern humans. He takes a sip of his coffee, which doesn't do the trick. Eventually, he repeats.

"Kentucky. Goblins?"

"Yeah," Henry smiles like that makes all the sense.

Brendan chuckles. "They made of eleven secret herbs and spices too?"

"Eleven herbs," Henry whispers to himself, "eleventh episode," and slaps his forehead. "It all makes sense..."

"Actually." Poppy's head bobs. "Though they're called Goblins, evidence suggests they were extraterrestrial—"

"That means aliens," Henry explains.

"I know what an E.T. is, little brother. I live with one."

"And it's one of the few recorded instances where armed civilians fought in open conflict with extraterrestrial lifeforms."

"Uh-huh." Brendan scratches his head. "Did anybody, I dunno, manage to get photos of these Goblins? Or, like, shoot one of the goobers and keep the body?"

"No..." Poppy chews her lip. "But there are drawings and—"

"Look," Brendan nods for Henry to budge up, and he obliges. "I gotta admit, as soon as you two goofballs started this nonsense, I figured you'd give it up in a week. Two tops, but you're sticking to it, and I can respect that."

"Thanks." Poppy blushes.

"You kids want a nickel's worth of free advice?"

"Yeah? Oh, wait!" Poppy whips out her digital voice recorder and turns it on. "Okay."

"This Kentucky Goblin thing, the Mothman, and...what did you cover last time?"

"Morgawr," Henry says like it's an actual word.

"It's a lake monster," Poppy adds.

"Any evidence? Wait, no, let me guess, nothing conclusive?"

"Lake monsters are," Henry preens, "by their very nature, elusive."

"Sure, yeah, lots of places to hide in a lake... Anyway, goofballs, you're covering all the things others have done to death. You want to make a splash, you gotta find a USP."

"What's a mailman got to do with paranormal podcasting?" Henry scratches his head.

"Unique selling point, you goober," Brendan rolls his eyes and wonders how they're related. "Find something only you two can do. Do stories the others aren't talking about: local legends, that sort of stuff."

"Yeah, like what?" Poppy asks.

"You guys are kidding me, right?" He looks at the two of them dumbfounded. "There's so much weird stuff that happens around the Bay Area. Look, have you ever heard of," he leans in and brings his voice to a whisper, "The Dogman of Buena Gardens?"

Henry's and Poppy's eyes meet, and they burst into laughter.

"Welcome, truth-seekers, to another episode of *Laughing at the Dark*," Henry leans into one of two mics hooked up to his laptop. They're in his bedroom, walls plastered with blurry poster-sized photos of Bigfoot, Champ, El Duende, and artists' impressions of The Flatwoods Monster. A giant corkboard covered in a mess of printouts dominates one wall, string linking newspaper articles to low-resolution photos and screen captures from forums.

"Where we ask the questions everyone else is too afraid to," Poppy adds.

"Like, if a vampire bites its lip, is that the same as drinking its own pee?"

Poppy shakes her head, throwing her arms in the air and silently asking why.

"Or are octopi just the spiders of the sea?" Poppy follows.

"And this week, truth-seekers, we have something special for you."

"A true story," Poppy teases.

"From just along the coast, in shiny San Francisco."

"Picture the scene," Poppy nods, and Henry presses play on some soft, lo-fi beats. "It's the middle of the night. Young Himiko fought with her mom and ran off chasing a stray dog. She finds her way to Buena Gardens, the little dog yipping like a guide." She gives Henry a signal, and he plays some stock dog-barking audio. "She comes across a whole pack of dogs and a strange man, his face covered with a hood. When she looks beneath that hood, guess what she sees, Henry?"

"A black void? Nothingness? The end of the world as we know it?"

"No, she—"

"Jared Leto?"

"Worse." Poppy clears her throat. "It's not a human face, nor is it an animal's. Rather, some strange combination of both, for he is the Dogman of Buena Gardens."

"I still think Jared Leto would be worse."

"This story comes from a Reddit post. A user posted this photo, Henry." Poppy opens a still, badly shot image.

"Woah, that's something, fellow truth-seekers! Poppy's just shown me a photo of a man cloaked in rags, dog-like snout poking through."

"This is—"

"It's like Lassie wanted to play *Assassin's Creed*," Henry jokes, "like if the Emperor was just a Beagle." He snorts and then puts on a croaking, menacing voice. "Yes, come to the dark side; that's a g-o-o-o-o-d boy."

"The story of Himiko is just one legend surrounding this mysterious cryptid. There are many others like this one from..."

"I don't wanna look, I don't wanna," Henry says in the diner, a hand over his eyes. He peeks through a slot in his fingers, squinting at Poppy. "How's it doing?"

She purses her lips and pops her eyes.

"It's bad, right? I knew we should have done something famous. Stupid Brendan, betcha if we did the Bell Witch, we'd be rolling in downloads."

Poppy clucks her tongue.

"How many? Don't tell me, no, do—"

"We got—"

"No. Yes! Argh!" Henry buries his head. "I hate this."

"Fourteen downloads."

"Fourteen?" Henry raises his head, locking eyes with Poppy as she slowly nods. "Four," he breathes, "teen. Fourteen!" Henry leaps off his seat, arms in the air in celebration. "We got fourteen downloads!"

"I'll give you kids fourteen up-whacks if you don't simmer down!" Mr. Powers calls from behind the counter.

"We got fourteen downloads," Henry sings as he does the floss, "we got fourteen downloads! Mr. Powers, two orders of victory pancakes if you would, my good sir!"

The cook grumbles but goes about making the order all the same.

"Listen to this." Poppy waves for Henry's attention as he rides the pony back and forth across the diner. "It's from our Instagram. 'I thought I saw the Dogman once, but it was just @benkissel1 eating a footlong in a single bite'—from @drfantasty."

Henry stops mid-dance.

"No. Gosh. Darn. Way!"

He leaps back into the booth, snatching the phone from Poppy.

"Hey!" she protests as Mr. Powers comes over with two plates of pancakes covered in syrup, fudge sauce, and ice cream.

"I have no idea what victory pancakes are, so that'll have to do. What's got the pair of you so giddy?"

"Only the crème de la crème of paranormal podcasting, *The Last Podcast on the Left* commented on our Instagram."

Mr. Powers stares at them, and Poppy takes her phone back.

"Those are words, sure, but heck if I know what any of them mean."

"When we're famous, do you want a photo of us for the wall Mr. Powers?" Henry asks as he shovels ice cream into his mouth.

"Sure, that's a swell idea," the cook says as he leaves them. "Been meaning to redecorate the bathroom."

"Our Insta is blowing up now. It's insane." Poppy scrolls. "We're getting tons of comments."

"How many likes?"

"I dunno, lots of people like the whole local legend angle. They keep saying it felt authentic."

"Yeah, but how many likes!"

"I dunno; why does that matter?"

"'Cause!" Henry says with a mouthful. "If we get lotsa likes and followers, we might get sponsored."

Poppy ignores him. "I think your brother was right. People are responding way more."

"My brother said that?"

"Yeah, he said it would make listeners feel more connected if they could identify with the subject." Poppy smiles. "People are sharing their own stories about spotting the Dogman in our comments. How wicked is that?"

"We're never gonna be world-famous podcasters if it's just Bay Area listeners," Henry says as he digs into his pancakes.

"Why do we need to be world-famous?" Poppy puts down her phone and stares at him. "I thought this was about having fun and being part of the paranormal, cryptid hunting community?"

Henry rubs the fingers of one hand together.

"I've got it!" He gulps down a ball of vanilla ice cream and then holds his temples as the brain freeze hits.

"Ha! Serves you right." Poppy sticks out her tongue.

"Do a poll? That'll get people involved."

"You're right," Poppy admits. "That'll prompt a good discussion."

"And make sure we're doing what's gonna get us the most likes," Henry adds.

Polly makes the poll, though it sits uneasily with her. They've both arrived at the same stop via different routes, and she has a sinking feeling that their final destinations are miles apart.

Henry had trouble sleeping. He was too excited at the prospect of making it big with their thirteenth episode. Especially with Halloween approaching, he knew it was the right time, and with the momentum behind them, they could boost their podcast into the charts.

He'd go to bed rehearsing his promo spots for Spring-Heel'd Jack Coffee or Raycon Buds so much he dreamt about them—so much that he'd wake up in the middle of the night and immediately reach for his phone.

Wincing against the sudden brightness, Henry squints as he scrolls through the poll results. There are the usual things, like Wendigos, the Dyatlov Pass, and then troll suggestions like his mom.

"Joke's on you," Henry scoffs. "My mom's as scary as they come."

A couple of suggestions begin to stick, people pointing out you can pick up a lot of strange number stations and radio frequencies from the Bay Area. Others suggest paranormal games like Charlie Charlie or calling cursed phone numbers. Those ideas begin to simmer as he flicks through and then stops on one response that catches his eye.

The user picture shows someone in a hoodie, face obscured with darkness and overlaid with static. Their suggestion is a jumble of numbers and letters.

"WhY D0n'T YOu do A Liv3 shOw frOm the oLd B34CON t0W3R?"

Henry's eyes widen and his cheeks strain against an impossibly cheesy smile.

"I think it's a creepy idea," Poppy says as they walk to school the next day. The town to their right, the ocean to their left.

"I know, right?" Henry hitches his backpack like he's ready to go.

"Not in the way you're thinking." Poppy looks to the ground. "How did they even know where we lived?"

"Huh?"

"Don't you think it's weird that whoever sent that suggestion knows we live in Beacon Beach?"

"Oh," Henry waves her concern away. "I geotagged the post and turned our location on."

"What?" Poppy stops dead, staring as Henry walks on, oblivious. "Henry Kaneda, you did not make our location public!?"

"Yeah." Henry shrugs. "Can't be anonymous and famous."

"Ohmygod, that's like the dumbest thing ever!" Poppy approaches and then slaps Henry over the back of his head.

"Ouch! What was that for!"

"What if some creep came for us? Like a stalker or kidnapper?"

"It's fine; you're just being paranoid."

"I'm para—seriously!? I can't believe the person who doesn't want an Alexa in his house 'cause she's secretly spying for the CIA thinks blasting our location on social media to a whole world of creeps is a good idea! You're the most paranoid person I've ever met!"

"Me, paranoid? Who told you that?"

"This is asking for it," Poppy groans and sits down on the bench below the World War II memorial.

"No, look, it's cool." Henry fishes out his phone. "The dude's all Cicada 3301; check it." He shows Poppy the user's profile. There is a seemingly random smattering of generic photos with captions that don't relate to the subject. "I think it's like a code or something, but I can't figure it out."

"This is a bad-bad-bad idea." Poppy buries her head in her hands.

"It's gonna be awesome," Henry insists. "It's the best idea I've ever had."

"This is the worst idea you've ever had," Poppy shivers as she and Henry stand at a high, razor-wired gate. A heavy, chunky padlock holds it closed. Age and years of kids sneaking through have bent the metal enough to form a small gap.

Henry shrugs off a heavy backpack, letting it fall to the ground gently.

"I can't hear you over the adoration of all our future fans."

Henry squats and squeezes through the gap with a grunt.

"Guess you gotta cut down on victory pancakes."

"This," Henry hops to keep his balance on the other side and pats his belly, "is the body of a champion. You may not like it, Poppers, but this," he points two fingers at his gut, "is what a winner looks like—oh, damn it!" He spots a tear in his shirt.

"Don't you mean whiner?" Poppy giggles and passes the bag through the gap. She follows a second later and wishes they'd gotten stuck.

In all the years she's lived in Beacon Beach, she's never dared to go beyond the fence. She tells herself it's not because of any ghost stories. The old army base is where the older kids go to smoke and drink—she doesn't want to mess with them. Or, worse, get caught and have her parents think that's what she's doing.

"Come on." Henry hefts his backpack on, its weight almost knocking him off balance. "Let's get this show started."

He leads the way alongside the one building still standing, a once-white brick bunkhouse with half the roof collapsed. Along the wall, someone spray-painted "Bonko Lives!" with a horrific graffiti-art clown leering over the words. Poppy tries not to look at the clown or the black, skeletal tower looming on the rise ahead.

It stands against the moonlight, fog hanging from limbs like wispy pieces of torn cloth.

"Do you have a script or something?" Poppy asks, trying not to listen to the way the stairs creak even before they set foot on them.

"Script? We don't need no stinkin' script," Henry jokes as he begins the climb. He stomps down like he has no fear that the rotten, eighty-year-old wood could crack beneath his footfalls.

"What shenanigans do you have in mind, Henry Kaneda?" Poppy follows him cautiously.

"You'll see," Henry cackles.

"I swear, if there's an Ouija board in there, I'm gonna hurl you and it over the balcony."

"Why would I do that?" Henry pants as he reaches the top, droplets of sweat beading his face. "That's so 90s," he winks. "I got something way better in mind."

Henry pushes the door open to the room at the top, brushing aside a pile of crushed beer cans.

"I'm surprised no one's up here, given it's Halloween." Poppy pinches her nose at the stench.

"Yeah, lucky us." Henry unloads his bag and begins unpacking their gear.

"Not the word I would use." Poppy clears a space for them that seems a little less filthy than the rest of the tower. "Kinda weird, isn't it?"

"Huh?"

"Like, if this was a communications tower, where's all the radio stuff?" She gestures around, and Henry agrees there's a distinct lack of old equipment.

"Maybe they took it with them when they shut down?"

"Maybe," Poppy says but doesn't think so. "Feels more like a watchtower to me."

Henry turns on the laptop. "What would the army be watching here? Think they were spying on the town? Oh! Maybe it was an MK Ultra thing?"

"Nevermind." Poppy doesn't want to think about it. Something about the lines of ruined buildings below unsettles her. "What's the plan?" She sits.

"We are gonna do a live stream of us calling cursed phone numbers from the spookiest location in Beacon Beach."

"Shut up." Poppy jerks right back to her feet. "No way, nope, not doing that."

"Relax." Henry waves her concerns away as he hooks up their mics. "I called most of them myself already, and nothing happened. This'll really sell the *Laughing at the Dark* angle, put us on the charts."

"I don't like it." Poppy folds her arms across her chest.

"Please, Poppy." Henry hits her with a sudden sincerity. It's disarming. "We're here, it's all set up, and I promise if something really weird happens, we'll pull the plug."

"You promise?"

"Of course. Besides, we'll go viral for sure if that happens!" Henry gestures for her to sit down and holds out her headset.

"Great." Poppy puts on her headphones and waits for Henry to start the live stream. He gives her a silent countdown, lowering the fingers on his right hand till he makes a fist, then points to her.

"Hey, truth-seekers! Horrific Henry Kaneda here with my co-ghost—"

"Poppy Poltergeist," she chimes in, cheery in voice alone.

"And you're listening to a special episode of *Laughing at the Dark*, where we ask the questions everyone else is too afraid to."

"Like, if Henry's not afraid of anything, why did he sleep with the lights on for a week after seeing *The Conjuring*?"

"And tonight, oh, we have a spooktacular special for you all. We're coming to you live from the top of the old Beacon Beach Army Base radio tower."

"One of the most haunted spots on the whole coast."

"Where the spirits of dead soldiers are said to radio into the night, calling to their lost loved ones."

"And that's exactly what Poppy and myself are gonna do, folks." Henry takes out his phone. "I see you there in the chat, guys. Once we get a few more people in, we'll call some spooky, cursed phone numbers."

"For the record, I am not a fan of this idea."

"Nice," Henry mutes himself and whispers, "way to sell the idea you're scared."

"I'm not faking," Poppy says as she mutes.

"The first number we got here, truth-seekers, comes from a Reddit post that claims the number contacts another dimension. It's never been traced to the source, and people hear something different every time they call, ruling out a pre-recorded message."

"Couldn't it be, like a twenty-four-hour stream or something?"

"The OP says he and his friends have tried calling it simultaneously and heard different things, so that's just what we'll do. You got your phone ready, Poppy?"

"I don't like this," Poppy groans and takes her phone out. "Do I have to?"

"Yep, the number's on-screen. Folks, we're putting it in the chat, if anyone else wants to join in. Okay, you ready?"

"No," Poppy half-hides behind her hand, "but go."

Their phones dial the number, but there's no ringtone, just silence.

"Looks like this one's a dud," Poppy says, and Henry shushes her.

"I can hear something; listen." Henry sends the audio to the laptop, and it goes out live to their audience too.

The sound that comes through feels like it's from miles away, like a rhythmic blast of foghorns from some massive grounded ship on an abandoned shore. It feels like it's alive, as though it's not a horn at all but the call of some vast creature.

"That's so creepy," Poppy whispers.

"I know." Henry bites his lip with excitement. "Do you—"

A scream cuts them off, a woman's, somewhere distant, but with so much pain and fear, they feel it in their spines. Henry panics and ends the call, almost dropping his headset.

"What..." Poppy feels cold sweat stick to her clothes.

"The actual heck was that!" Henry bounces with excitement. "That was so freaky. I'm calling it back—"

"No, don't," Poppy begs, but it's too late. Henry redials the number and then waits. Nothing. No ringtone, no foghorn, no woman.

"That's weird." Henry looks up. "Hey, check yours."

Poppy, realizing her phone's still on call with that number, picks it up and casts it to the laptop.

"See? Nothing. No, wait. Do you hear that?"

Click click-click click,

Click, click click-click-click click,

Click click click-click,

Click, click-click, click click, click click click click-click.

"I couldn't hear that before, but through the headset, yeah, that's weird."

"It just keeps repeating." Henry mouths along with the clicks. "I wonder what dimension you called?"

"I dunno." Poppy ends the call. "And I don't wanna."

"Aw, chicken," Henry clucks. "Okay, so the next one apparently connects you with a demon who'll tell you one random fact about your future. Could be the day you die, could be what you'll have for dinner three Tuesdays from tomorrow."

"Tacos," Poppy interrupts. "It's always Taco Tuesdays at my house."

"Well, let's hope the demon doesn't tell you that." Henry gets his phone ready.

"I'm not sure I wanna call a demon." Poppy looks at her phone but doesn't pick it up.

"I'll do this one; you do the next one?" Henry suggests.

"Depends." Poppy narrows her eyes. "What's the next one?"

"No spoilers," he winks.

"Urgh." Poppy crosses her arms. "Fine."

Henry dials the demon number and throws up some devil horns, sticking his tongue out as it rings. Something picks up on the other end, though only static silence follows.

"Is there—"

"Hen-ry Kan-e-da," the voice on the phone rasps, struggling with the expressions as though English isn't its first language. As though its mouth was not made to form human words. "You wi-ll fi-nd the tr-u-th an-d be de-s-troy-ed." The line clicks dead.

"The f—"

"Henry!"

"F-fun was that!" Henry hits redial.

"We're sorry, the number you're looking for is not in service. Please, contact an operator for further assistance."

"Wait, no, I just called it!"

"Maybe you only get one fortune told?" Poppy suggests.

"You call it."

"No way!"

"Come on. I wanna see if it works again." Henry snatches Poppy's phone and starts tapping the number.

"Henry, I said no!" She reaches for her phone, but Henry keeps it away. He hits the mute button. "Look at the chat, Poppy, they're loving this!"

"I don't care, Henry! I don't want to call that number; it scares me."

Henry hits send, and Poppy feels immediately overcome with dizziness.

"We're sorry, the number you're looking for is not in service. Please, contact an operator for further assistance."

"Seriously!?" Henry's face drops. "For real?"

Poppy breathes a sigh of relief, then snatches the phone back from Henry.

"Don't ever do that again," she warns him.

"Uh, Poppy," Henry points to the laptop, "you must have hit redial."

They can hear a ringtone. Something picks up, and more static silence follows.

"Po-pp-y-"

"Nope!" Poppy hangs up. "No way I'm listening to that."

"Aw, come on!"

"What's the next one?" Poppy glares, on edge.

"Chill, would you." Henry mutes. "The chat's starting to turn on you."

Poppy calms herself, takes a deep breath, and nods. "Okay, folks, we have one more cursed phone number, then we're calling it a night."

"Pun intended?"

"Come on, Henry, my head's ringing. Tell us about the last one."

Henry draws in an excited breath.

"This is the big one, truth-seekers. After scouring the internet's dark corners, I've come across a number that lets you speak with the dead, but only if you call from the place they're haunting." Henry puts the number into his phone. "And it's Poppy's turn to make the call."

Poppy looks from the phone to Henry and the big, stupid grin across his face.

"No."

"You said—"

"I said no to an Ouija board; what makes you think I'll literally call the dead!?"

"But you said—"

"I don't care." Poppy pulls her headset off. "I'm out."

"But the live stream, the chat—"

"I don't care. I quit!" Poppy tosses the headphones to Henry as she stands up.

"You can't, I mean, folks, we're experiencing technical difficulties." Henry sets off some preset spooky effects. "Probably some interference from the spirit world. We'll be right back."

The chat's a blur of words and laughing emojis.

"Poppy, come on!"

"I've had it, Henry. I can't do this," she wipes tears from her eyes. "I'm not screwing around with real dead things. This was just supposed to be for fun; now I'm really scared."

"I know; look, it's just a goof. You don't really think these numbers do anything, right?" Henry holds his arms open. "It's just an act; think of the follows and likes we'll get."

"Henry, if you respect my feelings half as much as you do strangers on the internet, you'll put that phone away and call it a night."

"But—"

"We're done." Poppy storms away, slamming the door to the tower behind her.

"Poppy, wait!" Henry calls after her, shoving his phone into his back pocket. "I'll stop, I promise!" he yells down after her, but it's too late. She marches down, into the fog, without looking back. "Please, Poppy, come back."

Silence and fog are his only answer.

"Damn it." Henry kicks the railing next to him, then drops down onto the top step, burying his face in his hands. Too distraught to think of how he can set this right or notice that as he sits down, with his phone in his back pocket, his butt hits send.

We'll Be Right Back After These Messages...

Sparks fly from the pointed edge of a metal crucifix held against a whirring grindstone.

The 20th Century Fox logo appears and fades into bright light streaming through a stained glass window. A young priest kneels in prayer, shoulder-length scruffy hair falling over his unshaven face.

"Father, I beg of ye," he prays in a heavy Irish accent.

"He's not listenin'," responds a gruff, terrible impression of an Irish accent. The young priest turns and looks upon a tall, strong-jawed older priest—bare, muscular arms covered in tattoos. He meets the senior priest's piercing blue eyes as he hands the younger man a sawed-off shotgun and says, "It's down to us to do the Lord's work."

"This fall," an overly-dramatic narrator announces, "Evil says its prayers!"

The senior priest is slammed against a gnarled, old tree—pinned in place by a floating woman in white, tendrils of her robe acting like spider's legs. Her face is an ashen, gaunt screaming horror. He flicks his hand, a bottle of holy water falls from his sleeve, and as he cracks it open with one hand, the spirit wails.

Cut to: the younger priest, his back to a wall between hastily boarded up windows. Many clawed, hairy arms reach through the gaps.

"They didn't teach this in Sunday School," he gulps with a bladed, metal crucifix held to his chest.

"Starring Robert Sheehan," the narrator announces, "and Gerard Butler!"

The senior, tattooed priest blasts down a door with a shotgun in one hand and a crucifix in the other.

"And Brendan Gleeson as The Monsignor."

A big, bearded priest whips two automatic pistols from beneath his cassock and starts blasting.

"*The Last Holy Man*! Based-on-the-novel-by-Jamie-Stewart. Rated PG-13, book your tickets now!"

A dark-skinned hand reaches, picking ripe, luscious fruit from a tree. The shoot pulls out to show a dense, healthy orchard growing in a desert.

"From environmental fortifications..." a soothing, authoritative narrator begins.

Swarms of locusts flutter within large, hanging nest farms as a woman in a white keepers suit tends to them.

"...to sustainable protein."

Scientists in blue shorts kneel by a tank containing a sick-looking shark.

"From conversation projects..."

A CGI image of an apple, with code running across its surface, appears.

"...to the future of enhanced foods."

A doctor in a white coat appears, standing before a pristine white backdrop with a logo in the corner—a simple seed, half white, half blue, with the words SEED Corporation below.

"The SEED Corporation. Fortifying the Future."

A motorboat moves slowly across a lake mired in fog—filmed by a passenger with a handheld camera. It's packed with teens and young people, eager and excited. Till it stalls, and the chatter dies.

One guy leans over the side, investigating some strange bubbling in the water—then leaps back as a creature explodes from below.

Everyone on the boat backs off as a hulking man in black, save for a creepy wooden mask, climbs aboard carrying a long, dirty machete.

"No-no-no-no-no!" The guy who leaned over crawls backward, pushing up against the crowd, trying to get away but with nowhere to go. A few people leap into the lake.

The camera shakes as it follows the wooden-masked man, and he leers over the cowering one and brings the machete up close.

"Please!"

The wooden-masked man grabs the edge of the machete and bends it.

Confused, the man on the ground snatches the blade and flexes it himself.

"Dude! It's rubber!"

The rest of the boat erupts into laughter as the cameraman turns the lens on himself, sticking his tongue out.

"What's up y'all! Dill here from *The Real World*, and we kickin' it large with an all-weekend party on spo-o-o-oky Black Stone Island in Cherry Lake. We gonna be live—"

"Till I get ya!" The wooden-masked man jumps into frame, hugging Dill.

"Uh-oh!" Dill fakes being scared. "Check us out Live this Halloween. Peace!"

We Now Return to The October Society.

Around the Hallow Fire, the October Society waits for Morgan to continue.

"That definitely didn't follow the script," Holly jokes.

"Can't imagine Henry's happy with how things went," Chardea adds.

Rascal nibbles loudly on his haunches.

"Let's just say," Morgan continues, "Henry wasn't taking it well..."

"Damn it!"

Henry kicks a small pile of empty cans, missing a flicker of something on his laptop. Something like a face, but hollowed out and contorted painfully to inhuman proportions.

The chat doesn't miss it though. Words and shocked emojis cascade across the screen.

Henry's phone buzzes. He answers it without looking.

"Poppy?"

"Henry." A robotic voice speaks in fragments. "I am glad. You took. My suggestion."

"Who is this?" Henry gulps.

"Henry. I am. Your biggest. Fan."

Henry's eyes dart to the racing chat.

"I did this for you. Henry," the voice on the phone says, off-rhythm by a fraction of a second.

"You did?"

"Yes. I can't wait. To be. A guest. On your. Show. Henry."

"Wait—"

"I am. On. My way. Henry."

"What!?"

Henry bounces from window to window, scanning the foggy, moonlit edge of the forest. He nearly drops his phone and catches it against his chest as his eyes land on the hooded figure at the bottom of the tower. Its face, cloaked in shadow, tilts up to meet him.

"Is that you out there?"

"Hello. Henry," the voice says as the figure waves slowly, rigid arm locked in place.

Cursing silently, Henry considers calling the police. But it's Halloween; they'll think it's a prank, or he'll get busted for breaking into the base (the thought that he's just blasted that over the internet doesn't even occur). Even if they believe him, there is no way they will get to him in time.

Henry turns back to the window, and the hooded figure now stands on the first corner of the staircase.

"I am. Excited. Henry."

If only Poppy were still here, she'd know what to do. At least he wouldn't be alone; they could—alone! That's it; he's not alone at all.

Henry dashes to his laptop and fidgets with the headset, jamming it on all wrong.

"Guys! Listen, I know this sounds like a prank, but it's not. We got the idea for this livestream from a user, and the creep's here. Coming for me, look!"

Henry lifts the laptop and holds it to the window, moving it around to try and capture the approaching stalker. The feed shows it standing a few more corners up, waving like its arm is moving through tar. Henry's face fills the screen, a low angle showing the panic in his eyes, sweat on his face, and snot up his nose.

"If something happens to me, please call 911, reupload—" Henry yelps as the door bangs open. The laptop clatters to the floor, followed by his headset.

The stream shows the stalker's basic sneakers and dark jeans as they walk toward the screen. They pass and kick the laptop so it turns to show Henry cowering in the corner. He holds out his hands, a feeble defense, and a wet spot forms on the floor below him. The mic still picks up his voice, but the acoustics are off, lagging.

"Please don't hurt me! I'm just a kid!"

The hooded figure steps into the shot, pausing between each step.

"Don't you. Want. To be. Famous? Henry."

"Please!" Henry begins to cry.

The hooded figure turns, creeping its face toward the screen, showing the livestream there's nothing under that hood apart from a black, empty void. Its attention crawls back to Henry.

"I'm sorry! Poppy, mom, I'm sorry!"

The figure squats on its haunches and carefully unfurls its hood.

Henry's heart races as he lays eyes upon a black sheen that catches the moonlight. Henry holds his breath as the hooded figure reaches up, places a hand on the back of their head, and pulls the blackness forward till it hangs around his neck like a scarf.

"Happy Halloween, goofball," Brendan smirks.

"H-h-h-h," Henry struggles to say even a single word as Brendan brushes his hair back. "Brendan!" Henry finally shrieks. He looks around his brother, and even from across the room, he can see the chat flood with crying-laughing emojis.

Brendan hops over to the laptop and flashes a thumbs up to the stream.

"Thanks for watching, folks! Gotta get your host home now before his mommy kills him." Brendan holds his hand to his mouth like he's telling a secret but speaks even louder, "not to mention get him a clean pair of pants. Don't forget to like, follow, subscribe, and have a Happy Halloween!"

Brendan cuts the stream and powers down the laptop. The reflection on the blank screen shows something moving in the fog beyond the tower window. Something huge.

"Oh boy," Holly chuckles. "Betcha Henry wasn't too happy after that."

"Getting what he deserves, if you ask me," Chardea adds as she runs a finger slowly across Rascal's sleepy head. She notices Braden's oddly quiet and asks, "What's crawled up your butt?"

"Nothin'," Brendan snorts defensively. "Just not a fan of cruel pranks is all."

"Since when," Chardea laughs. "Wait, is this 'cause I got you last time when you were working on some dumb song?"

"Wait, what?" Holly giggles. "Did Bwaden get a-scawed?"

"I have no incident of the memory to which you are referring," Braden huffs and crosses his arms.

"Yeah, Holly, he was singing something dumb. What was it," Chardea clears her throat and lowers her voice. "Yo, yo, my name's Braden, and I'm maddin' for..." Chardea trails off as she realizes what Braden's song was about. "I, uh, can't remember how it goes."

Holly's and Morgan's jaws drop as one, and their heads snap to each other as they both come to the same conclusion.

"Braden—"

"Has—"

"A—"

"Crush!"

"Lies and hearsay." Braden sinks into his seat.

Chardea watches as the two girls tease him, as Holly resorts to tickling Braden, their innocent joy framed by flickers of the Hallow Fire.

She knows who he was singing about, just as she knows it's too late.

There's no denying the connection between Holly and Braden. Instant best friends. And it's not like she ever liked the little dweeb. Why does it feel like she's lost something special, then? Something she never had but misses all the same?

"What happened next?" Gwennie asks, keen to move on with the story and away from this display.

"Henry," Morgan says as she takes her seat, "was about as pleased with the situation as little B-dawg here."

"Less of the little," he grumbles.

"Even if he got his wish. Everyone was talking about the prank, it went viral, and there was nothing Henry could do to escape it. He stares at the title of a YouTube video..."

Podcast Kid Pees Himself - Scare Prank Video! Must See!

"I didn't pee myself," Henry moans and slams his laptop closed. "Floor was already stained."

He doesn't even want to look at his phone. Since Halloween, his inbox has blown up, but there's not been a message from the one person he wants to hear from—Poppy.

Henry climbs into bed, curls up, hugging one of his pillows, and tries to force himself to fall asleep. He's back at school tomorrow, and as much as he's dreading the relentless teasing coming his way, at least at school, Poppy will have to talk to him. He hopes.

He twists and turns, shutting his eyes tight, but sleep won't come. His notifications are off, but Henry can still hear them. The comments, the messages, the—

GACHI-GACHI.

Henry's eyes pop open at the notification. Ringtones, in the small hours of the morning, hits the ear wrong—like a chuckle in an empty graveyard.

GACHI-GACHI.

Henry slaps his bedside table, searching for his phone, and knocks over everything else first. Only as he unlocks the screen and his eyes squint against the brightness, spotting the Do Not Disturb icon, does Henry remember it's on silent.

GACHI-GACHI.

It's not coming from his phone, but the window beyond.

Henry's hand trembles as he sits up and reaches for the curtain. He takes a breath, bites his lip, and yanks it back. First, one eye, then the other, Henry unclenches and brings himself to look—at nothing. Just darkness.

Even on a cloudy night, Henry can usually see the silhouette of the hills and Beacon Tower, but it's like a solid wall of black—one that moves.

Henry scoots up against his headboard, dropping his phone as something yellowish-white moves past the window. A row of jutting, box-like shapes follows. As they pull back, Henry realizes what they are, though it's too impossible for his mind to accept.

Teeth. Massive, crooked teeth, crammed in a jaw as wide as his mom's truck.

GACHI-GACHI.

The giant skeleton rattles as one pointy, bony finger reaches toward the window. To Henry's eye, it moves slowly, as though underwater, and yet covers the distance in a second.

He can't speak, frozen to the spot. All Henry can do is watch as the tip of the great skeleton's finger lifts his window effortlessly. Its hand moves into the room, breaking down to fit and clacking back together as it crawls through the air.

GACHI-GACHI.

Henry's rubber legs suddenly spring to life, and he scrambles for the door. He doesn't even make it halfway before the skeleton wraps its clunking hand around him and pulls him out through the window.

"Help!" Henry screams, the scent of morning dew and burning ash hitting his lungs.

GACHI-GACHI.

The skeleton cackles, the sound clunking through hollow bones as it tilts a massive, misshapen skull back and opens its crooked jaw wide. Henry dangles from one foot, staring down into the void within the monster's throat.

It drops him in, he squeezes his eyes closed, and everything goes black.

Henry jerks awake in his bed, slapping around, and only manages to hit himself. He leaps out of bed and rushes to his window—it's closed tight as early morning light comes through. He looks to the hills, thick with morning fog, and can see the rough shape of the Beacon Tower. And something else, just as tall, almost entirely enveloped in mist, standing next to it.

The school bell rings, and Henry pushes through a sea of kids in no hurry to get anywhere.

"Poppy!" he yells, sleepless eyes catching sight of her. If she hears him, she pretends that she doesn't. "Poppy, listen—oof!"

Henry runs into another kid, a big guy, who shoves him away with one hand.

"Watch it, Pee-Pants," the kid laughs, and the rest of the corridor joins in.

The very thing Henry had been dreading all weekend happens, and he doesn't care. He needs to tell

Poppy about what he saw. She disappears into her homeroom class, and even though Henry's in another one, he barges in anyway.

"Mr. Kaneda?" the homeroom teacher scowls. "What are you doing here?"

"Poppy." Henry ignores the teacher. "Look, I'm sorry, but we have to talk."

Poppy takes a book from her bag and makes like she's reading it.

"Poppy, come on—"

"Mr. Kaneda," the teacher growls.

"Please—"

"MR. KANEDA!" the teacher yells, making Henry flinch. "Please keep your lover's quarrel to the playground and kindly get your rear out of my classroom."

"Please talk to me at lunch," Henry begs as the teacher marches him out of the room to a chorus of giggles.

Behind her book, Poppy's face turns red.

Moments later, Henry slumps down on his desk, burying his face in his arms as his homeroom teacher begins roll call.

"Gables?" the teacher calls, and a quiet voice pips her response.

"Gachi?" he asks, though his voice is wrong; it sounds more like bones clicking.

GACHI-GACHI.

"Oh no." Henry jerks up, eyes darting around the classroom. The teacher points at the board, mouth moving, but nothing comes out. Everyone else quietly studies, oblivious to the sound.

GACHI-GACHI.

Henry cranes his neck towards the window, eyes squeezed tight. He dares to look, popping just one eye open, and breathes a sigh of relief to see the usual misty playground.

"Must be my imagination."

GACHI-GACHI.

The words fill the room, echoing from the corridor.

"Oh, crap," Henry gulps as bony fingers the size of small desks curl around both sides of the doorframe. The skeleton's face fills the gap, leering in with hollow sockets fixed on Henry.

GACHI-GACHI.

"Gachi—get the heck outta here," Henry panics, but he's paralyzed, unable to lift his hands from his desk.

The skeleton twists its head, dislocating its gawking jaw as it contorts its massive skull through the door. Bones clatter and crack, then spill through the gap like a tide of clunking yellow rocks. They begin to reassemble as they fill the room, recombining into a vaguely humanoid shape that curves along the wall, across the ceiling, and surrounds Henry.

The other students, and the teacher, continue their silent pantomime of normalcy.

Henry shakes in his seat as the grinning skull hangs over his head, as its fingerbones clack into some semblance of hands and begin to reach for him. He looks up and—

—screams himself awake, scaring the life out of everyone in his homeroom. Only for a moment, though. As soon as their hearts stop racing, the laughter comes, and Henry sinks into his seat.

"Poppy, please, you gotta listen to me!" Henry yells as she weaves through the cafeteria.
"I made myself clear, Henry. We're done."
"Yeah." One kid throws a tater tot at Henry. "Leave her alone, Pee-Pants!"
"Will you please listen to me for one minute?" Henry begs, and Poppy comes to a halt.
"If I do, promise you'll leave me alone if I ask."
"Promise!" Henry jumps in front of her. "Honestly, you're not gonna believe this—"
"Oh, I bet,"
"But ever since that night in the tower, I've been having these dreams, only they seem real. About this massive skeleton that tries to eat me only, I wake up and—"
"Skeleton?"
"Yeah, but like the size of a building. Bigger!"
"I can't believe this." Poppy hangs her head. "You're just dreaming about *Attack on Titan*."
"No! Seriously!"
"I can't do this anymore, Henry. I'm through with all this spooky horror stuff, and you promised you'd leave me be if I said so."
"But—"
"Didn't you?"
Henry goes silent for a moment. "Yeah."
"Please leave me alone and never speak to me again." Poppy bites back the tears and walks away.

Henry lets her go, unable to hold his own, and almost wishes the giant skeleton would show up and swallow him whole.

Out on the field, in gym class, Henry finally feels the exhaustion catching up with him. He lulls around in the outfield, making out like he's taking part but almost falling asleep on his feet. He fights it as much as he can, slapping his face now and then.

The sun sits behind gray clouds, and though it's late afternoon, the mist still lingers, merging with the horizon. There's a break in the sky, and Henry has to shield his sensitive, tired eyes from the glare. As it passes and Henry's vision returns, his arms drop to his side, glove hitting the dirt.

Two impossibly long bones jut from the treeline at the edge of the field, weaving in and out of the fog. The mist's so dense it rises halfway up the giant's rib cage. Its neck cranes over, three sizes too long, while slender arm bones hang so low they might reach its toes.

It just stands there, hollow eyes fixed on Henry from afar.

"What do you want!?" Henry yells.

The giant raises one arm, bones creaking like a dozen falling trees, till it points towards the Beacon Tower.

"What—"

"Heads up!"

Henry snaps awake to see a fastball fill his vision and knock him out cold.

Holding a compress to his head, making it feel paradoxically on fire and frozen, Henry questions his life choices and sanity. The stark, clinical light of the nurse's station brings him some cold, sobering clarity.

Monstrous, soul-hungry skeletons can't possibly exist, but the shiner coming through over half his face sure does. He's so tired. All he wants to do is go to sleep, yet he can't. What if, this time, the skeleton eats him and he doesn't wake up?

Henry lies back and winces.

"How did you do it, Henry Kaneda!"

He almost leaps off the bed.

"I know you can't edit to save your life, so you must have gotten someone." Poppy holds her phone out, screen forward. "I just can't figure out how on a livestream."

"What are you talking about?" Henry groans.

"I wouldn't have noticed it if people didn't keep commenting the same timestamp and after your crazy rant at lunch." Poppy thrusts the phone at him, and Henry takes it.

He looks at the comment Poppy's left it on, a timestamp followed by scared face emojis.

"Click it," Poppy orders, and Henry obeys.

It jumps the video to a frozen moment, just before Brendan reveals himself.

"Seriously, Poppy, I don't need to see this again." Henry tries to give her phone back.

"Look at the window behind you."

Henry squints at the screen and focuses on the dark folds of moonlit mist fogging up the window. He nearly drops it when he makes out the leering, hollow-eyed giant skull. Once Henry knows it's there, it's all he can see. There's almost an innocence to it, a complete lack of malice that makes it worse.

"I didn't do that." Henry shakes. "I didn't even see, dream, I dunno what, the thing till after that."

"I was afraid of that." Poppy snaps her phone back. "You're a jerk, but you're not evil."

"Thanks, I think." Henry dabs the swelling with the compress.

"Gimme that." Poppy takes it from him and holds it firm to his eye, ignoring the winces of pain. His wound only adds validity to his claims that he's seeing this thing. "Better?"

"Yeah." Henry smiles. "Thanks, Poppy."

"Good, 'cause we've got work to do."

"Urgh," Henry throws his head down in defeat. "It's no good." He's lying on his bed, laptop open in front of him, while Poppy sits on the floor, cross-legged, on a tablet.

"I can't find anything about a Beacon Beach army base, never mind anything that'll relate to a massive dream demon skeleton."

Poppy's too in her zone to pay any attention.

"Stupid Freddy Krueger *Power Rangers* rip-off."

"That's because it wasn't an army base." Poppy ignores Henry's joke and meets his eyes. "It's, um, here." She holds her tablet out, and Henry takes it.

"Oh," Henry gulps. "Beacon Beach Internment Camp."

"They—"

"I know what they were. My great-grandmother was in one. During the war."

"I had no idea." Poppy finds herself at a loss, torn by the desire to comfort her friend and somehow apologize for a horror carried out generations before they were born. "I guess the town doesn't want to advertise that."

"Nor does my family," Henry adds. "The Kanedas have lived in Beacon Beach for about a hundred years, and all my folks say is shikata ga nai."

"Huh?"

"It can't be undone." Henry pauses. "I had to ask."

"How is it you don't speak Japanese?"

"How is it you don't speak Polish?"

"Fair point. Wait, you said your great-grandmother..."

"Yeah?"

"The one in the retirement home by the shore?"

"Yeah?"

Poppy stares with a slack jaw.

"What?"

"Oh, I dunno, maybe we should visit her!?"

"Why?"

"'Cause I can't find anything that could explain this freaky giant skeleton thing. According to the records," Poppy takes her tablet back without Henry even noticing, "yeah, five deaths in all the time it was in operation. Natural causes, or so they say."

"Yeah, 'cause you can trust the government to tell the truth. They're still denying Bigfoot visited the White House in 1976."

"Let's go see your great-grandma, then."

It's a quick bike ride through the mist-dappled streets of Beacon Beach. Henry and Poppy ride down a waving hillside road that curves towards the shore and a jumble of brightly colored condos stacked together on stilts sticking out over the sand.

"So about my great-grandma," Henry says as they make their way through a brightly decorated hall. They stop before the door to an open room. Curtains flutter in the breeze, and a shrunken woman bundled up against the fall chill sits on the balcony.

"Yeah?" Poppy asks.

"She doesn't speak English."

Poppy slaps her forehead.

"We'll just Google Translate it if we need to." Henry leads the way. "Come on."

Great-grandma Kaneda is delighted to have some visitors. It melts Poppy's heart seeing the woman's smile with every part of her wrinkly face.

Henry bumbles through small talk with her, and Poppy tries not to laugh as the older woman scowls, then laughs as Henry corrects his broken Japanese.

"Okay, um, here goes." Henry scratches his head and tries to piece together enough Japanese to make himself clear. "Hi-baba, um, gaikotsu? Like, oki gaikotsu?"

Great-grandma Kaneda stares at Henry like he's crazy.

"What are you asking her?" Poppy stares.

"If she knows anything about the huge skeleton."

"Henry!" Poppy slaps her forehead. "You think she's gonna know about the giant skeleton thing!? Ask her about the camp, dummy."

"Okay." Henry turns back to his great-grandma. Her eager, glassy eyes move between Henry and Poppy in anticipation. "I dunno how."

"Show her this." Poppy takes her tablet out, passes it to Henry, and he holds it so the older woman can see. She squints, trying to make her eyes focus.

"Oki. Gaikotsu," Henry repeats.

"Henry—"

"Oki? Gaikotsu?" great-grandma Kaneda croaks, slowly raising one hand to point at the screen. "Dame, dame, unn!" She looks at Henry, eyes suddenly alert. "Gashadokuro..." she says like a warning, shaking her head so violently her cheeks wobble. "Gashadokuro!"

The commotion brings staff running, and they politely ask the kids to leave. They go, but the older woman points her shaking finger at the pair of them, raving. "Gashadokuro! Dame, Gashadokuro!"

"Well, that was a success," Henry quips as he gets back on his bike. "No new info, and nearly gave great-grandma a heart attack."

"No way," Poppy blurts out.

"Not literally, but—"

"Shut up and read." Poppy shoves her phone in his face. "I Googled what she kept saying."

"Gashadokuro," Henry reads, "no freakin' way. A Yokai born from the bones of those who died in wars. If they're not given proper burial rites, their anger can ferment, and as their flesh rots away, their bones combine into one enormous skeletal mass with a burning grudge against the living." Henry looks up. "What is it with ghosts from my family's homeland? They've always got a grudge. Can't we have just one Casper?"

"That's what you're seeing in your dreams."

"Yeah, but it says here they wander the countryside feeding on the living."

"So? Look at the picture."

Henry scrolls down to see old Japanese artwork depicting a massive skeleton the height of a pagoda leering down at it.

"That's him, sure, but why hasn't Giga-Skeletor been stalking Beacon Beach for the last eighty years?"

"Your stupid phone call!" Poppy snaps her fingers. "When you called the third number. The direct line to the beyond?"

"I didn't." Henry takes out his phone and brings up the call log. "See!"

"Um, you called it for like twenty minutes."

"What!?" Henry whips the phone around. "I didn't, I swear! As soon as you left, I put it in my pocket and—oh..." Henry trails off, clenching his face.

"What did you do, Henry?"

"I might have, sort of, maybe butt-dialed the beyond."

"Henry Kaneda!" Poppy whacks him. "You did not summon a freakin' demon with your stupid butt!"

"Technically, according to the website, it's a Yokai—"

"Yokai, your butt, you moron." Poppy swings at him some more.

"Look, it was an accident," he smirks, "and it's behind us, so..."

"I'm gonna kill you," Poppy sighs. "After."

"After what?"

Henry's face lights up before she says it.

"*Laughing at the Dark*." Poppy holds up a finger. "One night only, livestream special - Return to Beacon Tower."

Later that night, the two of them stand before the loose gate to the internment camp; the tower on the hill waits for them silently against a cloudless sky.

"You ready?" Poppy asks, turning a digital camera on and linking it to her phone.

"Ready," Henry nods.

"Going live in five, four," she counts down the rest silently, then gives Henry the go signal.

"Hey there, truth-seekers, and welcome to a special live edition of *Laughing at the Dark*, only this time we're not joking. Come with us as we contact the restless dead of Beacon Beach's darkest corner—the forgotten, shameful World War II Internment Camp."

Poppy follows Henry with the camera as they go through the fence and make their way to the tower.

"See, fellow truth-seekers, back when Japan sided with the Germans during the Second World War, some galaxy-brains thought it would be clever to round up all the Japanese-Americans living in the States."

They climb the tower, Henry leading the way.

"Something happened here, though. Something The Man doesn't want known. So, truth-seekers, I'm about to call the same number from last time, the direct line to the beyond, and see if the forgotten ghosts of the Beacon Beach Internment Camp have anything they want to say."

Henry brings up the number and hits send. He turns on the speakerphone and holds it up for the camera. The line connects, and, at first, there's just silence. Then a whispering rises to a clamor: the words, unclear, a mix of Japanese and English run through with panicked screams. A crackling, like fire, follows with sharp snaps of breaking wood.

"So many people," Poppy gasps.

The entire watchtower shakes.

"What was that?" Poppy spins the camera around, scanning the fog-laden view. "You felt that, right?"

The tower trembles again.

"Is that..." Poppy points the camera back to Henry, slowly walking towards the window. "Henry?"

Something huge bursts through the window, turning that side of the tower into shards of glass and wood splinters.

"Henry!" Poppy screams as the shockwave knocks her back. The last thing the camera sees before it hits the ground is something like a massive bony hand wrapping its clicking fingers around Henry, lifting the boy out the window.

He puts up no resistance. Henry lets the Gashadokuro lift him to its gaping maw and drop him within.

The scent of ash and bone hits his lungs. He breathes it in, refusing to recoil, and falls until he doesn't—until he finds himself standing in the dark.

The world fades in slowly.

He's in a long bunkhouse, plain brick walls lined with uncomfortable metal cots on either side filled with multiple generations of families. They speak mostly Japanese and English.

A spark flickers in the corner of the room, catching Henry's eye, and he watches as it becomes a flame—as it spreads along with panic. Some run, while others try to combat the fire, but it continues to grow, pushing the trapped prisoners to the back of the room. It reaches the top of the bunkhouse, the flimsy wooden supports, and down the roof comes.

Henry's lying down now, the one unburned body in a pit of blackened, quiet bones. Dirt lands on top of him till the world's nothing but darkness and buried anger.

Henry opens his eyes, and he's lying on the ground, somewhere in the middle of the camp, on top of weedy grass and surrounded by broken fragments of charred brick foundations.

He looks up into the fog and sees the faint outline of the Gashadokuro, nodding gently.

"Henry!" Poppy screams. "Henry!"

"I'm here," he coughs and then finds his voice. "I'm over here!"

Poppy comes running, camera in hand.

"What happened up there! I thought you were dead! I saw it; we all did." She catches up and doubles over, gasping.

"Are we still alive?"

"Yeah."

"Good." Henry starts to claw at the ground. "Keep filming."

He digs, attacking the ground with boundless, furious energy till his fingernails bleed.

"Henry?"

"It showed me," is the only explanation Henry gives as he continues, caking himself with wet earth.

"What did? The Gashadokuro? I thought those things were made from war victims?"

"It was." Henry stops and lets Poppy aim the camera into the hole.

"Oh my god," she gasps as she frames a fractured, rotten skull.

"There you have it." Henry looks back to the Gashadokuro, and the faintest hint of a smile touches his face as the skeletal giant fades back into the fog. He turns and looks into the camera. "The truth."

The fog turns bright as morning comes. It drifts through the streets of Beacon Beach as it always has. This morning, it carries the voice of a newscaster between the pretty wooden houses that face the ocean from their silted bases.

"A shocking discovery made by two young podcasters last week has unearthed a shameful dark secret—a mass grave at the former Japanese Internment Camp in Beacon Beach."

The mist crawls along the shore, touching the retirement home, and whispers to the one person left in Beacon Beach who lived through that dark time. A peaceful smile spreads across her sleeping face.

"As of yet, the number of dead has not been determined, but experts are working hard reconstructing the remains and plan to use DNA sampling to help identify and hopefully bring closure to the families of those involved."

It curls around the World War II Memorial, where the plaque at the bottom has been amended. It reads: In Remembrance of Those Lives Lost for Liberty Beyond This Shore. And Those On These For Ignorance.

"An investigation has begun into..." the newscaster trails off as the fog finds its way to the diner, tickling the glowing sign and pawing at the window. It waves to the two young people inside, the girl testing the boy with a *Learn Japanese* textbook. Neither of the children senses the fog, and that's as it should be.

"From that day on, the fog never returned to Beacon Beach." Morgan finishes her story. "Not like it had. Brighter days came to the town, freed from the shadows of its past."
The Hallow Fire crackles.
"Wow, that was powerful," Chardea speaks for the others, Morgan's story rendering them speechless.
"It makes me sad." Morgan rubs her arms. "Thinking of all the evil people do to one another."
"In many ways," Toby adds, "humanity is far worse than the monsters they imagine haunt them."
"Godspeed, giant skeleton buddy." Braden salutes. "Godspeed."
"Yeah." Morgan tears up. "I'm sorry."
Chardea moves to rise, cross the circle, and comfort the girl in the kitsune mask, but Holly beats her to it. And then she watches, curiously, as the girl in the dragon mask puts one arm around Morgan, and they link fingers with the other hand.
"We should." Holly squeezes Morgan's hand. "It's time."
"Yeah," Morgan nods. "Um, kinda didn't want to say because we didn't want to feel like we were rubbing it in anyone's faces."
Chardea looks to Braden, still piecing it together, and doesn't get why the boy's nodding so encouragingly. Does he know something she doesn't?
"Holly and I are, um, we're dating." Morgan shrugs nervously. "Weird time to tell you guys, but yeah."

Gwennie stands and approaches the two girls silently. The air is heavy with dread for a moment; even after her apology, they all know her wounds run deep. It's why Holly and Morgan kept their romance a secret.

"I'm so happy for you both." She breaks the silence and, with a slight hesitation, hugs them.

"Finally!" Braden cheers. "I've been sitting on this for weeks!"

"Seriously!" Chardea scoffs. "How did you not fart this out after two minutes?"

"Because I," Braden taps his chest, "am a gentleman."

"Honestly, if it wasn't for Braden," Holly interrupts. "I was way too shy to say anything to Morgan, and he sounded her out."

"For a second, I thought Braden was into me." Morgan giggles.

"That must have been horrifying for you," Chardea jokes, but her beating heart says otherwise.

"Good luck to both of you." Gwennie squeezes them again, then heads off into The Dark.

"Good evening, all." Toby nods as he stands. "And congratulations."

Holly and Morgan stand, holding hands. They look to one another, giggle, and say their farewell—heading off into The Dark together.

Rascal does a big stretch and gets ready for his third evening nap.

"See ya next time, Char-Char." Braden waves and turns to leave.

"Braden, wait," Chardea calls after him, but when he stops and looks back, the things she wants to say won't come. Instead, she says, "that was a nice thing you did for Holly and Morgan."

Braden shrugs. "No biggie. Night, Char-Char."

She waits till he's gone, till he's too far away to hear the croak in her voice.

"Night, Braden."

Roll credits.

Episode Six

Revel in this night, this evening of dark magic and midnight wonder, for you never know when the magic fades. You're young, perhaps? Perhaps not? There comes a time when that which brings you joy loses its glow. All magic fades, my friend, and even the wicked charm of Halloween isn't eternal.

Did you not feel an autumnal enchantment as you lit that jack-o'-lantern? Do your seasonal books sit in a pile, unread? Is the thought of an all-night monster movie marathon no longer enticing?

If so, perhaps you'll understand the emptiness of young Gwennie's heart. And what follows.

Chardea's tanned hand hesitates before she knocks on a wooden door. Only for a second, till she raps against it three times, her mask hanging around her neck.

"Just a second!" Braden yells from within. The sound of things hurriedly being hidden follows, along with crashes and Braden complaining as he breaks something. "Just a second!"

The door creaks open, and Braden leans against the frame nonchalantly. "Yo, Char-Char, what's the haps?"

"I need to talk to you about something." Chardea rolls her eyes. "I can't believe I'm saying this, but can I come in?"

"But of course, mademoiselle." Braden bows and steps aside. Chardea shudders and regrets her choice not to find a hazmat suit as she steps inside. "Welcome to my crib."

There's little to no floor space visible inside Braden's den, the parts that aren't covered in comics taken up by soda bottles and bags of potato chips. A Mayan pyramid of empty coke cans dominates one corner. The walls, likewise, barely have gaps between posters for movies and bands—all ones Chardea would consider retro. She didn't expect Braden's little pocket of reality to be clean, but this is beyond what she could have imagined. An old NES is hooked up to a TV, and the main menu screen reads The Legend of Zelda.

"Can I interest you in a fine beverage, or perhaps some oar deserves?"

"You mean—nope, nevermind." Chardea sighs. "There's something I need to tell you. Something I don't want the others to hear, not yet anyway."

"I'm all ears." Braden throws himself down into a massive lime green beanbag, sending a cascade of spilled chips flying. "Is this where you confess your undying love for me?"

"I—" Chardea's heart skips a beat. "No. It's Derek."

"What's up with the D-Man? You speak to him again?"

"That's just it." Chardea screws her face up as she clears away some junk and Braden's mask from the bottom of a bunk bed. She sits on the very edge. "I haven't."

"What, like tonight?"

"I mean at all." She sighs. "I've been lying."

"Woah..."

"I didn't want anyone to worry, but it's been eating me up inside. Plus, Gwennie, and it's just, like, something's wrong. Really wrong."

"I know what you mean." Braden gets up and takes a seat beside her. He notices she's shaking and places his hand on hers. Chardea tenses up, then lets Braden's fingers entwine with hers. "So what are we gonna do about it?"

Chardea smiles. "I don't know. But, as weird as this sounds, and if you ever repeat it to anyone, I'll deny it, I'm glad you said we."

"'Course." Braden smiles back. "We're friends."

"Yeah," Chardea looks away. "Did you mean what you said before? That you never had any?"

"Yeah." Braden's shoulders slump. "Nobody really liked me before you guys, you know. It's probably why I try so hard, but I just end up annoying people even more."

"You don't annoy me." Chardea gives him a sideways glance. "I mean, you do, but I'd miss it if you didn't." Her throat goes dry. "I hope you know even though I'm mean to you…like a lot…that doesn't mean I don't like you."

Braden squeezes her hand. "That's how I know. You're not afraid to be yourself. No fake stuff, just Char-Char."

"Braden?"

"Yeah?"

"I—we better get going." Chardea hops off the bed before she says something stupid. "It's getting late, and Gwennie's up."

"Yeah." Braden follows. "Awesome."

"There you are!" Gwennie chirps as Braden and Chardea join the rest of The October Society. "Been waiting for ages, so we have."

"Sorry," Chardea says to the rest of them. Holly and Morgan share a seat, Rascal weaseled between them. Their hands are interlocked like hers and Braden's were just a short while ago.

Toby sits beside Gwennie, hands steepled as he waits.

"Come on then." Gwennie's surprisingly eager. "Let's get started."

Chardea fumbles in her bag and hands Gwennie the black book before taking her seat.

"So tonight, I have a story for you that's about being afraid. We're all scared of something, aren't we? Not being liked," she looks at Braden. "Or being let down," she looks at Chardea. "But for some of us, what we're afraid of has already happened, and it's only by accepting that fear, learning to embrace it, can we do anything about it."

Gwennie clutches the black book to her chest, closes her eyes, and speaks. "My October Fellows, we make our own fears, but horrors lurk within..."

The Fear Factory

Kindness is not the experience of those who do not belong, and no one knew this as much as the Horned Boy.

He sleeps in a small bed, under a blanket too short and so moth-eaten it does nothing to save him from the cold. He shivers, and a small cloud of fog slips from his lips, dissipating past a blackened eye and unwashed brown hair that flops over a pair of tiny horns jutting from his forehead.

Growlers rattle on cobbles, horses clop, and drunks chant; the city sings its lullaby for the sleeping boy. Till the sound of a door slamming and shuffling, stumbling footsteps snap him awake like a shot. They bring back bitter recollections of how the black eye came about.

"Freak!" the drunk man calls, slurring. "Wh-where are ye, Freak!"

The Horned Boy knows there is little point in delaying. He rises from his filthy bed and pads toward his father's call.

"Freak!"

"I'm here," the Horned Boy says and realizes his mistake as the large man's swooping hand strikes his cheek.

"You forget your manners, Freak," he burps, foul warmth spilling forth. "Even a mangy cur can be taught," another belch, "to heel correctly."

"Sorry, sir, I'm sorry." The Horned Boy bows low as a red welt rises across one side of his face. He knows better than to look up at the man. The defiance he'll assume, the sight of the boy's horns, or both, will infuriate him further.

Before the horns, there was a time when such violence was a rare occurrence. Though they barely break the skin and reach less than an inch from the boy's head, they've pierced the Horned Boy's world irrecoverably. Their growth brought disgust and horror, heated arguments into the wee hours punctuated with slaps. His mother, no longer able to take the abuse and disgusted at the child she bore, left one afternoon with no notice, no farewell, and no looking back.

Unable to accept his share, the man blamed the Horned Boy entirely and visited violent retribution upon him whenever the mood took. And it often did.

"Why is it colder in than out, Freak?" the drunk man demands to know, kicking the ashes of a vacant fireplace. "Have ye wasted all my coal?"

"No, sir," the Horned Boy insists. In truth, they've not been able to afford the luxury in weeks, not with his father caught in a cycle of temporary dock work followed by weeks of pub crawling. The Horned Boy would like to work and help alleviate his father's burden, but he is forbidden from going outside. His father resents that the boy does not contribute and yet will not allow him to be seen, less others see what a poisoned, disgraceful child he is.

"It doesn't matter," the man slumps in his chair by the cold hearth and stares into the sooty darkness. "We're to be evicted come the morn."

"What does that mean, sir?" The Horned Boy sits on the floor; he knows his place.

"It means," the man swallows a wave of warm bile surging up his throat, "that rent's past overdue, and we're to be turned on the streets."

"But, where will we go, sir?"

"I've signed on to a merchant ship, Freak, and leave port two nights after tomorrow." He does not say what's to become of the Horned Boy, and the lad doesn't dare ask.

The man nods to himself and stands. Barely able to balance, he stumbles forth several steps before righting himself. He fights with his belt, freeing the flaked leather from his waistband and wrapping each end around a knuckle.

A whipping is one thing, but how his father holds the belt tells the Horned Boy worse is to come.

"Ordinarily, I'd send ye to the workhouse." His grip tightens. "But I can't have my good name sullied by those devilish intrusions."

"I don't understand, sir," the Horned Boy says as his father moves to him. "Where else am I—" his words are taken as the belt snaps around his throat, lifting him off the ground. His father pulls the belt taut, and the Horned Boy's face flushes red.

"Don't fight me, Freak. It'll soon be over." Suddenly, his excessive drunkenness makes sense. But, though he may have found courage in liquid, it's dulled his strength. The man struggles to keep the Horned Boy in his grip. "I said stop fighting!"

His brace weakens, and with that comes slack. The Horned Boy turns into it instinctively and drags one of his horns across the man's chest. It tears his clothes and flesh, leaving behind a rough slash in the man's jacket and a steady trickle of blood. The shock and pain cause the man to push the Horned Boy away, reaching for his wound, and the child falls to the floor, gasping for breath.

The man looks at the blood on his hand and swoons. Only his fury keeps him alight, and his vengeful eyes set upon the Horned Boy curled up on the floor.

"Beast!" the man screams, gripping one end of his belt. "Ungrateful filthy beast!" He swings it overhead. The buckle whistles through the air as it descends on the Horned Boy in a wicked arc—cracking across the child's back.

The Horned Boy cries out, eyes turning red and falling upon his father. The man winds up from another swing—drunken, sadistic glee dances across his face, and something else, too. A long-hidden desire now realized, his blackened soul revels in the violent end he's about to bring to his tainted son. It's the last thing the Horned Boy sees before—

A steam whistle blares through The Factory; it could be heard from miles away, but not a soul was around to hear it. The Factory stands as a lump of rotten, misshapen, and moss-strewn brick topped with a smattering of uneven chimney stacks that spew black bile into the sky above an endless forest.

The Horned Boy wakes to the whistle's second blast as it drags him from his nightmare. Always a fragment of the same one, an episodic venture into the heart of his suffering.

He rises; the horns on his forehead, now several inches longer, branch into antlers that poke through long strands of greasy hair. His flimsy, stained pillow lies torn and shredded.

A face hangs upside down from the bunk overhead, a kind one hidden almost entirely by fine, shiny black hair.

"Mornin'," the hairy boy says. He notices the torn pillow and furrows with concern. "You're not having nightmares, are you?" he whispers, glancing around to make sure no one hears him. "You know—"

"I'm fine, Scratch," the Horned Boy insists. "No nightmares," he lies and pokes one of his horns. "Hard to sleep with these bloody things, that's all."

Scratch drops to the floor, landing on his haunches. "I hope so. You know what happens if you have nightmares." He paws relentlessly at his hairy face.

Across the room, two more boys stir from their bunks.

It had been so long since anyone who knew them before The Factory said their names that all four had forgotten them. They named one another instead.

A small, round lad with an almost flat, upturned nose snorts as he plops chubby, stout legs on the floor.

Though time at The Factory didn't feel like it passed quite the same, they knew Snout to be the most recent bunkmate, but none of them are sure since when.

A pensive, fidgeting boy perches on the bunk above Snout, waving his arms as though to wake them all up.

Ruffles was there before the Horned Boy and earned his name through a near-constant state of jittery alertness.

The Horned Boy refused all attempts to assign him a name, but together, they were known as The Odds. As a rule, The Odds were separated from the rest of The Factory's workers as much as possible.

The Horned Boy runs a finger across his pillow. He tries not to think about the damage those horns have caused, but it's inescapable.

"Better hurry," Scratch says as the other Odds make their way to the door. "Don't want to miss breakfast."

The Horned Boy places a hand on his forehead, gently touching the hardened, cracked skin around the base of his horns. He brushes aside his greasy hair and discounts the idea of washing it anytime soon—there's no point. Every inch of The Factory is filthy, and it's impossible to stay clean.

He follows the others. Ruffles leads the way, ensuring they stay an appropriate distance from The Norms.

More than a hundred children work in The Factory, and though The Norms are almost entirely resentful of The Odds having a room to themselves, none of them would want to bunk with them. The Odds' bunkroom stands alone at the far end of the dormitories, separated from Norms' bunkrooms by a series of closets and lavatories. The four pass these and a giant pinned billboard reminding the workers of one of The Factory's rules: close your doors! The fabric's edges curl, stained and soaked with the same gray ooze that seeps from most of the ancient, dirt-blackened brickwork. The worn and stained drawing shows a dark doorway with two leering eyes and sharp tendrils of shadow crawling into the light.

All the children march past it, Odds and Norms, without paying attention, yet come night, they'll all do as it says.

The Odds sit at their table in the cafeteria, separate from The Norms but only by distance—and not far enough that one can't spit across it. They eat the same thing for each meal; a pale yellowish gloop doled out by strange, slug-like creatures.

The Beadles ran The Factory. Each the same height as a small adult, creatures comprised of jaundiced, rolling flab. No necks, only folds of drooping flesh, and their beady eyes—which gave them their nickname—sat buried in sagging mounds of skin. The only distinction between one Beadle and the next were the uniforms they wore, dictating which part of The Factory they maintained.

Children line up, holding bowls and stepping forward as a Beadle in a stained apron doles out a gloop from a dangling nozzle fixed to a churning vat of grayish, yellow slime.

Above hangs a vast tapestry—a simplistic rendition of the forest surrounding The Factory. Eight sharp, jagged lines break above the trees, coming together under a round, fanged head that stares down at the children. Only two words are sewn into the tapestry, almost the size of the forest and the spider-like creature itself: IT WAITS.

Everyone in The Factory knows it's out there, beyond the fences, just as everyone knows someone who knows someone who was eaten by it. It's one of the reasons they stay at The Factory, do their work, eat their gloop, and follow the rules.

Ruffles looks up from his bowl and his slurp turns to a near choke to see the Horned Boy without his pin. He chokes on his words, and the other Odds look at him, confused. Ruffles slaps Snout on the chest, then points to the Horned Boy.

"You forgot your pin," Snout hisses, looking around carefully to make sure no one hears. There is no danger. Despite his sensitive ears, even Snout would have trouble making out anything over the din and guttural guzzling that echoes through the cavernous cafeteria. Though it's not one of the other children hearing that worries Scratch.

"Oh," the Horned Boy touches the blank space on his shirt where the pin should be. "I must have left it in our room," he says with little concern. There's something else bothering him.

"You have to wear it!" Scratch growls in a panicked whisper. "Else, The Darkling will take you."

"I heard," Snout snorts, "that if The Darkling comes for you, it'll take everyone around you too. Even if you gots yer pin on."

The other three Odds quietly touch their pins and say a silent prayer to ward off The Darkling.

The Horned Boy looks to a table packed with Norms, busy pouring their gloop down their throats. All except one Norm, who stares at The Odds with a sideways sneer. It's more than a little unusual that one of The Norms would even look at The Odds, never mind do so with such challenging bravado.

"Can I help you?" the Horned Boy calls to the Sneering Lad.

"Aye," the lad rises and crosses the cafeteria, stopping just short of The Odds' table.

There are chalk lines on the floor, spotted with grime and slime, marking separate areas for each bunk. They are not to be crossed during meal times—ever. The Sneering Lad stays on his side of the line and dares the Horned Boy to approach.

"I was just wondering, how is it that they let the animals eat here with the people?" The Sneering Lad turns to his bunkmates, looking for praise and finding more apprehension than he would like. "Isn't there a trough or a sty outside for you beasts?"

"Oh, there is," the Horned Boy rises. The rest of The Odds urge him to sit back down. He approaches the line, looking at the shocked faces of The Norms and gormless Beadles. "But the thing is, your mother's taken the whole thing up, so they had to let us inside." The Horned Boy throws his arms up. "I know, standards these days."

A chorus of suppressed tittering and giggles sweeps across the hall.

"I'm not afraid of you." The Sneering Lad rises to the Horned Boy's challenge.

"Is that so?" The Horned Boy comes close to crossing the chalk line.

"I might be new here, but I've been in many a workhouse before," the Sneering Lad boasts. "And I've seen much worse than you. Freak."

That single, solitary insult brings a lifetime of pain and suffering to the surface. It takes all the Horned Boy has not to cross that line and gore the Norm with his horns.

The Sneering Lad jumps back, sliding on the slick, oozy stone beneath his feet and falling hard on his backside. The laughter that spreads this time is raucous and prompts the Beadles to interfere—they hurry around the room, urging silence, while two take the Sneering Lad in their sickly arms and drag him away.

"I'll get you for this, freak!" he warns, and the Horned Boy doesn't listen. "I'll get all you disgusting freaks!"

After checking the roster, The Odds take up their post for the day in Processing. They stand on either side of a rusting, slime-smeared conveyor belt that carries lumps of a strange, black rock.

Ruffles operates the release, pulling a lever that lets some of the rocks land on the belt. Scratch turns a grating wheel that moves the belt, causing the rocks to jitter towards a large piston. Snout pushes down a stiff lever, causing steam to hiss and a press to crash down on the rocks, and the Horned Boy, the strongest of the four, resets the press. As it rises, it leaves behind tiny, shining black crystals shot through with lightning streaks of yellow. They resemble reverse cat's eyes, and though no one who works in The Factory knows what the gems are, they don't need to. Their job is to process, package, and load the refined rocks for collection.

It's exhausting work, but there are worse jobs. Gloop bottling, for one, though why anyone would willingly purchase the vile, vaguely meaty syrup escapes all who work in The Factory.

Some two hours into their shift, Ruffles begins to hobble from one foot to the other.

"Are you alright?" Scratch ponders.

"I need the loo," Ruffles grunts, "terribly so."

"That's not allowed!" Snout grunts, the whites of his eyes expanding. "You'll have to hold it till lunch."

"I can't," Ruffles complains, all in a flurry.

"Well, go in the corner," Scratch suggests, glancing at the disinterested Beadle standing on the walkway above, supposedly on the crow, but the creature looks half asleep. "Can't make this place smell any worse."

"Just go," the Horned Boy says. "I'll cover for you."

Ruffles looks up to the Beadle, then to the Horned Boy.

"Maybe I should ask..." he says but only stares at the Horned Boy expectantly.

"I'll do it," the Horned Boy sighs and glances up. "Excuse me!" the Horned Boy yells. "Can my mate here go to the bog, please!?"

The Beadle slowly turns, then looks at the Horned Boy with one droopy eye. After what feels like an age, it nods once, so slow it seems to be bowing at first. Its globulous cheeks hang like empty pockets, and when it raises its head, they sit differently.

Ruffles hops happily, waving a thank-you to the Horned Boy as he shuffles away on long, skinny legs. Time passes, barely noticed with the Horned Boy filling the role of two, and it's not till the steam whistle blows for lunch that the remaining three Odds realize their friend has been gone a long time. Too long.

It doesn't take the Horned Boy and the others long to find their lost friend. They need only follow the sound of laughter and jeers bouncing off the oozing walls of The Factory. It leads them to the lavatory, and crowds of gawking Norms move aside, skittering in fear when they realize The Odds are so close.

A gaggle scarpers from within as the Horned Boy approaches, and one all but crashes into him. The Sneering Lad looks upon the Horned Boy, meets his eyes, and states coldly, "Shame we didn't have a river to drown it in."

A large hessian sack writhes on the cracked, blackened tiles of the floor, covered in dark, wet patches. It reeks worse than the lavatory itself. Desperate, muffled squealing comes from within.

"Ruffles!" Scratch yelps and bounds over. He tries to take hold of it, but the trapped Odd within only lashes out. "Ruffles! It's us, friend!"

Scratch manages to get his paws around the top of the sack, but it's tied too tight for his fingers, and he doesn't want to use his teeth less he tastes whatever foulness the sack's soaked in.

"Your horns are sharp," Scratch says to the Horned Boy. "Come cut him free!"

"I...can't." The fear of what those horns can do, their grim potential, paralyzes him.

Likewise, Snout cannot bring himself to action though he's held in the grip of far more self-centered fear. What if the Beadles come and blame them for putting Ruffles in the sack? What if it earns him a trip to the cellar?

As though the thought summons, a Beadle appears and barges into the lavatory. It pays no mind to The Odds, save for the one struggling within the sodden sack. Instead of freeing Ruffles, it simply takes hold of the sack in its filthy, swollen hand and drags it away. It squeaks across the tiles, the dampness leaving behind a wet trail.

Snout and the Horned Boy step aside and watch as the Beadle drags Ruffles away. His wailing continues long after he's gone from sight.

The three Odds look to one another, say nothing, and follow Ruffles' frantic screams.

Through the halls of The Factory they go, chasing the cries of their friend. Eyes dare to look upon them, but none dare to comment. They pass more signs warning the workers to close their doors, that danger waits in the forest, and others encourage them to work hard and be safe.

The Odds come to a halt at the same time as the Beadle, in the middle of a long, wide hallway, while the Beadle stops before a caged, barred gate.

Taking a key from its belt, it unlocks a panel and pushes a button on the wall beside it. Some ancient grating machinery comes to life. Cogs clunk and chains rattle above the door as something rises in the shaft beyond it—an elevator.

"No," Scratch whines as Snout shakes his head in disbelief.

"The cellar," the Horned Boy says and watches helplessly as their friend—still screaming within the stained hessian sack—is dragged into the wrought-iron cage that descends into the darkness below The Factory.

We'll Be Right Back After –

"No!" Gwennie screams, drawing us back to the Hallow Fire. Four stunned faces look upon her, hidden behind their masks. "Let me finish," she insists, staring boldly into the fire, holding her ground as it crackles and relents.

The others sink lower in their seats, and Rascal lets a low growl slip from his muzzle as Gwennie continues.

"It wasn't the thought of what was occurring to his friend in the basement of The Factory that haunted the Horned Boy's dreams that night. It was a fragment from the same nightmare as always; what was frightening him."

Rain clinks off tin roofs; it gurgles through gutters choked with soot and cascades down the walls of a crooked alley. It hits the cobbles hard and splashes up under a broken cart the Horned Boy shelters beneath. The torrent weaves through uneven cobblestones in miniature rivulets, swirling with drowned insects and sodden, dead rats.

The Horned Boy looks at an oily, stiff rodent and considers eating it. A powerful hunger turns his stomach, but a shred of dignity remains, and his desperation has not reached such a low to overpower his revulsion.

Not yet.

The cart, at least, provides him respite from the cruelty and barbarism of the city. Hidden from sight, his growing horns can't draw the eye of those who would do him violence. Or so he thinks.

The door atop a rickety staircase towards the back of the alley clatters open, and for a brief moment, dark, soot-stained brickwork glows from the warm, red light within—jeers and hoots spill into the night, and then grunts of indignant dissatisfaction.

"We're goin'. We're blooming well goin'!" A boorish man stumbles over his words and feet as he and two others follow.

The Horned Boy prays these men, who smell like his father, go on their merry way without paying him attention.

The trio bumbles past the upturned cart as one of them declares to the world at large, "Nature calls, lads!" He unburdens himself and adds a foul stream of sickly yellow to the downpour.

Beneath, the Horned Boy pushes himself as far under as he can, too hurriedly, and bucks the cart.

"The Devil was that!" the man yells. "Who's under there?"

The Horned Boy says nothing. Hands grope in the gloom, and though he cowers, they find him all the same.

"There's someone under here, lads!" the man declares as his dirty hands wrap around one of the boy's horns. He pulls and drags him out into the night. The three drunk men stare in stupefied awe at the small, skinny boy with antler horns dangling in the man's arms.

"Please, sir, I don't want no trouble," the Horned Boy pleads.

"What is the name of all that's holy is that," one of the men squints, lips pulled back in a disgusted sneer.

"Looks like the Devil himself," the other adds.

"No, lads, no, this is no Devil." The man holding the Horned Boy aloft lifts him higher, using the distant glow from a street lamp to get a better look. "This is one of them carnival freaks—" The Horned Boy tenses at that word. "What's the name of that sort who's put up down by the Two Sisters?"

"Pelma somethin' or other," answers one of his mates.

"Aye, reckon they'll pair a fair coin for this one."

"Please," the Horned Boy tries again. "I don't want no trouble, sirs."

"I don't like how it's talkin'," one of the men says.

"Aye, feels like an affront to God," the other adds. "Say, ain't the bishop down at Saint Bart's payin' for blasphemous books to burn? Might have a spot on the pyre for this thing and a few shillings for us?"

"No! Please, no!" the Horned Boy begs. He knows this bishop and barely escaped their last encounter with just a wicked scar. He'd read about how houses of God were sanctuaries for the lost and found that to be entirely fiction in his case.

"'ere, might be those toffs down Huntington Way would pay to mount this thing's head over their snotty fireplace? My sister does the housework for those stiffs and says the walls are covered with heads of beasts."

"No!" the Horned Boy panics, and the fear rushing through his veins pushes him to action. He struggles, and the man holding him loses his grip. One hand comes free, and the Horned Boy falls, unwittingly driving the liberated horn into the man's shoulder.

He roars as he stumbles, back hitting the wall, and the Horned Boy falls to the wet cobbles. Heavy trickles of gutter water rain down on the man, and a gout of something red joins the torrent. His hand grasps the wound and comes away slick and dark. Eyes widen in horror and then set upon the Horned Boy with rage.

"Get him!"

The Horned Boy takes advantage of their shock and barges between the other two men. They leap aside, afraid of what those horns might do, and by the time any of the three drunks have the wherewithal to pursue, the boy is long gone into the night.

He shelters where the Two Sisters Rivers meet, beneath a stone arch bridge older than the city itself.

His stomach growls with exertion brought on by his flight, and a bloated, upturned rat drifts close along the surging black water, drifting ashore.

The Horned Boy can smell the rot, made infinitely worse by the foul polluted waters of the river, and a war wages in his stomach. The need to feed rages against deep-rooted disgust. Just as the former wins over, a voice calls from the road beyond the tunnel.

"I wouldn't eat that if I were you, lad."

The Horned Boy cranes his neck from under the bridge and shields his eyes from the rain.

A tall man sits atop a carriage drawn by a single horse with fur darker than the night itself. Cloaked in a black, hooded oilskin from head to foot, with a scarf covering everything under the hood save for eyes that seem to glow.

"Here," the tall man opens his coat, and for a brief second, the Horned Boy can see pockets stuffed with all kinds of strange goods. The Merchant's hand dances across glimmering vials, a case of black gems run through with yellow lightning, and bottles containing living lights.

He takes a fresh, red apple from one pocket and offers it.

"I have no money." The Horned Boy steps from under the bridge, ready to snatch the offered apple should the Merchant withdraw.

"It's a gift," the Merchant rasps.

"I don't trust gifts," the Horned Boy states, and the Merchant stares at him, silent for a moment, before erupting into throaty guffaws.

"Here." The Merchant tosses the apple to the Horned Boy. "Payment, then, for a fine laugh on a foul night." The Merchant flicks the reins, and his horse clops on.

The Horned Boy bites into his apple, the bitter tang filling his mouth and soul so much that he pays no mind to the unusual gait of the horse. He doesn't notice that it trots on six legs.

"Wait!" the Horned Boy calls after him, and the Merchant calls his carriage to a halt. Bottles and jars clink within, along with caws and snorts of living things. "Are you hiring? I can work, sir."

"Sorry, lad, this here's a one...man operation." The Merchant pauses, just long enough for disappointment to settle in the Horned Boy's heart. "Might be I know a place." He moves aside and pats the space next to him.

The Horned Boy scrambles, apple clenched between his teeth, and clambers up.

"Thank you, sir!" he says with a mouthful.

"Don't thank me yet." The Merchant nudges his horse on, and it carries them through the pre-dawn grime of the city. "Nothing's free, lad. Even a gift given is in expectation of something. I know of an opportunity, yours for a fee."

"I don't have any money."

"Ah, but you have something far more valuable. Your name."

"My name?"

"Yes, lad. Trade me your name, and I'll take you to a place where work can be found. It won't be fun or pleasant, but it's a roof over your head and food in your belly."

"But, what can you buy with my name?"

"Trade isn't always about money, boy. Sometimes it's about moving things around, opening up opportunities."

The Horned Boy considers the offer, but not for long. What use has he for a name he's rarely heard spoken and means so little? An easy price to pay to escape this dismal existence, so the Horned Boy extends his hand.

"Deal."

He wakes in silence, slathered in a cold sweat and torn fabric, with shreds of straw stuck to his pasty face. The Horned Boy looks at the pair of bunks across from him, one of them empty.

It's impossible to hear anything over the clinking of cooling machinery and the wind howling through the halls of The Factory, and yet the Horned Boy imagines he can. He imagines the terror-filled screams of their friend, Ruffles, suffering whatever torture the Beadles are inflicting down below.

All the children in The Factory know that screams in the night earn them a one-way trip to the cellar. Some say the sound calls the creature in the woods, while others believe the scent of bad dreams draws The Darkling. The Horned Boy weighs these monstrosities against his friend's suffering in his restless mind.

He casts aside his sheets, but before the Horned Boy's feet even hits the tiles, Scratch whispers, "Where are you going?"

"To find Ruffles."

"You can't," Snout snorts.

"I can't just lie here. I'm not asking you to come with—"

"I'm in," Scratch leaps to the floor, landing in a silent squat.

"You two are mad!" Snout complains, then throws aside his bedsheet.

"No." The Horned Boy holds a hand up. "One of us has to stay and make it look like we're still asleep if the Beadles make the rounds."

"Oh, thank God," Snout sighs. "I mean, I can do that."

"Come on." The Horned Boy leads the way, him and Scatch forgoing their shoes to be as silent as possible. As they crack open the door to their bunk, The Odds discover stealth was a wise choice.

A Beadle waddles its way down the hall. It stops and lurches toward one of the main bunkroom doors and yanks down a viewing slot. It glances through and grumbles something in the same gibberish all the Beadles speak. Seemingly satisfied, it hobbles to the next door and yanks open its viewing slot.

Its progress is painfully slow, and at the intersection ahead, the two Odds can see a second Beadle stumble through its rounds.

"There's no way past them," Scratch complains as he deals with an itch above his eye. "And, how are we supposed to get a key from them without getting caught?"

"We need a distraction." The Horned Boy looks around the hall, and an idea occurs to him as his eyes land on the linen room. He crosses to the closest Norm bunkroom and carefully opens the slot. Unlike The Odds, The Norms all have single beds, each with a set of wheels. It makes sense; much easier to cart a screaming child away in their bed than drag them. It begs why The Odds don't have such a setup, though it's not something the Horned Boy considers for long—not when the situation provides him with a solution to both problems.

A few minutes later, the Horned Boy layers torn linens atop his head, covering the knots of his antlers to make them better resemble Devil horns.

Scratch gets cold paws. "I don't want to get someone else in trouble; what if they're taken below?"

"That's the plan." The Horned Boy covers himself with a sheet. The effect is somewhat comical in the light, but he's sure it will suffice in the dark.

"But—"

"Trust me. I'll pick one who deserves it."

The Sneering Lad snores, scowling at something in his sleep as a shadow rises over him. A gentle nudging causes him to stir and a more vigorous one to wake. As bleary eyes focus, they settle upon a nightmarish visage looming overhead. A Devil, strips of torn flesh dangling from its horns and wicked frame. It leans in, breathing heavily, reaching with one crooked hand.

"D-D-D-Darkling!" he screams. "The Darkling! Help!"

As others jerk from their slumber and eyes turn to the Sneerling Lad, none are quick enough to catch the horned specter slip under the bed.

The Horned Boy clings tight to the frame below.

Lights clunk across the dormitory and three Beadles barge into the room, gibbering.

"The Darkling!" the Sneering Lad screams. "You saw it? Right!? It's here!"

Children close to the Sneering Lad recoil, afraid of catching his madness.

The three Beadles unfurl hidden restraints from the bed frame and bind the struggling boy's arms and legs. He's no match for Beadles' bulky strength. All he can do is yell.

"The Darkling! It's here!"

One of the Beadles stomps on a brake, and another begins to drag the bed towards the door. The Sneering Lad wrestles against his restraints, calling out his desperate warnings as his bunkmates watch in frozen silence.

Below the bed, the Horned Boy holds fast, unsuspectingly carried through the halls of The Factory. They stop when they reach the wrought iron gate to the elevator, and a moment later, the Horned Boy hears the Beadle turn the key.

The ancient machine cranks to life once more, and the Sneering Lad's cries reach fever pitch as the doors open. He breaks down into sobs as they close behind them, and the three of them begin their descent.

"I don't know if I like him doing that," Chardea interrupts. "That was cruel." The Hallow Fire seems to agree with her.

"The world is cruel," Gwennie defends.

"Sure," Braden agrees, "but a good guy does better. Or tries to."

"Sometimes there isn't better." Gwennie stares into the Hallow Fire, and despite its warmth, what she says next brings a chill to them all. "Sometimes, there is no such thing as good. That's something the Horned Boy already knew, but what he found down there..."

The elevator clunks through pitch darkness until a pale light leaks through the bars. A voluminous din drowns out the metallic grinding and the Sneering Lad's whimpers. So much noise, so many screams—it's a cacophony of cries piling on top of one another.

The elevator descends into a vast panopticon, and the Horned Boy watches as floor after floor of caged cells goes by, some dark but others filled with flickering lights. Greasy pulsating tubes trail across walkways, snaking below like mechanical roots of some industrious tree.

Coming to a jarring stop, the Beadle gibbers as it heaves open the door and then drags the bed along a rusted metal bridge. Every rise on the floor causes the bed to shake and the Horned Boy's grip to falter. He almost falls but hangs on and quietly sighs with relief when the wheeled bed sails onto smoother, even tiles.

From the depths below comes a bellow, something chuckling with delight, and all the Horned Boy can see of the source is a vast, bulbous shadow.

They come to a cell. As soon as the Beadle pushes them into the center of the room, it gets to work. It leaves the bed beside a set of bellows attached to an eyeless gas mask. The Beadle takes two grimy tubes from the station and forces them down The Sneering Lad's throat, making him choke on his screams.

It flicks a switch, and yellow gloop pulses through the tubes. As the Sneering Lad fights in vain, the Beadle fixes the gas mask over his face and turns the bellows on, immediately muffling the boy's screams. Only the Horned Boy can still hear them, but they're coming from outside the cell now and sound like they're moving away.

A projector comes to light, cycling through horrific images. A woman made of candle wax, dripping hand reaching forth; two children joined at the forehead, one long mouth with too many teeth shared between them; a man with arms down to his feet, floating in the air as he screams; a raggedy creature of torn flesh and twisted horns—

The Sneering Lad panics at the sight of that one. He pulls on his restraints as the tubes carry his screams into the pit below.

Gibbering, the Beadle fidgets with the projector. It pulls out a cartridge, and the screen turns blank. For a moment, the Sneering Lad calms to a simmer only to boil over as the Beadle jams in another cartridge, and the ragged creature returns.

The Sneering Lad's grunts escape the mask, but his wails echo far beyond the room in a disconcerting stereo. The word "Darkling" bounces in the void.

The image of The Darkling clicks to another—reaching out towards the screen—and the Sneering Lad gives in to the fear.

A dark stain appears close to where the Horned Boy clings. Wetness and a foul smell follow, but he holds till the Beadle wanders from the cell.

Emerging from his hiding place, the Horned Boy takes in the complex brass concoction fixed to the Sneering Lad's face. It wraps around the boy like some mechanical insect, and the Horned Boy takes pity for half a heartbeat. He considers removing the device and setting the Sneering Lad free. Then he recalls why they're here in the first place and that his friend is someone in this dungeon—it's all this boy's fault, so the Horned Boy leaves him to his fate.

He creeps by several dark cells till he comes upon a lit one. Hope floods his heart that Ruffles will be within, and when he pulls himself to the bars, it's all the Horned Boy can do to not vomit over the side.

The thing within the cell, once a child, is but a dry, hollowed-out husk. Desiccated and devoid of color, alive in body alone.

Snippets of screams haunt the void; half of one escapes a tube that worms between the Horned Boy's feet, only for the rest to sound several floors below. It's so confusing and the sight within the cell so alarming that the Horned Boy overlooks the Beadle until he backs up against the creature.

Before he can run, thick, flaccid, yet impossibly strong arms wrap around him. They lift him, bracing him against the creature's chest.

"Bring him to me." A slurred, somehow simultaneously deep and shrill voice demands from below. It silences the Horned Boy, and the Beadle carrying him complies. He's back in the elevator, descending to the bottom—the pit easily the size of The Factory itself. However, despite the strange machines, tubes, and cells, something about it is infinitely more ancient. It was here before The Factory, and it'll be long after.

A sickly yellow shape comes into view, glimpsed through the bars and in flickering firelight. The elevator comes to a jarring halt, and as the Beadle cranks the gate open, the Horned Boy's eyes struggle to take in the creature that lurks beneath The Factory.

It's a vast, yellowish blob of indeterminable folds oozing globs of slime-like sweat. A small segment of the creature's underbelly protrudes, coarse and caked with bedsore-like calluses. It curves up with rows of tiny, human hands that twitch greedily. The rear end of the great Slug connects to a funnel-like machine, operated by a team of Beadles pumping levers that send a viscous yellow gloop up a tube towards The Factory.

The only other human aspect of the monster is its face, the size of a child's, complete with bobbed hair that rests above a constantly shifting mound of glistening chins.

"Well, aren't you a naughty boy?" The Slug speaks in a voice belonging to both a booming monster and a small girl. "Tut-tut-tut."

"Where is my friend!" the Horned Boy demands.

"You're not afraid?" The Slug sniffs the air. "No! You are, just not of me." The Slug slouches down, bringing its human face toward the Horned Boy. Folds of slimy flesh burp, polluting the air with greasy vapors as one of her tiny hands pings his antlers. Giggling, she adds, "but you do fear someone."

"I don't—" the Horned Boy sees something flash before his eyes—the man whose shoulder he stabbed in that rain and fifth-strewn alley so many years ago.

"Oh, I think you do." The Slug chortles, flecks of grime peppering the Horned Boy's face.

"I don't," he insists, and a memory of children running in fear from him comes back.

"Be true to yourself, boy." The Slug smirks.

"I—" the Horned Boy recalls a belt around his neck, pushing against his father. He sees his escape, his father's pursuit, and things go blank. Suddenly, the man is on the floor clutching a badly bleeding wound, and the Horned Boy catches sight of himself in a broken mirror above the fireplace. His face slick with blood. The Horned Boy runs, and yet no matter how fast, he cannot escape what he fears most—himself.

The Beadle releases him at the Slug's nod, and the Horned Boy drops to his knees.

"I can take it from you if you wish," she slurs, rising and gesturing to the machine behind her—a complex mess of dials, valves, and metal that vaguely resembles a screaming face. "The Factory can do so."

"The Factory? Not you?"

"Oh, no, poor boy, don't you understand?" The Slug comes close again. "I was just like you once upon a time. A freak!" She grins at the twitch this brings to the Horned Boy. "I, too, did not belong, so they chased me into this forest."

"Who?"

"Who!?" the Slug rages, twisting so violently that the entire pit shakes. "The Normal people. The Norms!" she spits.

"Then why keep us Odds here too?"

"To keep you safe, my child. You have no idea what this forest does to our kind. The black iron of this place keeps the magic at bay. It truly is dangerous out there."

"Seems like it's dangerous in here too. Maybe you want to keep us prisoner? To harvest our fear?"

"Oh, you are clever." The Slug chuckles. "Yes, it is true. The propaganda, division, and silly things like a pin protecting you from nothing are all devised to stir nightmares. Nightmares, the machines within The Factory refine."

"The Darkling isn't real?"

"Oh, it is. The Waxen Woman, The Shared Grin, and The Floating Man are all real, though perhaps not as you've come to know them."

"Why? Who would buy nightmares?"

"There is a growing market for fear. The light of reason is chasing the dark away, and those whose existence depends upon the shadows have needs. Needs only The Factory and I can meet."

"The gems...the gloop..."

"It is called synchronicity, my child. A Factory capable of turning fear into a commodity, a freak whose slime induces nightmares—it was meant to be. Somewhere out there, a young girl suddenly finds herself afraid of talking fish heads, while another dreams of a grinning pale face in the dark. A boy develops a sudden fear of deep water. Now, my child, if you wish, I can take away your fear."

"You can do that?" the Horned Boy asks. He's tempted, even knowing what would become of him.

"Oh, yes, such a potent fear will fetch a high price indeed."

"And I'll become hollowed out?"

"Is it not better than living in fear?"

"Where's Ruffles?"

"Why, you already know. Your friend took my offer right away."

"No—" The Horned Boy thought of the vacant husk he saw before getting caught.

"He's much happier now," the Slug contends. "Now, I will have your fear, child. The easy way," she nods to three Beadles that line up behind the Horned Boy, "or the hard way."

"How are you any better than The Norms who chased you here?"

"They did this to me! I—"

"Spread fear and dread through the world; you're so much worse."

"I only sell it! What the buyers do with it is none of my business!" the Slug glowers. "Take him!"

"You're right," the Horned Boy says as one Beadle puts an arm around him. "I was afraid of what I am. What I've done, what I can do."

"Oh?"

"But not anymore!" The Horned Boy leans hard to the side and jams his right antler through the head of one Beadle. It staggers away, collapsing into a mound of rags and slime.

The Slug wails like the blow struck her, and the Beadle holding the Horned Boy releases him. He wastes no time. Turning, he gores the one behind him and charges toward the elevator.

"Stop him!" the Slug commands, pulling and hurling globs from her mass. They splat in the dirt and begin to form blank faces with stumpy hands. He's already in the elevator as new Beadles form, oozing through the bars too late as the Horned Boy heads up into The Factory once more.

As the light vanishes and he enters the enclosed shaft just before The Factory, something cracks through the stone and brick. They crumble away, revealing pulsing slime beyond, and the Slug's face forms from the crud.

"You can't escape!"

The elevator carries him higher, and another segment of brickwork explodes as her face reforms.

"I am everywhere!"

The Horned Boy's at the top now, and the Slug's face breaks through the masonry.

"I AM THE FACTORY!"

Scratch and Snout are waiting for him.

"Where's—"

"He's gone." The Horned Boy puts a hand on each of their shoulders. "We have to get out of here. This whole place is a monster."

"But the forest—" Snout complains, and the tiles crack beneath them. The Slug's face shapes itself in the pulsing slime below.

"IT'S DANGEROUS OUT THERE!"

"Okay, let's go!" Snout and Scratch nod and follow the Horned Boy. As they race past the dormitories, he comes to a halt. "What are you waiting for?"

"We should warn them," the Horned Boy says.

"The Norms?"

"Why?"

"Because we're not monsters."

The Horned Boy yanks a pipe from the wall. "Follow my lead." His friends do the same, and they storm into the nearest dorm. "Wake up!" the Horned Boy yells. "This Factory is eating you alive!"

The Norms sit up in bed, confused and scared. They watch as the Horned Boy swings the broken pipe against rotten bricks, and as they crumble, vile slime oozes through. Gasps of shock and disgust spread.

Scratch and Snout do as the Horned Boy does, breaking holes in the walls all over the dorm. Faces begin to form in the muck, the child-like girlish face of the Slug.

"Stop it!"

Screams follow, panic spreads, and the Horned Boy nods to his companions.

"We're leaving; you can come with us or stay here."

The Horned Boy tosses his pipe down and strides calmly towards the door. Scratch and Snout follow first, but a stream of Norms soon join them. Not all, but some, and the Horned Boy leads the procession through the halls, out towards the main gate.

The sun creeps up from just below the treeline, it's almost dawn, and the Horned Boy's exodus pauses before The Factory's giant black iron gates. Murmurs spread among the children. Whispers of the creatures they know to live in the forest.

"I can't promise you safety," the Horned Boy speaks. "There is danger beyond these gates. You can either embrace that fear and live or turn back and wait to die."

"We're with you," Scratch says, and Snout nods.

The Norms, however, are not. Some of them peel off quietly, others shamefully, but one by one, then all together, they back down. Though they linger and make excuses, there's not one of them who can find within themselves the bravery to step out into the unknown.

He does not feel pity for them. The Horned Boy understands, but he's already given too much to his fear.

I am not afraid, he tells himself as he pushes through the gate, and his friends follow him beyond those black iron bars.

They're not long through them when a familiar carriage comes clopping up the road.

"Well, well, well," the Merchant says. "Look who it is. Grown some, eh? Got some friends now, too, always knew you had it in you."

"What do you mean?" The Horned Boy is confused.

"Oh, nothin'. Things are changing a might, and about time too. Say, reckon it's time to return that which you traded."

"My name?"

"Aye, lad. Have it back." The Merchant speaks his name, and the Horned Boy feels a change come upon him. "Hunter."

He nods. "Feels good to be me again."

"Aye, shame I don't have anything for yer mates."

"It's fine. I'll share mine with them; we'll be the Hunters Three." Hunter turns to his friends. Scratch's nose grows and his eyes glow yellow; he becomes more of a wolf with each passing second. Snout's teeth twist into long, powerful tusks.

The Merchant's eyes smile above his mask. "That's heartwarming, that is."

"Thank you," the boy whose horns are growing says, and when he turns back to his friends, he is a child no more. "Let's go," the Stag says and leads the way.

They venture into the dark forest, the Stag, the Wolf, and the Boar, free now and forevermore from fear.

"Free from fear," Gwennie repeats as she stares into the Hallow Fire. "Free from fear…"

"Gwen, you okay?" Chardea asks, feeling a sudden chill.

Rascal growls.

Gwennie turns to Toby, meeting his eyes.

"Be free from your fear," Toby tells her.

Gwennie nods and hurls the black book into the Hallow Fire.

"Gwennie, no!" Chardea yells, but it's too late.

The Hallow Fire surges, consuming all the tales within the book in an instant.

"Why!?"

"What the heck's going on!?" Braden leaps to his feet and races past Holly and Morgan, who hold tight to one another. He goes right past Toby to Gwennie. "Why did you do that!?"

"Because," she sobs. "I had to die to meet the only boy I'll ever love, and this way, I can see him again."

"That's not how this works!" Chardea joins Braden. "Gwen, you've got to be ready—"

The Hallow Fire sputters like it's choking.

"I want to be, though!" Gwennie screams in Chardea's face. "He said it would work!"

"Who!?"

Toby begins to chuckle, and his blank-faced mask crumbles. The face behind it doesn't belong to the polite, awkward boy they've come to know. It's twisted, grinning with sadistic glee.

"Poor Gwennie. Love will make you do some foolish things, won't it?"

"You, who are you?" Chardea puts herself between Gwennie and Toby.

"Do I have to spell it out for you? I mean, I already have. Infecting your little tales, had you paid close enough attention, you'd have seen this coming. Haven't you felt October slowly dying? Soon enough, Halloween will fade from your hearts."

"You were one of us!" Chardea screams. "We let you in!"

"You did, yes, so let ME tell you all a story—a true one. See, once upon a time, my October Fools, all the children lived in fear of The Dark. But then something happened. They started to tell stories. Words were spoken by candlelight, over dancing flames, and each tale fed it!"

Toby throws a glare at the Hallow Fire—it sputters again and begins to dwindle.

"It thrived on their hope, devoured their despair, and grew. Oh, how it grew. As the light of reason drove the dark things into MY realm, it came too. The Hallow Fire, this parasite. Don't you see!? It feeds off you and steals from me. It's the true monster here! I'm here to save you all, to return you to The Dark."

"No way that's happening!" Braden lunges for Toby, and the tall boy swats him aside with ease, sending him crashing to the dirt.

Rascal snarls, baring all his tiny teeth. He leaps from his chair, darting toward Toby, and launches himself at the boy with unbridled fierceness. Toby catches the dog by the neck, mid-air, though that doesn't stop Rascal from snapping away.

"Honestly, of all the Guardians there's been, you have to be the most pathetic."

"Don't you dare hurt him!" Chardea warns.

"Or what?" Toby whips his arm aside and sends Rascal sailing into The Dark. There's a painful thud and a weak yelp somewhere far off.

"You're a monster." Tears well in Chardea's eyes.

"I am THE monster." Toby holds his arms out. His face begins to crack, just like his mask, this time revealing nothing but a swirling void within. "I am The Dark, and it's time you children remembered to be afraid!"

Tendrils made of midnight creep from beyond the clearing, crawling toward the Hallow Fire. It's almost gone, burnt out on consuming the tales so quickly.

Holly and Morgan feel the shadows wrap around them first, and before they can call out, The Dark yanks them away.

"Holly!" Braden yells and scampers after them, only to halt by the edge of the clearing.

"I'm sorry," Gwennie sobs. "He said it would; I didn't want this. I—

"Gwennie—" Chardea reaches for the girl as The Dark takes her. Chardea's vengeful eyes turn to the shadow boy, almost entirely shed of his human disguise.

"She doesn't have to be alone," The Dark sneers. Its voice comes from all around. "You can join her."

Chardea's eyes are drawn to the Hallow Fire, not little more than an ember. It's barely alive, but still, maybe it's enough. The Dark fears it, after all. She reaches in and grabs the last remaining spark of the flame and shoves it in The Dark's face.

A thousand nightmares scream at once, and the last of Toby evaporates into black fog.

"Look out, Char-Char!" Braden yells, too late, as shadows creep on Chardea. They envelop her from behind, causing her to drop the last ember as they tear her mask away.

"Keep it alive, Braden. I know you can do it."

The last thing Braden sees before she's pulled into The Dark is her smile and her mouth whispering three words lost against his pounding heart.

Then she's gone, leaving Braden alone with the final ember of the Hallow Fire. He snatches it up and waves it against the encroaching dark, closing in on all sides.

And then the ember goes out.

Roll credits.

Credits

Thank you, once again, for tuning in to *The October Society*. It's good to have you back, and if this was your first time, welcome.

Writing a book is scarier than anything that lives in The Dark. You pour your soul and heart into something that a few will love and others will discard without thought. It's been a journey since last year, and I couldn't have made it alone.

To the talented people who helped make this book look good, Bret Laurie for editing, Matt Taylor for his interior art, and Derek Eubanks for his cover design, thank you. You fellows make me look good, and more than that: you're good people whose friendship and contentment brighten my days even when I'm lost in The Dark.

To the two best friends I could ever ask for, Craig Walker and Casey Smallwood, thank you for being there from beginning to end and beyond.

To all my friends through this adventure, Rob, Jamie, Kelly, Cass, Sam, Harriet, Loki, Leeroy, and everyone else who's made me feel like I can do this, thank you.

To those who uplifted me, Andrew Robert of DarkLit Press, who has taken on my next project and Nikki @apagecastingwitch, for shouting to the world about a particular clown book and helping it reach more readers than I ever imagined possible, thank you.

To the kid from my class who used to tape *Are You Afraid of The Dark?* and then sell bootleg VHS tapes to us, and my mother for eventually caving and getting us SKY so I could watch it (though she just wanted to watch *Buffy*, let's be honest here mum), thank you.

And, lastly, to Dexter. For being a (mostly) good boy.

Keep a weathered eye to the horizon, me hearties, for the next time you hear from me, I'll be spinning ye a tale of pirates and dinosaurs, *Of Black Flags and Devil Birds*.

Special Guest Appearances

The *Twin Peaks*-esque TV show in the Episode 4 commercial break is based on the novel *Mississippi Blue* by Brittany Johnson. It's a must-read if you want an indie book that punches up, feels like one of the big fellows, and isn't riddled with terrible fart jokes.

The Last Holy Man trailer in the Episode 5 commercial break is an inaccurate adaptation of Jamie Stewart's *The Woman Under The White Tree*. The town of Marybell, from his novel *Montague's Carnival of Delights and Terrors*, also features in the Episode 3 *Haunted Hunters* commercial alongside Kelly Brocklehurst's Summerland from her story *Dance With Us*.

Thanks for letting me include you, and I encourage anyone reading this to seek those mentioned above out—they're some of the strongest voices in indie horror and well worth your time.

Post-Credits

The school's basement floods as the boy wades through the rising water.

A pipe bursts, pouring more, and the tide rises against his legs, reaching his waist.

The broken TV flickers across the room, high on a shelf with the image of a campfire, though each time the feed cuts to static, it comes back weaker. Still, it calls to him, and though it makes no sense, the trapped boy knows this is a way out.

He pushes on, the water rising rapidly to his stomach, but he's so close. Just as he reaches the TV, the campfire goes out—a second later, the TV follows.

With it goes the boy's hope. There's no escape now. The water reaches his chest and keeps rising.

Season 3 Teaser

The miniature Dachshund drags himself through The Dark, his back two legs splayed, and though they hurt, he won't let that stop him. He's caught a scent and must follow it no matter what.

His nose leads him along a trail scattered with the broken fragments of Halloween masks. He pauses by half a Devil and a smashed Pumpkin. Those smell like his old friends, but they're not here. He doesn't understand why.

Further on, he catches the scent of his newer friends from a discarded Dragon and a snapped Fox. He looks around, sensing many things moving in The Dark, but none of them are his friends.

There's one more scent, a powerful one—an unforgettable one. It leads the Dachshund further into The Dark, deeper than he wants, but he must. Even as the doubts creep in, as he feels wicked eyeless things watch him with an insatiable hunger. The Dachshund follows the trail as it leads him to a yellowed, chipped hockey mask lying in the dirt—almost covered entirely with crispy orange leaves.

The dog nuzzles the foliage aside and then whips his head at something only his large, sensitive velvet ears can hear. His head turns quizzically as he listens, and then he takes off—broken legs be damned.

He only slows as he comes to a tall, hollowed-out dead tree. Carefully, keeping a wary eye, the dog approaches and sniffs at the crack in the rotten bark. His eyes light up, and with all his might, the Dachshund puts those board paddle paws to work, scratching and digging at the tree till he breaks off a chunk.

It's not much, just big enough for a hand to push through.

The Daschund licks the fingers as they pet his chin.

Producer's Notes

Episode Three - The Song of Sorrow touches on a very serious subject. We debated not including it, given how upsetting it may be for some. As someone who was that kid, like Holly and Pete, who didn't see a way out at one point, it wasn't an easy episode to produce.

However, a good friend said to include it "because if you were that kid, maybe you can show another one there's a better way out."

There is. Believe me. I know you can't see it, but it's there, and things will get better.

Say something. Talk to someone and let them know how you're feeling. Don't suffer in silence and let the Lords of Sorrow win.

Episode Six - The Fear Factory contains multiple scenes and references to child abuse.

Support:
www.childline.org.uk/
www.thecalmzone.net
https://suicidepreventionlifeline.org/
https://www.stopbullying.gov/
https://988lifeline.org/
www.bullyingcanada.ca/get-help/
www.canada.ca/en/public-health/services/suicide-prevention.html

The October Society

Were

Derek

Chardea

Braden

Gwennie

Rascal

Morgan

Holly

Toby

The October Society

Will return…one last time.